"Super Mom is funny, sexy, heroic, and touching."
—J. A. Konrath, author of *Rusty Nail*

Super praise for
Melanie Lynne Hauser's
Super Mom novels

"Only a very talented writer and a super woman could have written *Confessions of Super Mom*. Not only does Melanie Lynne Hauser make it believable, but she makes her hero resonate with all mothers. Bravo, I look forward to reading more super adventures!"

—Sharon Baldacci, author of *A Sundog Moment*

"Hauser takes elements of classic superhero legend and adapts them into a uniquely American kind of magical realism—her Super Mom novels are funny, knowing, and charming, but best of all they show great insight into the hearts and habits of contemporary families."

—Timothy Schaffert, author of *The Singing and Dancing Daughters of God*

"*Confessions of Super Mom* is a contemporary romp . . . a must read for every super mom out there!"

—Tasha Alexander, author of *And Only to Deceive*

"Like its title character, this debut novel has a secret identity. . . . It's unexpectedly poignant and packs an emotional punch despite the cheery veneer. . . . At the heart of this story is a narrative about a lonely, wronged woman who just wants to do right by her children and stand up to an uncontrollable world." —*Publishers Weekly*

continued…

"Moms everywhere will wish they could be like the Super Mom of Melanie Lynne Hauser's charming, funny, and heartfelt novel . . . and will ultimately realize they already are."

—Pamela Redmond Satran, author of *Suburbanistas*

"Melanie Lynne Hauser is funny. *Confessions of Super Mom* overflows with laugh-out-loud and read-out-loud moments." —Knight Ridder

"[This] fun twist on the superhero tale comes packaged with a socially responsible message." —*Booklist*

"Hauser's quirky characters sparkle brightly as a newly Swiffered floor, and her writing shines like freshly polished glass."

—Meg Cabot, author of *The Princess Diaries* and *Queen of Babble*

"What a delightful debut! . . . Hauser has penned a chic, witty celebration of motherhood, and it moves faster than a speeding bullet. I can't wait for the next adventure." —J. A. Konrath

SAVES THE WORLD

Melanie Lynne Hauser

NEW AMERICAN LIBRARY

New American Library
Published by New American Library, a division of
Penguin Group (USA) Inc., 375 Hudson Street,
New York, New York 10014, USA
Penguin Group (Canada), 90 Eglinton Avenue East, Suite 700, Toronto,
Ontario M4P 2Y3, Canada (a division of Pearson Penguin Canada Inc.)
Penguin Books Ltd., 80 Strand, London WC2R 0RL, England
Penguin Ireland, 25 St. Stephen's Green, Dublin 2,
Ireland (a division of Penguin Books Ltd.)
Penguin Group (Australia), 250 Camberwell Road, Camberwell, Victoria 3124,
Australia (a division of Pearson Australia Group Pty. Ltd.)
Penguin Books India Pvt. Ltd., 11 Community Centre, Panchsheel Park,
New Delhi—110 017, India
Penguin Group (NZ), cnr Airborne and Rosedale Roads, Albany,
Auckland 1310, New Zealand (a division of Pearson New Zealand Ltd.)
Penguin Books (South Africa) (Pty.) Ltd., 24 Sturdee Avenue,
Rosebank, Johannesburg 2196, South Africa

Penguin Books Ltd., Registered Offices:
80 Strand, London WC2R 0RL, England

First published by New American Library,
a division of Penguin Group (USA) Inc.

First Printing, March 2007
1 3 5 7 9 10 8 6 4 2

 REGISTERED TRADEMARK—MARCA REGISTRADA

LIBRARY OF CONGRESS CATALOGING-IN-PUBLICATION DATA

Hauser, Melanie.
Super mom saves the world / Melanie Lynne Hauser.
p. cm.
ISBN: 978-0-451-22036-3
1. Motherhood—Fiction.   2. Heroes—Fiction.   I. Title.
PS3608.A876S87 2006
813'.6—dc22   2006029846

Set in Bembo
Designed by Spring Hoteling

Printed in the United States of America

To my parents—thanks for providing all the books.

CHAPTER 1

What happens when a normal, PTA-fearing mother of two teenagers suddenly finds herself thrust into a new career at the tender age of forty-one?

And what if that career happens to involve an entirely new wardrobe, including high heels (which she hasn't worn in decades) and underwire bras (ditto)?

Furthermore, what if the job description includes keeping the world safe for democracy and engaging in hand-to-hand combat with really evil villains with unusual names?

Well, apparently she starts hearing voices.

At least, that's what happened to me, after a full six months on the job as the newest kid on the superhero block, that maternal dynamo known as—

Super Mom. (That's me.)

I'd just come home from yet another busy day of fighting crime. I stumbled up to the back door tired, cranky because I'd forgotten my key, but then realized I didn't need it because the extra set was dangling from the doorknob, practically sending out an engraved invitation to any interested evil villains to c'mon in and take their best shot at me. I sighed, pulled the keys out of the doorknob and pushed the door open with my shoulder, because it's old and it sticks.

"Who left the keys in the back door?" I called, stumbling over the pile of discarded tennis shoes, flip-flops, snow boots, and chunky platform wedges just inside the door. None of which were mine. I flipped on the kitchen light, only to shield my eyes from the devastation—the open cabinets, dirty dishes, and globs of peanut butter—that greeted me. "Well, I have had it," I muttered, tightening my Apron of Anticipation around my waist, preparing myself for one more final, epic battle between good and evil.

(I'm good, for those keeping score.)

"Martin," I called, my hands on my hips. "Pick up your shoes! Kelly, get that backpack out of the way! Has it occurred to anyone around here to close a cabinet door lately? And what have I told you about turning out these lights? Money doesn't grow on trees, you know!"

I was met by a menacing silence that set my Super Mom Sense on high alert; I whirled around, tense, ready for the onslaught of an enemy more terrifying than any villain imagined—*teenagers.*

(They're evil. In case you're still keeping score.)

"Mom, I'll just have to put them on again tomorrow, so what's the use? Jeez!"

"Mother, please! I'll get it later when I do my homework! Have you tried lifting that thing, anyway? Do you want me to put my back out by bringing it all the way up to my room?"

I tugged on the offending backpack, crammed full of high school textbooks; even with my superpowers I couldn't lift it. So I kicked it out of the way and sighed dramatically, just in case anyone was paying attention to me. Then I trudged upstairs, untying my Apron of Anticipation, shaking out the dirt and cookie crumbs that had settled into the pockets—and bumped into two huge piles of laundry in the hallway. Stepping around them, I tripped over an empty soda can somebody had left in the middle of the hall—only to discover that it wasn't really empty.

My chest started to vibrate. I clenched my fists, reared my head back, and felt my mouth almost split my face in two.

"All right! That's it! I have had it, I cannot live in a pigsty anymore. No allowance this week, do you hear me? No allowance!!!!!!!!"

My Mighty Roar thundered through the house; mirrors shook, dishes rattled, and I cringed, just waiting. Sure enough, I heard a huge crash accompanied by the tinkling of shattered glass.

"Mom, that's the second picture this week!" My children confronted me at the foot of the stairs, their arms folded over their chests, twin pillars of martyrdom.

"Can't you learn to control yourself?" Kelly arched one golden eyebrow.

"Now who's going to clean it up?" Martin shook his head.

"Sorry," I mumbled. "Sorry. It just—came out." I took a deep breath, worked up some quick tears, and pulled another weapon out of my arsenal. *Super Guilt Trip.*

"It's just that I've been a little busy today, fighting crime and all," I whispered, wiping my eyes with the corner of my apron. "I'm sorry if I seem a little cranky—but I did stay up late last night doing all this laundry. But never mind." I sighed and sat down on the top step, showing off the cuts and bruises on my hands, hitching my costume up to reveal a giant gash on my knee from an earlier battle. (Me vs. The Ice Cream Man from Hell, who was notorious for driving away with little kids' change and not giving them their Push-Ups. I won. Just in case—you know, the score thing.)

"I'll find the time to put it away for you," I said with a groan. "I'll just have to get up earlier tomorrow, go without my own breakfast, maybe let an evildoer or two slip through the cracks—but that's fine, I don't mind. That's what mothers do, you know. . . ."

"Oh, please." Martin grinned in that patronizing way he inherited from his father; Kelly shook her head.

"Come here, young lady." I sat up straight, my Super Mom Sense—which alerted me to the first sign of a child in trouble—tingling the back of my neck. "What on earth have you done to yourself?" I grabbed a hunk of her glossy blond hair—which was shot through with bright pink streaks—and yanked on it.

"Ow! Oh, that." She shrugged. "Vienna thought it would look cool, so she did it for me after school. It's no big thing, Mother, so stop looking at me like I pierced my tongue."

"Vienna? Tell me, what kind of person names their daughter after a city? And if Vienna thought it would look so cool, why didn't she put one in her own hair?"

"She did. It's purple."

"Oh."

"I'm hungry," Martin interrupted. "There's nothing to eat. When's the last time you went to the grocery store?"

"Well, excuse me, I was a little busy saving the world. But there's plenty to eat. I think I counted fourteen boxes of cereal."

"There's nothing good."

"Why don't we go out to Wally's Pizza Station? We haven't been there in ages. Remember how much you love the little train that brings the pizza to the tables?" I perked up, feeling the burden of being a superhero and a mother of teenagers slide off my shoulders; we always have a good time at Wally's Pizza Station. Plus you get free breadsticks.

"Mother, really. I wouldn't be caught dead in that place." Kelly twisted a pink strand of hair around her finger and admired it.

"It's a little lame," Martin agreed. "Can't we just order in?"

"I guess. . . ."

"Forget about me, I'm going to Vienna's to study. She's picking me up in a minute."

"She can drive?"

"Yes, and she's a safe driver, so don't worry."

"Kelly, I'm not so sure, I hardly know her and I've not met her parents and—"

My daughter narrowed her gray eyes at me, put her hands on her hips, and hit me with her best shot, simply by asking a question. The Question. The Question that punches every parent in the gut no matter how many times it's asked—and answered: *"Don't you trust me?"*

And the thing is, I do. So far. But sometimes it seems that by saying so, I'm giving her permission to run off and do some terrible, unspeakable thing. Like knock off a couple of liquor stores with a sawed-off shotgun.

"I . . . well, of course I do . . . ," I stammered, helpless, my superpowers failing me.

"Thanks, Mom!" She granted me a quick kiss on the cheek. Then she ran off to unearth the perfect pair of chunky wedge shoes from the pile downstairs.

I studied Martin, who, being the younger sibling, knows far too much. If he wasn't my son, I might have to kill him. "What are you looking at?"

"Nothing." He grinned. "Don't forget to order the pizza— pepperoni."

"Right." I sighed as he retreated to his lair to do whatever it is he does when I'm not around. Then I surveyed the piles of laundry surrounding me: faded underwear and mismatched socks and bras held together with safety pins. I plucked out a pair of sweatpants, T-shirt, comfy bra (meaning no underwire) and retreated to my own lair to change clothes and wonder what Wonder Woman was doing tonight. Probably getting a deep-tissue massage from some man-slave.

As for me, I trudged downstairs, grabbed a broom and dust-pan and swept up the glass from the broken picture frame, then called for the pizza delivery. I made quick work of the kitchen, taking full advantage of my ability to clean with the power of ten thousand Swiffers, which was by far the most practical of the superpowers I had acquired since suffering my Horrible Swiffer Accident last fall. (Swiffer, by the way, is a remarkable cleaning product that I heartily endorse. And which was not responsible for my Horrible Swiffer Accident, as I had violated the warranty by negligently pouring dangerous combinations of household cleaners in the reservoir and inhaling their fumes due to im-proper ventilation.*)

When I was done with the dustpan I put it away, in the cab-inet under the sink. But as I did so I knocked something over—I heard a metallic thunk—so I knelt down, reached past the five dozen paper bags, neatly folded, that I keep in there for no ap-parent reason other than genetics (there are five dozen identical bags underneath my mother's kitchen sink), and grabbed the knocked-over can. I pulled it out, saw that it was a very old can of shower cleaner, chuckled a bit at the idea of me, Super Mom, using a plain old commercial household cleanser, and was about to toss it in the trash when I heard a little "chirrup."

I stopped, looked around, shook my head, and then started toward the trash again.

"Purrupp," chirped something. Something *adorable*, because it was the cutest, brightest little sound you've ever heard.

---

* Just a little legal mumbo jumbo that Procter & Gamble "suggested" I use from now on.

"Did somebody bring a puppy home?" I called. Neither of my children answered. I bit my lip, opened the cabinet where the trash can was stored, and dropped the can—

Only to hear a slightly anguished "ooohhggoooogoooo . . ." as it fell into the trash can, down, down, down. . . .

And that's when *I* yelped.

"God, Mother, get a grip," my daughter said as she regally made her way across the kitchen and picked up her backpack with ease. "Are you starting to talk to yourself now?"

"No, but . . . I swear . . ." I looked into the trash. The can of shower cleaner—rusty along the edges, the label faded so that the Scrubbing Bubbles' eyes weren't quite so brightly black—lay nestled among Pop-Tart wrappers and yesterday's paper. "That *can* talked to *me*. . . ."

"Mother. Honestly. You are so losing it." But Kelly stopped to give me a hug before she ran out the door to the tune of one car honking.

"Kelly, when will you be home?" I ran to the door and called after her retreating form, just a gray shadow in the dusk.

"Ten!"

"Because I want you home by ten—oh! Well, then, make sure you are. Home by ten." I waved pathetically at my teenaged daughter as she got in a car driven by a girl I hardly knew, who happened to be named after the capital of Austria. And if recent history has taught us anything, it's that a girl named after a foreign city is going to be trouble. I told myself that it's not my daughter I don't trust. It's everyone else in the world.

I watched the car back out of the driveway. I couldn't tell if Kelly had buckled her seat belt. I also couldn't tell if Vienna was smoking a cigarette. I definitely couldn't tell if there were any open containers of alcohol or lusty teenaged boys stashed in the backseat, and because I couldn't tell, I could only begin to imagine.

Which is never a good thing to do on an empty stomach, a super-hero outfit within easy reach.

I wrestled with my conscience for a full twenty seconds. Then I threw some money down on the table for the pizza guy, ran upstairs, pulled on my costume again, and hit the streets in my brand-new Mom Mobile (complete with Super Paint-Color-Changing Panels, to protect my identity).

I may have even snickered with evil maternal glee as I kept a discreet distance behind the VW Beetle that was speeding my daughter away to points unknown. I definitely forgot how tired I was, how hungry, how my high-heeled pumps pinched my feet. I even forgot about the talking can of shower cleaner.

Because the truth is, a Super Mom's job is never done. Especially when her own children are involved.

"How was your session yesterday?"

"Birdie, you know I can't talk about it. Doctor-patient privileges, remember?"

"C'mon, you can tell me! I promise I won't tell anybody else!"

"Well . . ." Carrie, my best friend and coworker at Marvel Food and Fine Beverages, shut her register drawer and leaned across her conveyor belt. "Promise?"

"Cross my heart and hope to be smashed to a pulp by an evil archnemesis." I held up my hand, Girl Scout–style.

Carrie giggled, tugged at her straight black bangs, and adjusted her thick glasses. "You didn't hear it from me, but Robin, the Boy Wonder, is a total mess. Father issues, latent homosexual feelings, and a scary tutu fetish."

"Ooh! Freaky!"

"Shhh! Not so loud. But it *is* creepy, isn't it? He came to me just in time." She shook her head and blinked her little blue eyes like a mole.

"Carrie Peters. Psychiatrist to the superheroes." I smiled proudly. After all, it wasn't just anybody who could turn a thesis about superheroes and stifled childhood aggression into a thriving psychiatric practice endowed by the Justice League of America. (Although the JLA, not wanting the rest of the world to know that their superheroes have some pretty disturbing psychological issues, asked Carrie to keep her day job as a cover.) "Speaking of which . . . have you ever heard of a superhero seeing things?"

"What kind of things?"

"Oh, you know. Inanimate objects suddenly becoming—animate."

"Birdie, you're talking about a bunch of paranoid people, one of whom believes he can talk to fish, several who claim that they're interplanetary travelers, and one woman of very advanced years whose breasts continue to defy gravity even though she swears she's had no plastic surgery."

"So, you're saying . . . ?"

"That as a whole, you're a seriously messed-up bunch," she said with a professional cluck of her tongue.

"No fair." I pouted, more than a little hurt. I, too, was a card-carrying member of the Justice League of America (although I hated the picture on my ID card; my cape made me look fat).

"So," Carrie said with an elaborate shrug as she wiped down her conveyor belt. "How's Kelly been lately?"

"Fine. Although she has a new hairstyle."

"Really?"

"Yes. A pink streak running down the side."

"Kelly?" Carrie put down her dust cloth. "Kelly's hardly the pink streak type. Although pink was always her favorite color. . . ."

"I know. From pink clothes to pink hair." I tried to laugh as if I were one of those cool mothers who believed in allowing their kids to experiment with finding themselves. But Carrie and I both knew I wasn't.

"I suppose I would never have known. Chrissie hardly sees her anymore. . . ."

"I know, I know." I sighed. I'd been dreading this conversation for a month now. Carrie's daughter, Chrissie, and Kelly had been best friends since kindergarten. But now, it seemed, they'd grown apart. And as much as I grieved for the apparent end of their friendship, I was more worried about how it would affect Carrie's and mine. What happens to parents when their children aren't friends anymore? I didn't know, and I was afraid to find out.

"It's this Vienna person. Kelly is totally infatuated with her. I'm sorry—I hope Chrissie doesn't feel left out."

"Of course she doesn't," Carrie snapped, a bit too defensively. "She's perfectly fine."

"I'm sure she is. And I'm sure this will all blow over, and everything will be the way it was." I smiled, she smiled, and we both looked away.

"Isn't there anything left in this world that doesn't change?" I asked with an unexpected—melancholy—sigh.

"Well, let's see . . . oh, I've got it! Doctor Dan will always be an asshole!"

"True." I snorted, grateful for my friend—who *was* my friend, no matter what happened between our daughters—always ready to cheer me up with a well-timed zinger aimed at my ex-husband.

"And he'll always have a tiny penis. . . ."

"Carrie! Shhh! I should never have told you that!" We both giggled like twelve-year-olds, then we got back to work because it was five p.m.; Magic Hour at Marvel Food and Fine Beverages, when everyone stopped in on their way home from work.

I greeted the first person in line. "Hi, Mary! Going to the PTA meeting next Thursday?"

"Of course. I think our esteemed president would kill me if I didn't." Mary Denton nodded toward Carrie, who grinned.

"So, let me guess . . ." I scanned the items from her cart, the usual carrot sticks, lunch meats, cheese, spaghetti—and two six-packs of Gatorade and a case of PowerBars. "Is it baseball season already? It's only late March!"

"Opening day is in two weeks!" Mary beamed. "This year is going to be great! Jimmy might be starting left field. And with the new sports complex going up, who knows what will happen? Mayor Linseed even hinted that we might get the Little League World Series! It's all so exciting!"

"I don't know, it's not like we're getting a Krispy Kreme—now *that* I could get excited about!"

"But we need the revenue, especially since Super Mom shut New Cosmos down," Mary said.

"Well, she had a good reason for doing it. Children were getting very sick because of that junk food." I tried not to sound too defensive.

"But it was locally grown, patriotic junk food. And half the town lost their jobs when they shut the place down. So all the new construction for the ballpark is a good thing!"

I scowled, pausing in my scanning to look across the road, just past the empty headquarters of New Cosmos Industries, former manufacturer of patriotic junk food that had almost been the ruin of the children of Astro Park. In the distance inched, boldly and bravely toward the sky, a brand-new youth sports complex. The pet project of Astro Park's longtime mayor, Jon Linseed, it was the talk and hope of a town still reeling from the loss of its biggest—albeit evil-to-the-core—industry.

And what thanks had I, the superhero who had risked life

and limb to shut it down, gotten? A memorial trash can. I could see it now, standing on the corner of Elm and Taylor. Somebody had trampled the daffodils the Beautifying Committee had planted around it. And the trash can itself was covered by graffiti that declared "Super Mom Sukz." I made a mental note to stop by after work and take care of it. (Either correct the spelling or clean it up. Depended on what kind of mood I was in.)

"Mayor Linseed's coming to the PTA meeting on Thursday," Carrie said. "Apparently he has a special request. Related, of course, to the building of yet another shrine to sports while arts and academics in this country go to hell in a handbasket."

"Stupid mayor," I muttered. The trash can had been his idea.

"I bet he wants money," Carrie said.

"He's a politician, isn't he?" Mary asked with a wise sigh, pushing her cart out the door.

I didn't look up to see who was next. But I could guess from the plethora of TUMS, Rolaids, and Pepto-Bismol rolling down my conveyor belt.

"Coach Henderson." I greeted the man built like a drill sergeant, but with the kindest face—all creases and tired acceptance—I'd ever seen. "Ready for the start of the season?"

"It's gonna be a great one! And I'm not just saying that because I'm head coach!"

"I know." I smiled and took his money, proffered in a big paw of a hand. "But are you ready for the parents?"

Coach leaned in and whispered as only he could (meaning—everyone in the store could hear). "I'm never ready for the parents! The kids, they're great. But those parents . . ." He shook his head.

"Maybe it'll be different this year."

"I don't think so. The mayor is already pressuring me to field a championship team. It'll be more of a draw, he says—more revenue for the new complex. It's a shame, really. In my day we played in an abandoned lot, with rocks for bases. And we were happier than these kids, let me tell you—"

A loud *thwack* caused us both to jump; someone had thrown a huge bag of ice on Carrie's conveyor belt. We all watched as a mean-faced little man turned to a boy—who could have been anywhere between eleven and fourteen, because of his slight frame, coupled with big feet—behind him.

"What'd I tell you? What? It's not that heavy! You could have lifted it—you need to bulk up, remember? You can't let that little snot of a Denton beat you out for left field again!"

"And so it begins." Coach Henderson shook his head. "Little Brian"—he jerked his thumb in the boy's direction—"he's not a bad player. A little slow off the bounce, maybe, but not bad. And he's a good kid, too. But that father . . ."

"Yeah." We watched as "that father" grabbed a candy bar out of Brian's hand.

"What? No candy for you—I told you you have to lose five pounds. You're too slow. Too lazy. Too fat and lazy."

It grew quiet in the store. The only sounds were the rustle of bags, the steady hum of conveyor belts—and the constant berating of a boy who seemed to shrink with every word, every breath, his father expelled.

"Hey, Brian," Coach Henderson growled in his kind way, as Brian's father paused for breath and paid for the ice.

"Hey, Coach." Brian smiled, his pale, peaked face gaining a little color.

"Hello, Mr. Derringer." Coach's face darkened, but he still managed to give a polite nod to the boy's father.

"Coach Henderson! Well, are you going to come to your senses this year and start Brian? I admit last year he was lazy"—Brian winced—"but this year should be different. I'll make sure it's different, won't I, Brian?"

Brian didn't say anything; nobody did. Although Coach Henderson growled like a furnace getting ready to blast.

"Brian's a fine little player, Mr. Derringer. No need to make sure of anything. I'll see you at practice." Coach popped open a bottle of TUMS and poured some down his throat, crunching like mad as he grabbed his bag and trundled out the door—after stopping to give Brian a weathered, but kind, smile. Brian's eyes lit up, just for a moment; then they glazed over, as if a curtain had been pulled across them.

"Grab that ice, Brian. Are you happy now? Coach saw what a wimp you are. Now take that ice to the car and hold it on your lap all the way home. I'm turning on the air-conditioning, too." Mr. Derringer—who had a face like a ferret with sharp, pinched features not unlike his son's, only his were etched out of meanness, not sadness—pushed Brian toward the door, causing him to hit his thin shin against a grocery cart and tumble down, ice and all.

"Hey, you!" I couldn't help myself; I leaped over my conveyor belt and pulled the child up, since his father wasn't moving a muscle to help him. "There's no need for that. Are you all right, sweetheart?"

He nodded, his nose red, his chin quivering, trying for all his might not to cry.

"Excuse me. Who are you?" Mr. Derringer grabbed the ice—and Brian's arm.

"I'm—well, I work here, and—"

"Then keep your nose out of other people's business. Who do you think you are, Super Mom?"

"If I were you," I growled, narrowing my eyes into a Merciless Gaze, raising my right arm, "I wouldn't ask that question. . . ."

"Birdie!" Carrie appeared by my side and grabbed my arm. "Birdie, look, you have customers!"

"Yes, go back to your customers, miss. And I'll take care of my son. Do-gooder." Mr. Derringer spat this last and pulled Brian out the automatic doors; through the window I could see him plunk the bag of ice back in the boy's arms and stride away toward the parking lot, not looking back to see if Brian was following.

"Carrie, I swear . . ." I was trembling all over.

"Birdie, remember where you are—remember *who* you are. For now."

"I know, I know." I went back to my register and started scanning groceries—frozen peas, chocolate syrup, granola, Band-Aids, razors. I didn't look up, trying to concentrate on just being Birdie Lee, mild-mannered grocery clerk. I needed to get hold of myself; this was Little League season, after all. If I ran around flinging toxic cleaning fluid into the eyes of every parent I saw yelling at a child, I'd probably fling myself dry.

"I hate baseball season," I muttered anyway. "Thank God Martin never played."

"And thank God I have a daughter who hates sports," Carrie agreed.

"I'm so glad I'm with a kind man." I thought of Mr. Derringer and shuddered. "Not one of those frustrated ex-jocks living out their fantasies through their kids."

"You're lucky. You've got the last sane man in Astro Park."

"Well, let's not tell him. It might go to his head." Finally I was able to smile, trying to put the image of Mr. Derringer and his mean, pinched little face out of my mind. But there was an obstacle to this: the parade of juice boxes, PowerBars, and Gatorade rolling steadily down my conveyor belt, fortifications for Little League season. I sighed and reached for the next item in the endless stream of consumer goods. A bottle of Mr. Clean.

But then I gasped.

For just as I swiped his shiny butt over the scanner, Mr. Clean turned his grinning bald head, looked at me. And winked.

"Carrie—I—remember what I was saying about inanimate objects?" I stammered.

"Yes?"

"Well, this bottle of Mr. Clean . . ."

Carrie froze, a two-liter bottle of Pepsi in her hand. She turned to look at me, a concerned scowl on her face.

"What would be wrong with that bottle of Mr. Clean, Birdie?" she asked in her soothing, hypnotic psychiatrist voice. "That plastic bottle of perfectly ordinary cleaning solution you're holding in your hand?"

I looked at her, then at the stout woman in my checkout line, who was staring at me as I manhandled her bottle of Mr. Clean. I swallowed, tried to smile, and shook my head.

"Nothing, never mind. I must be tired, that's all." I placed the bottle—very gently—down among the rest of the items. Carrie nodded with approval—although her eyes, little blue stars magnified by her thick eyeglasses, did blink once or twice—and turned back to her own customer, as I continued to scan perishable and nonperishable items. But as I did, I couldn't help but feel as if someone was watching me.

And that feeling didn't go away until Mr. Clean was double—no, make that triple—bagged and put away in a shopping cart. Covered up by a giant bag of kitty litter.

CHAPTER 2

There were two places in my life where I felt safe.

One was on my family room sofa between my children, on the increasingly rare occasions when we were all home at the same time, watching TV together. It didn't matter what we watched. It didn't matter that they were so tall now I had to lean my head on their shoulders, instead of the other way around. It only mattered that we were all three together, me in the middle, Kelly and Martin on either side—a mom sandwich.

The other place where nothing could harm me, not even dastardly supervillains or flirtatious bottles of household cleaners, was wherever Carl Sayers happened to be. And tonight he happened to be in his split-level house, an absentminded professor's idea of domesticity. Not one plate matched, but he had an entire high school chemistry set in the basement; no framed family photos graced the walls, yet the periodic table was taped to the front of his refrigerator. He had a sound system worthy of a rock band; however, I had yet to locate the second beater for his handheld mixer.

The one splash of color among the bare walls and floors was a bright blue wooden stepstool decorated with cutout hearts, tucked away in a corner of his family room. In the six months we'd been dating, I hadn't yet gotten up the nerve to ask him where it came from. I was afraid to; I was afraid he'd say that it was left over from his ex-wife, some remnant of that life he couldn't bring himself to discard.

We'd brought our pasts, both of us, to this relationship—husband, wife, children. Sometimes it seemed so crowded we couldn't find each other; sometimes it seemed as if we had too much room, between my house and his house and my work and his work, and we had to cling together so as not to get lost.

I stood on the porch of his house, pressed the doorbell, and waited. A goofy grin split my face in two even as the door opened. And before I could see his face, I threw myself in his arms.

They were open, waiting for me. They always are.

"Hi," I said, talking into his chest.

"Hi," he said, his lips tangled in my hair.

"Missed you."

"Me, too."

I didn't want to move. I wanted to stay there, his strong arms about me, my face resting on his chest. I reached around him, feeling him—his sweater, his ropy muscles and strong bones, his solidity. Yet beneath the comforting, nerdy scientist exterior—always coiled, ready to spring—was his need, his hunger. For me.

I breathed in—vanilla and wood smoke. Today, the vanilla was just a smidgen stronger.

"Hi," he said again, pushing me away so that he could look in my face. He smiled, his brown eyes soft, his mouth bracketed by those deep lines—not quite dimples, but not wrinkles, either. They saved his face from ordinary cuteness, giving him stature.

I blinked, leaning up for a kiss . . .

"You're in my way," a disgusted voice said from behind him. A disgusted, cracking, adolescent boy's voice. Carl and I sprang apart.

"Hello, Greg," I chirped, my face tightening up into that

ridiculous, plastic smile I always pulled whenever I saw him—like a preschool teacher on Ritalin.

Greg Sayers stood in the hall, a slouching, hulking sort of boy with long black hair and brown eyes like Carl's. He was holding a sleeping bag and a backpack. He grunted.

"Greg." Carl looked at him. "Say hello to Birdie."

"Hello."

"Greg's going to sleep over at a friend's house tonight," Carl said in a forced, bright voice. "Aren't you, Greg?"

"You said I had to," Greg mumbled. Carl's face reddened; I looked at the floor. Mercifully, a car pulled up in front of the house and honked.

"Have a good time." Carl tried to hug Greg, who slithered out of his grasp.

"Oh—and Martin said to tell you hello!" I called as he stomped down the sidewalk. He stopped at that and turned around; I felt guilty for saying it. Because, of course, Martin had done no such thing. Martin would never do such a thing. Neither would Greg. Because they were each convinced the other was an alien life-form.

Greg opened his mouth, then shut it. He grunted again. Then he loped down the sidewalk.

"Well, I think that went better than usual!" I looked up at Carl.

"I think so, too!" He had an identical plastic smile on his face.

I leaned against him as we watched the car drive away. When it was out of sight, Carl planted a kiss on top of my head. We closed the door and walked toward the family room, holding hands, bumping into the narrow walls of the hallway.

"Do you think they'll ever be friends—Greg and Martin?"

"Nope."

"Oh, Carl, don't say that!" I tried to disentangle my hand

from his, but he wouldn't let me. He just held on, tighter, smiling as if he knew I'd give up eventually. Which, of course, I did. "Meanie," I growled, following him into the family room, where a fire was already burning in the fireplace. He laughed, reached down, and tilted my chin up to his, and all I knew were Carl's lips, his hands, and some impressive yoga-type move that ended in me lying across his lap with my back against a sofa pillow while he cradled me. He pulled back for a minute, just to brush the hair out of my eyes.

And that's when I noticed the blue-and-white baseball cap on his head.

"What—what's that?" I pointed.

"What?"

"That. That hat."

"Oh." He reached up and touched the brim. "It's my lucky hat! I wear it every baseball season!"

"Baseball?" I sat up and pushed myself off his lap, falling into one of the cracks between the sofa cushions. "But—you're a nerdy scientist!"

"So?" He took the cap off, bent it in half along the well-worn crease, and plunked it back on his head with a grin. And despite how adorable he looked—raffish and messy and young—I refused to grin back.

"Well, I didn't think nerdy scientists played sports!"

"Says who? I've played baseball all my life. Coached Little League ever since Greg was five, until last year."

"Greg plays baseball?" This I really couldn't believe. Lumpy, sullen, slow-moving Greg? The Greg who was also in cartooning club, just like Martin? The Greg who as far as I knew never left the house in the daylight because his skin was so white it looked like paste?

"Of course. Although this is his last year—fourteen's the cutoff age. Wasn't Martin ever in Little League?"

"No, soccer. When he was little."

"Soccer." Carl rolled his eyes and harrumphed.

"It's a sport, too, you know."

"Not like baseball. And besides, baseball isn't just a sport, Birdie. It's . . . it's . . . religion. America. Apple pie, hot dogs. . . ."

"I should have known. You've made me watch *Field of Dreams* eleven hundred times."

"Kevin Costner is God," Carl said, his brown eyes shining so reverently I almost expected to hear angels sing.

"I cannot believe this. I didn't know—how could I not know this about you?"

"Because it wasn't baseball season?"

"I guess."

"So—does it make a difference?"

"Suppose I said it did?" I plucked the cap off his head and plopped it onto my own.

"That would be tragic." From the lascivious light in his eyes, I knew I had to look pretty cute in the hat.

"Lucky for you, I'm not a sports snob." I wiggled back onto his lap, hooking my thumb through the belt loop of his jeans.

"Yes, lucky me." He buried his head in my neck; my body went on high alert, tingling and burning in all the right places. "Why is it when I'm with you, all I want to do is make out like a teenager?"

"I don't know. But me, too."

"Oh, hell, why fight it?" He leaned in again, my lips found his, and we necked on his family room sofa in front of a roaring fire. And it was bliss.

Times like this, when it was just the two of us, free from

children, free from responsibility, were so rare. It made each encounter heated, because we never knew how long it might be before we could again rub and tease, fingers tickling, prodding, until my breasts were swelling against his hand, his knee parting my legs, shirts and pants and underwear falling away on their own accord—the two of us rising and falling as one, wrapped together in a sheen of perspiration. Because it was so urgent, this lovemaking. Such hard work, it seemed, in the middle of it—would we make it? Would we succeed? Would it be worth it, in the end?

Ah, yes. Yes, it would be.

"Well."

"Well, yourself."

"That was . . . remarkable. . . ."

"Astonishing. . . ."

"Earth-shattering. . . ."

"Mind-boggling. . . ."

"Good," we both said, and sighed. And lay perfectly still in each other's arms, because we were old and needed to catch our breath.

"What's that?" I pointed to the coffee table, where a bottle of wine and two glasses were waiting. Along with a dry, crumbling maple leaf in a bud vase.

"Oh. Nothing. Just a little, uh, atmosphere." Carl pushed me off him, rather ungentlemanly, as he reached for his shirt and pants.

"Why, Carl Sayers!" I also grabbed my clothing. "I do believe you were trying to woo me!"

"Well, it worked, didn't it?"

"I think you're supposed to give me the wine first, then the other stuff happens—"

"I can't help it if you're easy." He grinned and pulled his sweater over his head.

We finished getting dressed; he got up to poke at the fire, the way men always need to do. But that was all right; I didn't mind his little shows of male dominance. After all, it couldn't be easy dating a superhero who could kick your ass, should she have a mind to.

"This is nice," I murmured when he sat back down and scooped me up in his arms.

"Hmmm mmmmm." He brushed my hair back from my neck, leaned down and inhaled me. Closing my eyes, I wondered how I smelled to him. Did he sometimes go about his day at the pharmaceutical company, doing normal, nerdy scientist/secret baseball freak stuff, and then suddenly stop, overwhelmed by a scent—the way the aroma of burning leaves on a cold night could make me weak in the knees with longing?

I opened my eyes and studied the coffee table. "That leaf sure is pretty. Very unusual."

"You think so?"

I nodded.

"It doesn't look familiar?"

"Not particularly."

"This leaf," he said, clearing his throat, "is from the park. Our park. The one where we first . . . you know."

"I know." And I blushed, remembering—the picnic table, a sheltering pine tree branch, the hard ground littered with leaves. Our nakedness, glowing with a brilliance eclipsed only by the full moon overhead.

"That first night, I tucked this leaf in my pocket. I don't know why, I guess I just wanted to take part of you home with me. . . ."

"You did?" All I could do was whisper; he wasn't fair. He caught me off balance, knocking me over with this perfect, poetic gesture. My chest felt heavy, so full of love there wasn't room for air. I buried my face in his arms so he wouldn't see my tears. How dear he was—how surprising, every day.

"Birdie." His arms tightened around me. "Do you have any idea how much I love you?"

I nodded. Then blew my nose on the sleeve of his shirt.

His arms wrapped even more tightly around me, and I was content. I could have stayed there the rest of the night; I couldn't think of any better way to sleep than cuddled up in front of a fire, Carl's strong arms about me.

I sighed and nestled against him. He reciprocated by suddenly sitting up and pushing me away.

"Carl—?"

"Birdie?" His voice sounded strange, strangled and panicky. He spun around and put his hands on my shoulders, almost shaking me. He looked so serious—no dimples around his mouth at all. In fact he was pale, even in the warm glow of the fire.

"Carl? Is anything wrong?"

"Yes—no—that is, I hope—the thing is—" He let go of me, reached for his wineglass, and drained it. "Birdie, you're happy, aren't you?"

"Of course."

"I mean, with me—what we've been building, these past few months?"

"Happier than I ever imagined being." I touched his face, so soft despite the chiseled jaw, strong nose.

"After all this time, ever since that night at the Harvest Dance, when I found out about your, well, you know—" He made a funny little gesture with his hands, and I knew he was referring to the night he found out I was Super Mom—the night he first kissed me.

I nodded.

"Well, then, if you're happy, and I'm happy—that is, we're both happy together, and happiness is very important—you have to admit that, then, and remember, I saved the leaf . . ."

"What?"

"What I'm trying to say is, well, why don't we make sure we're happy all the time?"

"Sounds good to me." I smiled. "So, how do we go about doing that?"

"By, well . . ." He reached to pour himself another glass of wine, but his hands were suddenly shaking too much to hold the bottle steady. "By, maybe, doing this forever. Like married people. Like that."

Suddenly I was shaking, too—not just my hands, but all over.

"Ma-ma-married people?"

"Married people," he said, suddenly—annoyingly—calm. He steadied my trembling hands, pulling them against his chest. I had to raise my face then, to see if this was real. There were tears in his eyes.

"So, marry me. Birdie, please? Please marry me?"

"Oh," I said, still staring at his tears, the room blurring and fading until the only things I saw were his brown eyes, glistening with hope. "Oh. Well . . . I . . ." One thought pushed its way into my head. One deep, profound thought—I opened my mouth, trying to give voice to it, but the air was suddenly too thick, too hot; no words could slice their way through it. No oxygen, either—I tried and tried to find a way to breathe.

"Toe . . . too . . . tah . . . ," I finally whispered as the room closed in around me.

Carl looked alarmed. He leaned his face into mine and opened his mouth; I couldn't hear his words, I couldn't understand what he was trying to say. I could only give him one last, lingering smile . . .

Before I passed out.

CHAPTER 3

Toenail clippings.

That was the profound thought—the words I tried to form before the room faded to black and I passed out on Carl's couch, hitting my head against the coffee table and spilling wine everywhere.

Toenail clippings. Doctor Dan's toenail clippings, to be specific.

Doctor Dan Lee was my ex-husband. Thankfully. It took me a long time to say that, but it was, finally, once and for all, true. He was a dapper man, a fastidious man. Appearance meant a great deal to him; it still does. Which is just one reason why we disappoint each other so profoundly.

But he had one deep, dark secret that no one ever suspected. Had I known it, I wonder if I would have married him. As it was, only my genuine, mind-altering love for my handsome doctor bridegroom—a love that had me brainwashed for too many years—caused me to overlook this secret; even guard it, fiercely, lest the world find out.

He cut his toenails in bed. And left the clippings in the sheets, where they lay in wait, ready to shred my bare legs without warning.

Even now I can't think of them—those little white half-moons—without feeling sick to my stomach. And over the years they came to symbolize all that was wrong with my marriage—and marriage in general; thoughtless, careless debris, left by one partner (the husband) for the other partner (the wife) to clean up.

So I'm afraid that's what I thought of, after Carl Sayers—who had kept a crumpled maple leaf reminding him of the day we fell in love, and put it in a vase as a gift to me—bared his soul and asked me to share his life forever.

Toenail clippings.

He was really sweet about the whole thing. He bandaged the cut on my forehead and waited as I zapped up the wine with a flick of my cleaning-fluid-filled finger, a whir of my sponge-like palm. (Red wine on carpet—on top of everything else, I couldn't do that to the poor man.) Then he followed me as I drove home in my little dented minivan (retired from super-hero service with the arrival of the new Mom Mobile). He kissed me on the forehead and never mentioned the fact that I hadn't answered his question. *The* question. It was still hanging in the air between us, this gigantic, clumsy *blob*, when he said good night. And that he'd call me in the morning to make sure I was okay.

I thanked him, leaned up to kiss him again, but he had already turned and was walking—almost running—to his car.

"Carl—"

He stopped. But he didn't turn around.

"Don't say anything now. All right, Birdie? Just don't say anything."

"But—"

"I'll call you tomorrow."

And when I went to bed that night the image I kept replaying, over and over in my mind, was of Carl resting his head against the steering wheel, just for the briefest of moments, before he slowly drove away.

I didn't sleep very well; I didn't have nightmares, exactly. Because I don't dream. I never have, not that I can remember, and I'm of the opinion that's not a bad thing. (Although it drives Carrie, who's such a Freudian, nuts.) But that night I kept imagining toenail clippings in the sheets; it got so bad I ended up sleeping on the floor, wrapped up in the bedspread.

The sun was high in the sky by the time I opened my eyes and unrolled myself. I threw on a sweatshirt and stumbled down the stairs, my bones cold and aching, and poured myself some coffee before going outside to grab the paper. But just as I was bending over to pick it up (my back making inappropriate creaking sounds), a noise in the backyard prompted me to tiptoe around the side of the house to investigate. That stupid little yappy dog from next door, probably. Why couldn't Mr. Shoemaker keep it locked up? It was always digging up our flower beds. . . .

But there was no little yappy dog. Only Martin, not little or yappy at all, sitting on the roof of the garden shed in the farthest corner of the backyard. It was his hideout, his refuge; the place he liked to go to escape the females constantly surrounding him. "I need to think man stuff," he once told me. And I nodded, serious, because I knew how important it was to him that I understood he was growing up. Needing room. Room to think.

"Hey, buddy," I called out. He was sitting cross-legged, his old green army jacket thrown over plaid flannel pajamas that were too small—his long white feet stuck out, and you could see his pale shins, dotted with dark hairs. They were man's legs, knotty and hard.

But his brown hair still flopped over in his eyes, like a puppy dog's. It was the only thing that kept him young, saved him from becoming a total stranger to me.

"Hi, Mom." His croaky voice was deeper these days. Didn't most boys' voices crack in adolescence? But Martin's hadn't; it'd just gotten lower and heavier, like someone had turned the bass up on the stereo.

"Whatcha doin' up there?"

"Nothing."

"Can I come up, too?"

He shrugged, which I took as a yes. I handed him up my coffee and climbed the ladder to the roof, inching across it until I sat next to him, careful not to touch any part of his new man body.

"What's up?" I panted. He handed me my coffee.

"Nothing."

"What time is it?"

"Eleven."

"A.M.?"

"Yep."

"Jeez. I've wasted the whole day. I didn't sleep well last night." I sipped some coffee.

"Why not?"

"Oh . . ." It all came back to me—the fire, the wine, the proposal. The passing out. "I had a headache. Honey, what do you think of Carl?"

"What do you mean?"

"I mean, you know. We've been together now for a while, and . . . I'm just interested in your opinion of . . . well, him. And me. Together."

"Like, what? Like as a couple?" His eyes—the absolute horror in them. He looked as if he might hurl himself off the top of the shed just to end this conversation.

"Well, yes, a little. I mean, mainly, though, the future. How do you see the future?"

"With Carl, you mean?"

I nodded.

"Does that include *Greg*?"

"Well, of course, naturally. . . ." Greg. I'd forgotten about him. When Carl proposed, I just thought of him and me. And toenails. Then this morning I remembered to add Martin and Kelly to the equation. But not Greg. How could I forget him? Except—maybe I wanted to forget him. Which made me a terrible, horrible person; a wicked stepmother-in-the-making.

"Stupid *Brady Bunch*," I grumbled.

"What?"

"Oh, you know. *The Brady Bunch*. They made it look so easy."

"You mean that Carl—that you and he—might—ewww. Did he get down on his knee and everything? Isn't he too old for that?"

"No, he's not. And no, he didn't. Never mind, I shouldn't bother you with all this, sweetie. I'm sorry."

"No, it's okay. I mean, well, *love*." He sighed and heaved his shoulders, and I almost laughed out loud. But something in his face—a shyness, a hesitancy, like a cloud—stopped me. "How old were you when you first, um, dated?" Martin addressed a tree branch as he said this.

"Well, probably about your age." I chose my words carefully, not sure where this was going.

"Really? Huh. 'Cause, well, I might be considering it."

"Considering it?"

"There's this girl. . . ." He sighed, a great, world-weary sigh. "She's got brown hair that's really shiny and smells like peaches. She sits in front of me in social studies. She likes gum."

"Oh. Gum?"

"I gave her some once and she said she liked it. So now I always bring an extra piece, only I'm not sure how to give it to her without seeming dorky. I mean, 'Hey, would you like some gum?' How lame is that? And what if she said no? I could put it on her desk before she gets there, but then she wouldn't know it's from me, would she? Unless I put a note around it, but that's too 'Hey, would you be my valentine?' I mean, I don't know, it shouldn't be this hard. It's just *gum*." He laid his head on his arms.

"Sometimes gum is very important," I said, managing not to smile. He nodded. "Maybe you should just give it to her without asking—maybe you can say, 'Here, in case you want some later.' How's that sound?"

He raised his head and squinted at me, his hair flopping into his eyes. I ached to push it back, but felt he wouldn't appreciate the touch of my hand right then. Not when he was thinking about a certain peachy brunette.

"That doesn't sound half stupid. Thanks, Mom."

"You're welcome." I tried to smile, but all I felt was despair. So it had happened. Somehow, I'd never dreaded the thought of Kelly dating. But with Martin, it was different. Some teenaged siren had come along to take my place as the most important woman in my son's life. First gum, then him—she was a grabber, this hussy. She'd take my son away from me; I'd be the lonely mother-in-law in all those telephone commercials, weeping over the gift of a phone call on Christmas morning.

I choked on a sob in my coffee; Martin patted me on the back until I stopped coughing.

"You all right?"

"Promise me you'll call now and then, okay? And maybe send me a Christmas card, if it's not too much—"

"Mom!" He rolled his eyes in disgust.

"I'm just thinking ahead. . . ."

"Well, don't. Jeez. You're freaking me out."

"Sorry."

"It's just gum!"

"Sorry!"

He sighed, shook his head, and moved away from me an inch.

I drank my coffee, wiped my eyes, and stared at the grass, just beginning to turn green after the dry prairie winter. I was aware of Martin beside me, grunting, sighing, not talking, but I was afraid, all of a sudden, to look at him. I was afraid of who I might see—not my little boy anymore.

"Oh, and I've been meaning to tell you," that not-so-little boy said. "I'm going out for Little League."

"You're *what?*" I spilled coffee on my pajamas, and almost said a bad word.

"I'm going out for Little League. Baseball. You know."

"Yes, I know—but why? What? How? You're— you're a— well, you're the indoor type, Martin, if you know what I mean. . . ."

"You mean I'm a nerd?!" His voice did crack then, and he turned scarlet.

"No, no, not exactly—but you've never played baseball before, sweetie, and from the sound of it, every other boy in this town came out of the womb with a baseball mitt in his hand, and . . . why? Why now?"

"Because. I just thought I might like to try it."

"This wouldn't have anything to do with a certain gum-chewing brunette, would it?" I consulted my coffee, too chicken to look into Martin's face.

He didn't answer.

"Aha," I said. And sighed. And wondered how much this was going to cost me.

"I just thought it might be fun," he mumbled. "And you're always telling me to go outside and play more. . . ."

"You're right. You're absolutely right. And besides, Greg's on the team, and this might be a good way for you two to—"

"That lame-o is on the team?" Martin jerked his head up, eyes glazed in horror.

"Yes."

"Oh, man!"

I watched him as he shook his head, his brow furrowed, wrestling with the decision. "I guess it'll be all right," he finally huffed. And my heart sank as we both contemplated what this meant. The desire to impress the opposite sex through excessive sweating winning out over the desire to separate oneself from a well-known "lame-o."

"I guess I'll need to take you shopping for a cup," I mused.

"Mom!" He inched away from me some more. "Gosh!"

"Well, it has to be done."

"Yeah, but we don't have to talk about it."

"But—"

"Mom!"

"Okay, okay." I sighed. "Hey—remember when I tried to fly?" I nudged him with my elbow, trying to get him to like me again.

"Yeah."

"Remember, you were my trusty sidekick?"

"Yeah."

"Want me to try again?"

"What?"

"I could try again. It's been a while. . . ." Although my bones immediately sent up a protest that it hadn't, actually, been that long ago. My bones practically jumped through my skin in their efforts to remind me how long it had taken them to recover from the last time.

"You want to?" He looked at me, nose wrinkling mischievously. "Think you're up to it, old lady?"

"Old lady! Okay. That's it." I drained the last of my coffee and shoved the cup in his hands. "Prepare to be dazzled."

"Bet you can't," he called as he scampered down the ladder—an excited little boy again, not a lovesick man. And so I had to go through with it, protesting bones or not.

"Yeah, well . . ." I stood up, tottering a bit. "Bet you're . . . you're . . . oh . . ." I looked down at him. He seemed farther away than the last time I'd tried this, back when I first discovered I was a superhero. It was only after I nearly broke my neck that Martin had informed me that not all superheroes could fly. (Batman, for instance. Although he has a butler and I don't, which I hardly think is fair under the circumstances, since I'm the one with kids and a day job.)

Now, as then, I stood up straight along the ridgeline, claiming my balance. I lifted my arms, felt the wind tugging at them, at me, so seductively—

And I forgot about Carl. And Greg. And questions, responsibilities, brown-haired junior high school temptresses. All I thought about were those tufts of clouds, above me now, but maybe, maybe, if I tried hard enough . . .

I pushed off, starting my usual tumble toward the ground. Then something happened—like a hiccup, or a burp. Some little hitch in the air, a moment when it felt like I wasn't falling at all but suspended on a current, and if I reached high enough I just might make it. . . .

But then the hiccup was over. And I was falling down, down, down. Into a heap at Martin's feet. I lay there and looked up at him; his eyes were shining.

"Did you see that? Did you? You almost made it. For a minute there it looked like you were going to fly!"

"No, you think?" I jumped up and brushed the dirt off my pajama knees. "I felt something—but it was probably just the wind."

"No, I saw it!"

"You saw what?" We both turned as Kelly came running around the side of the house, waving a small piece of paper. "What did you see?"

"Mom! She almost flew, I swear, Kel. You should have seen her!"

"That's great. Look!" She held up the piece of paper to his eyes. "Look!"

"What?"

"I passed driver's ed! I just found out this morning!"

"Oh, no, was I supposed to drive you? I overslept—"

"Vienna drove me. But Mom, look! I can officially drive! I can go get my driver's license!"

I looked. State of Kansas, it said. Instruction Permit. Kelly Lee. Received a passing grade in driver's education. Is now eligible to receive her driver's license . . . blah blah blah. It all boiled down to one thing—

My daughter. Twenty-five hundred pounds of metal and steel. Horsepower. Lots of narrow country roads.

I didn't exactly pass out. Not this time. But the sky did spin, along with the coffee in my stomach, and as Kelly continued to chatter, asking if we could go to the DMV, right this minute— she'd drive, of course—there were no words forcing themselves to the surface.

Because toenail clippings, first love, evil archvillains, athletic cups—it didn't much matter. They all seemed so harmless, compared to the dangers ahead.

CHAPTER 4

"Do you like my picture?" Kelly held up her brand-new driver's license. I looked at it—she gazed at the camera knowingly, her eyes level and wary, a tight smile on her face. She looked about twelve to me. Yet the state of Kansas had determined that she was qualified to drive a motorized vehicle all by herself. Without me in the car, to tell her what to do, to help her make the right decisions—to stop her from harming herself. And anyone else who happened to get in her way.

"You look beautiful, sweetheart. Although I'm still not sure about the pink stripe."

"It's a streak, Mother, not a stripe."

"Oh." I hugged her as we walked out of the DMV, resisting the urge to whip out some antibacterial hand wipes, because if ever there was a place that made you feel like taking one of those chemical showers, like in *Silkwood*, it was the DMV.

"You think? This is going to be with me for the next four years, you know."

"Kelly, it's fine just the way it is."

We walked toward my little dented minivan, and I handed her the keys.

"Don't you think I need my own set, now?" She held herself so still and serious, like a ballerina—her shoulders level, her legs turned out, her hand, holding the car keys, outstretched in a graceful pose. She looked like she was waiting, but not restful; on the verge of a great leap, an intricate series of steps, dizzying, head-spinning pirouettes.

"I suppose you do," I said, trying not to smile at her loveliness. "We can stop on the way home."

"Okay." She nodded, allowed a small smile to escape, then got into the car—into the driver's seat. I buckled myself into the passenger seat.

We'd driven like this a hundred times before. I'd gotten used to, sort of, not being the one in charge. The first time had been traumatic; when she turned the ignition on, I had to reach over and touch her hand on the steering wheel, overwhelmed by the idea that *she* was driving *me*, instead of the other way around, the way it had been her entire life. But still. I was required, I was necessary; the state of Kansas decreed that she must always be accompanied by a licensed driver over the age of twenty-one.

Until now.

"Sweetie," I said, sniffing, courageously not giving in to the urge to curl up in a fetal position and bawl my eyes out—and wondering how many more emotional, potentially life-changing events I could endure before I simply exploded into a quivering mass of maternal Jell-O. "Do you realize what an important day this is?"

My beautiful daughter smiled, nodded gravely—licked her lips, reached up and plucked a snazzy pair of sunglasses from the visor, and slid them on. She rolled down her window—even though it was fifty degrees out—and crooked her arm so that her elbow hung carelessly outside.

"Let's rock and roll," she said with a Girl Scout's grin.

"Oh my God." I buried my face in my hands. She turned up the stereo and put the car in gear—

And we were off. Roaring toward her future, me hanging on to the dashboard and trying my hardest not to cry.

"Use the wiper fluid, Kelly, the windshield's a mess." We drove past a big truck, which hit a bump and sprayed dirt and tiny pebbles everywhere.

"It's okay."

"But you can't see."

"Sure I can."

"But, Kelly—"

"Mother! You have to trust me." She kept her eyes on the road, but managed to shoot daggers at me anyway.

"But—"

"Mother!"

"Oh—wait a minute!" I spied a familiar building about a block ahead, on the right. "Turn into this parking lot!"

"But, Mother . . ."

"Please?"

She sighed. But she turned into the parking lot— remembering to signal at the very last possible minute, just as I was opening my mouth to remind her. She parked the car carefully—a comfortable three inches away from the car in front of her—then turned off the engine.

"Why are we here?" She looked at the plain brick building— and at the red Dodge Viper in the prime parking space at the entrance. Then she frowned. "What's up?"

"Nothing's up," I said with a brave smile. "I just thought that we should share this moment with your father."

"Really?" She removed the sunglasses, revealing dancing little-girl eyes. "Daddy?"

"Well, don't you think so?" I smiled and smoothed her hair, trying to sort out the tumble of feelings that had started up as soon as I'd seen the familiar building from the road. Was it merely because I felt an obligation to force my ex-husband to share his children's lives? Or was it more? Something, perhaps, having to do with the events of the night before and the way my stomach gave a queasy heave every time I thought of the words "Do you take this man to be your . . . ?"

I'd done that once before, you know. Taken a man—the man who spent most of his time in this very medical building, as a matter of fact.

"So let's go in and say hi—I'll bet he'll be tickled to see us!" Although this assurance was more for me than for Kelly, who was already scampering ahead, opening the door that read "Dan Lee, MD—Dermatology."

I followed more slowly—after first turning around, pointing my right hand, and zapping the windshield clean—every step making me pause and adjust myself. Was my hair right? My collar straight? My shirt buttoned all the way? Lipstick—I hadn't put on lipstick before we left. But would he notice? And why did it matter if he did or he didn't, after all these years?

Because he had ended the marriage, not me. And his rejection would be with me, always. Sneaking up on me when I least expected it. Just like, oh, *toenail clippings*.

"Daddy!" Kelly ran inside, where Doctor Dan—tall, Nordic, with floppy hair just like Martin's (only Dan's was blond, and thinning)—was standing in the waiting room, talking to a nurse. Kelly threw herself in his arms—even if they weren't quite ready for her, I couldn't help but notice. He patted her on the shoulder and kissed her ear.

"What a pleasure!" he said, not in his usual false, hearty way. He actually sounded as if he meant it. It *surprised* me—and

I hadn't been surprised by Doctor Dan in years. I had to touch a wall, just to get my bearings. "What brings you two here?"

"Kelly just got her driver's license," I said, trying on a friendly smile. "We thought you'd like to see it."

"Oh." My smile wasn't exactly returned, but he didn't freeze me with those glacial blue eyes of his, either. "Well, thank you for thinking of me. It's—nice." He looked at me, his blond head cocked, sounding almost as surprised as I was.

We locked eyes for a moment, blinking, as if we hadn't seen each other for a very long time. Suddenly we both turned to Kelly, each grabbing an arm.

"Can you believe how big she's getting?"

"My little girl! Driving?"

"Sixteen last month!"

"Where has the time gone?"

Kelly beamed in the unfamiliar twin spotlights of parental attention. "I'm not a little girl anymore, Daddy!"

"Nonsense. You were just twelve. And what's this?" He traced the pink streak with his finger and looked at me, one eyebrow raised. I shrugged.

"Daddy! It's just a little hair paint."

"Well, it looks smashing."

Kelly glared at me. I successfully refrained from kicking Dan in the shins.

"So, um, how's the practice?" I surveyed the purple-and-gray waiting room, decorated in the latest modern fashion by Doctor Dan's second wife, Dixie. A few teenagers with acne waited nervously, uninterested in the *House Beautiful* and *Architectural Digest* magazines scattered about. "Looks busy."

"It is."

"Is that a new painting?"

"Yes."

"I see the fish tank has a couple of new goldfish."

"It does, indeed. I'm surprised at your interest, Birdie."

"What do you mean?" I smiled, pleasantly, I thought.

"I mean you never asked these kinds of questions when we were married, did you?" Those blue eyes turned glacial; I shivered, then, even as I welcomed the sudden—familiar—chill.

"I don't know what you're talking about."

"I think you do."

"Well, I guess we should be going now." I tried to smile at Kelly, whose brightness had faded; she was chewing a fingernail, her long blond hair hiding her face. "I have things to do. . . ."

"Right. Like folding paper bags at the 7-Eleven." Dan snorted.

"It's not the 7-Eleven and you know it. It's Marvel Food and Fine Beverages, and I'm a head cashier." I tried to keep my voice from rising, but didn't succeed—quite a few acne-scarred faces turned our way.

"Yes, well. It's a fine occupation, I'm sure. And so much more important than letting me enjoy time with my daughter."

"Excuse me, since when were you the one complaining because you couldn't spend time with your family? You've never had time for us—them—oh, you know what I mean!" I opened my purse, searching for my car keys, so angry that red wavy lines blurred my vision.

"You never let me in, Birdie. You stayed home and had your family and never wondered about me. In the beginning you did. But not once the kids came." Doctor Dan's voice got husky; he turned away from me and grabbed a chart off the reception desk.

I opened my mouth—but then didn't know what to say. I was stunned that he remembered that; stunned that he could still be angry about what went wrong with our marriage. *He* was the one who had walked out, after all. *He* was the one who had defined our marriage, labeled it one bitter, horrible mistake. I'd gotten used to that—thrived on it, to be honest.

"Mom?" Kelly parted her curtain of hair and looked at me, curiosity in her gray eyes. "What does Daddy mean?"

"I— I— don't know, that is— I—"

"Nothing. Nothing, Kelly." Dan turned around, although his face was hidden by the chart. "I was just thinking—it's nothing. It's in the past, anyway. Isn't it, Birdie?" His eyes met mine, then, just long enough to make my head hurt and my heart tremble.

"Ye-es? It is . . . that is, of course it is. It's all in the past."

"And the past can't be forgotten. Can it, Birdie?"

"No— I mean, I suppose, but—how's Dixie, by the way? Busy with the town council?"

"Oh, yes." His voice was flat and dry. "Busy as a bee. All this sports complex nonsense."

"Yes, it's quite the hot topic these days— Well, we really should be going. Tell Dixie we said hello."

He looked at me, his head tilted quizzically, his wispy blond hair flopping into his eyes, just like Martin's. He opened his mouth to say something but then clamped it shut, consulted his watch, and started back toward his office. But his shoulders sagged, just a little; so very odd for the Doctor Dan I thought I knew.

"Wait," I called, unaccountably touched—not to mention confused—by this whole strange encounter. "Actually, we don't have to run home just yet. Don't you want to go for a spin with her? It's a nice day for a drive. . . ."

He didn't turn around. "I don't know. . . ."

"Mom, Dad, here's the thing." The words burst out of Kelly in an unaccustomed rush; she snatched the keys I'd been searching for out of her pocket and dangled them, like a prize. "I was really hoping to drive home alone. You know, I just got my license and it would be nice to really use it, and I promised Vienna I'd pick her up and take her to the mall."

"What? Vienna? But, Kelly, I had the whole evening planned. I thought you could drive Martin and me to Wally's Pizza Station and . . ."

"Mother, please, let it go. I want to go out with my friends tonight. But the thing is, how would you get home?" Kelly wouldn't look at me, but she did train her eyes on her father. Who turned around and met her level gaze with an identical one.

"Well, I suppose *I* could drive her home. . . ."

"That would be great. Is that all right with you, Mom?"

"Wait a minute, I don't know, this is all so sudden—I don't want to inconvenience you, Dan, and Kelly, I really would have appreciated not having this sprung on me right now. Right here." I jerked my head toward her father.

Kelly didn't bat an eyelash. "But Dad said he could drive you home," she replied.

"Really, it's fine," Doctor Dan said, setting his chart down on a counter. "I can take a small break. That is, if it's all right with you. . . ."

"No, yes, I mean, I just don't want to take you away from work. . . ."

"Okay," Kelly said with an explosive sigh. "Dad will drive you home. Can I leave now? I have my cell phone. And yes, I know the rules—only one minor in the car with me for the first six months. I'll only drive Vienna, I promise. And we won't have the radio on too loud."

"But— sweetie, I— I guess?" I wasn't ready for either of the things that had just developed. Kelly driving alone. Dan driving me home. But looking at them both—Kelly with her eyes shining, car keys in her hand, and Dan with his face carefully bland

and noncommittal, which worried me in a way I couldn't put my finger on—I didn't feel like I had any choice in the matter.

"Oh, thanks, Mom!" And Kelly swooped in and gave me a quick kiss before fluttering away like a hummingbird and doing the same to Dan. Then she darted out the lobby door, Dan and I exchanging a quick look before we both took off after her.

"Wait, sweetheart—just wait a minute!"

"Kelly, hold on, give us a chance to—"

"See you!" We both chimed in. We stopped just outside the door and watched as our daughter slid into the driver's seat of my car. She carefully adjusted the rearview mirror and accidentally turned the windshield wipers on. I started to say something, but Dan stopped me with a hand on my arm.

"Let her go," he said gently. I nodded as she backed out of the parking lot and headed into traffic, stopping to switch on her turn signal first. I bit my lip so hard I tasted blood, and the salt of the tears sliding down my face. Because my little girl was gone. Joining the traffic heading up and down State Road 46, pulling away, out of my sight, before I could take a steady breath.

I wanted to run after her. I wanted to cast my cleaning fluid in a long, wide arc, strong enough to bring her back to me. The one thing I didn't want to do, however, was cry. Not standing next to Dan. Not like this.

"It's all right," he said, even though he couldn't see my face, which I kept turned away, watching the hectic road my daughter had just embarked upon. I nodded, every muscle in my face working overtime to stop the tears. But when he put his arm around my shoulders and said, in a voice I'd tried to forget ever existed, a voice that called to me across a wide canyon of years and hatred and bitterness, "You've done a good job with her, Birdie. You've done a terrific job with our children," I did burst into tears.

Tears of sadness, tears of regret. For all the things I didn't want to remember, but was afraid to forget. Then I allowed my ex-husband to put me into his car and buckle me up, all brisk concern and action, so that neither of us had to talk anymore. And then he drove me home. He didn't stay; he didn't walk me up to the front door. He did, however, honk at Martin, who was sitting on the front stoop in his brand-new baseball uniform, awkwardly doing that thing where you throw the ball into your glove, over and over.

When he saw us, he jumped up—dropping the ball, which rolled underneath the azalea bush. He scrambled underneath the bush to retrieve it, then ran to the car.

"Finally! I'm almost late for practice!"

"Oh—oh, I don't have the car," I said, my heart sinking. Realizing that this was just the first of many times I would be saying that sentence.

"Get in, sport," Dan said. "I'll take you."

"Really, Dad?" Both Martin and I stared at Doctor Dan.

"What about your patients?"

"They can wait. My boy needs a ride to baseball practice. That comes first."

"But—you—" I didn't have time to stammer out what I was really thinking, because Martin yanked open the door, pulled me out, plopped himself inside, and they roared away. Without a backward glance.

But standing alone in my empty driveway, I did say what was on my mind: "Who are you, and what have you done with my ex-husband?"

Crabby Mr. Shoemaker, who chose that moment to step out on his porch to shake out a rug, harrumphed.

I shrugged, turning to go inside—only to realize that I didn't have my keys, and so I was probably locked out.

Another thing I was sure would happen many, many times in the weeks to come.

CHAPTER 5

Somewhere, in the back of my head, a nagging thought was buzzing. But I couldn't quite figure out what it was. I'd get ready to go out for an evening of crime fighting, putting on my Swiffer green fifties housedress (made out of treated dust cloths so wayward dust bunnies could stick to me), slipping on my black high-heeled pumps, tying my Apron of Anticipation around my waist, stocking it with all my goodies (and I finally got that endorsement deal ironed out, so I can now reveal that Wet Ones is the official Super Mom–approved brand of antibacterial hand wipes), and clasping my dish-towel cape onto my shoulders with two wooden clothespins. Oh, and never, ever forgetting to tie on my little black mask. (And of course, freshening my lipstick and curling my hair, because a well-groomed superhero is a superhero who might get her own comic book someday. Or a statue. Or at least her image printed on a toddler's sippee cup. Something a little more exciting than, oh, a *trash can*.)

And all the while, I'd think—there's something I'm forgetting. Did I remember to get the dry cleaning? Sign a permission slip? Something wasn't quite right; I felt unfinished. Like that time I went to a parent-teacher conference and I couldn't figure out why the teacher was staring at me until I went home and discovered I'd left a curler in my hair. (In my defense, it was way in the back of my head.)

I might have kept walking around, feeling the back of my head for stray curlers forever. Had fate—in the form of the monthly meeting of the Hawthorne Valley School District Parent-Teacher Association—not intervened.

"So where's Carl?" Carrie asked when I met up with her in the hallway of Jerome Siegel Junior High and High School the night of the meeting. (After first making an unofficial Super Mom pit stop, cleaning fluid bursting out of me, palms scrubbing like crazy, as soon as I confronted the unholy mess that was the boys' bathroom.)

"Carl? *Carl!*" I stood still, my stomach knotting itself up in a sick twist. Carl. Of course. That's what I had been forgetting. Carl Sayers—patient, kind, unbelievably sexy (particularly when he was wearing his favorite Bullwinkle sweatshirt and an old pair of jeans)—hadn't called like he'd promised the night that I responded to his marriage proposal by passing out in his family room, spilling wine everywhere and just generally ruining the mood for the rest of the evening.

"Didn't you guys come here together?" She turned to me, her little eyes blinking suspiciously behind her thick glasses. I gulped.

"What, did the two lovebirds have a fight?" Marge Miller sidled up to us and giggled, a plate of cookies quivering in her hand. (No PTA meeting can be held without cookies and punch. It's in the bylaws.)

"Not those two," Mary Denton chirped, joining us. "You're so cute together! Carl and Birdie sitting in a tree, k-i-s-s-i-n-g, first comes love, second comes—"

"Marriage," a warm, wry masculine voice finished. "Isn't that what normally comes next?"

I looked up, my heart suddenly threatening to burst out of

my chest. Carl was standing in front of us, his usual befuddled smile on his face, like he was just a little late getting the punch line to a joke. But he looked at me, and me alone. And there was a question in his eyes.

My throat went dry. I tried to swallow, so that I could at least say "Hello." But before I could, something tickled the back of my feet.

"Move it, move it, comin' through," a raspy voice announced. We all turned to see who it belonged to. Janitor Bingo, ageless fixture in Astro Park schools and town festivals, was stabbing at my heels with a huge push broom. Nobody knew his real name; he'd been called Janitor Bingo forever, due to his habit of crying "Bingo!" whenever summoned to mop up an overturned lunch tray (or nervous kindergartner's stomach contents). He'd been working for the town since the Nixon administration.

He growled and stabbed at my heels again, reminding me of the many rumors, mostly involving mysteriously disappearing, excessively sloppy schoolchildren, whispered about him. And what he did in his office deep within the bowels of the school.

"Oops!" I jumped out of his way. "I see they're working you too hard, as usual."

He stopped and leaned on the broom handle. "Hmmph. I wouldn't say that. Not much call for a janitor lately around these parts. That Super Mom, you know. She's keepin' things pretty clean."

"Oh!" I said, my voice too bright, my smile too wide. "Well, isn't that nice? More time for you to . . . do . . . whatever it is you do. . . ."

"Mebbe." His wide—and hairy—nostrils flared, as he scratched his grizzled chin. He fixed his one good eye—watery blue, red-rimmed—on me. (The other eye was glass, the result of an Unfortunate Toilet Plunger Accident in the Teachers' Lounge.)

"S'pose that's one way of lookin' at it." Then he grunted and pushed off down the hall, in pursuit of imaginary dust bunnies.

"Oh, look at the time! I bet the mayor's already here," Carrie grumbled as she shot down the hall, her little legs whirring like a windup toy's. Marge and Mary followed her, giggling and casting significant looks at Carl and me over their shoulders.

"Um, hi." I started down the hall after them, afraid to look at Carl's face just now. He fell into step beside me.

"Hi."

"How've you been?"

"Just peachy."

I looked at him, the sarcasm in his voice unmistakable. His hands were in his jean pockets, but I could see the outline of his fists through the denim.

"You didn't call."

"Nope."

"I wanted you to." And as I said it, I knew, for the first time, that it was true.

"Really?" He stopped. But he wouldn't look at me.

"Really."

"Oh." His face softened then; his jaw relaxed so that it didn't look as if he was chewing steel anymore.

But before either of us could say another word, there was a sharp crack of wood against a lunch table in the cafeteria; Carrie was calling the meeting to order with a rap of her gavel.

"All right, everybody, let's begin!"

I hurried to my place beside her; Carl took his usual seat near the back (so he could get in a quick catnap without anyone noticing).

All my fellow PTA parents took their seats. I switched on my tape recorder, since I was secretary and had to type up the minutes. And then I carefully reached into my Jolly Green Giant tote bag, pulled out the latest issue of the *National Enquirer*, and placed it on my lap safely out of Carrie's sight. (I, um, like to stay current on all the important magazines and newspapers available to the customers of Marvel Food and Fine Beverages.)

"Tonight I'd like to allow Mayor Linseed to say a few words before we get down to business," Carrie announced. "So without further ado, Mayor Linseed."

Everyone applauded as a short round man, red of face and bald of head—a Weeble in a gray pin-striped suit—pushed himself out of a student-sized chair and wobbled toward the front of the room, pausing now and then to shake hands and wave the "V" for Victory sign. The Honorable Jon Linseed, mayor of Astro Park for twelve years (and counting), smiled gratefully.

"Thank you, thank you, nice to see so many concerned parents. You're the ones who keep our schools running." His Honor broke into a huge grin, pressing his double chins deep somewhere within his chest. His Honor's cousin Jasper—the slight, fawning little man who shadowed the mayor wherever he went—laughed long and hard, slapping his bony knee. The official word was that Jasper was Mayor Linseed's bodyguard; the official rumor was that Jasper had gotten into some undisclosed trouble in the past, and this was the family's way of keeping him under wraps.

"And what about those Jaguars?" the mayor asked with a teasing shrug. "Huh? What a team!" Wild cheers and applause. The man was good; he knew his crowd. The high school basketball team had managed to put together a winning season for the first time in fifty years.

"The Science Club placed first in the National Science Olympiad," Carrie piped up.

"Well, well," Linseed said, stroking his chins. "I'm sure their parents are very proud. However, I'm here tonight to talk to you good people about what makes America great. And what, most importantly, can make Astro Park great again after Super Mom, unfortunately, brought about the demise of New Cosmos Industries. . . ."

"Why does everyone always blame me?" I muttered to no one in particular. "It was for their own good!"

"Baseball," the mayor continued. "That's right, baseball. America's pastime. Right here in Kansas, the breadbasket of America, we can build a grand cathedral for the hallowed sport of Little League baseball. I need your help, good citizens! But more importantly"—he gripped the sides of the podium with his sausagelike fingers, leaned over, and looked every PTA member right in the eye, one at a time—"the youth of Astro Park need your help!"

Jasper, seated in the front row, started to applaud, but the mayor cut him off with a look.

"We are in the midst of our most ambitious building project ever—the Astro Park-O-Dome Field—"

"It's got a dome now?" Carrie whispered. I shrugged.

"However, a stadium like this—a temple to youth sports— needs funds. We've done very well with the property tax hike, the sales tax increase, and the ice cream truck tax. Although after last week's incident involving one of the drivers and Super Mom, there's one less truck to tax."

"The man was evil! He deserved what he got!" I hissed to Carrie, who shushed me with a well-placed elbow to the ribs.

"But, parents, we're still in need. And that's where you, the PTA, come in!" His Honor's little brown eyes twinkled behind his rimless glasses. He was the kind of man who looked as if he should always be wearing a top hat.

"Your fund-raising prowess is legendary. Why, remember the Great Computer Drive of oh-three? You single-handedly equipped every classroom in town with its own computer. When the elementary school playground needed a climbing wall, who provided it? That's right, the PTA. When the driver's ed class needed new vehicles the year after the Thompson quadruplets turned sixteen, who came through? Again—the PTA!"

Modest smiles now, as we veterans basked in the glow of remembered battles, of bake sales and wrapping-paper drives of days past. We also hung our heads in remembrance of Judy Turner, who succumbed after working three days straight, with no breaks, alphabetizing wrapping-paper orders during the Holiday Marketplace Fun Fair of '04.

"So I'm asking you to focus your mighty energy on this— Astro Park's greatest hope. That future Joe DiMaggio who just wants a chance to steal second base on a professionally designed diamond surrounded by Tifway Four Nineteen Bermuda grass complete with drainage system, featured on a Daktronics color-matrix board so his proud parents, seated in their comfortable bleachers with Wi-Fi capabilities, can see the instant replay, while sipping their Frappuccinos from the Starbucks in the snack pavilion. In other words . . ." Mayor Linseed whipped out a startlingly white handkerchief and, touching it to one eye with a practiced sniff, said, "Think of the children!"

The crowd rose as one, roaring with approval as Mayor Linseed waved his "V" for Victory sign and shouted, "Vote for Linseed!" Everyone but Carrie, that is.

"Birdie!" She tugged at my sleeve and pulled me down. "Are you as nuts as they are?"

"But a Starbucks, Carrie! How cool is that?"

"What happened to good old-fashioned Gatorade?"

"Excuse me?" A timid voice begged for attention. "Excuse me?" Slowly people started to sit down, leaving a young girl with a mouth full of braces standing nervously in the center of the room. Her hands trembled as she clutched a notebook. But her voice was steady as she addressed the rotund politician in front of her.

"Mayor Linseed, I'm with the Jerome Siegel *Daily Planet*. I wonder if you'd like to comment about your family's ties to the old Parker Salt Company?"

"Excuse me?" He cocked his head. Jasper uncurled his sycophantic body and slowly turned to stare at the girl, his eyes unblinking.

"The Parker Salt Company. Isn't the new stadium being built on property formerly owned by this company?"

"What's your name, young lady?" Linseed asked it kindly, but I could see his shoulders stiffen and his pudgy fingers grip the podium.

"Lois, um, Blane," she stammered, and I smiled. I'd known Lois since she was a Brownie; she was the sweetest girl in Martin's class, always so meek and mild. Hardly the type you'd think would secretly dream of being her generation's Christiane Amanpour.

"Well, Lois, I applaud your journalistic instincts. They're absolutely right—yes, my grandfather was a major shareholder in the company. But I assure you, the sale of the property to the city was entirely aboveboard. In fact, I'd be happy to show you all the records pertaining to it." Linseed looked at Jasper, who started to raise a finger, then stopped. "Any other questions?"

"Well, no, then . . . I guess not. . . ." Lois turned bright red, and blinked several times. Then she sat down and bent her head over her notebook, her dark brown hair hiding her face.

"All right then, I must bid you fine people adieu. The city doesn't run itself, you know!" His Honor chuckled, his chins shaking, acknowledging the thunderous applause. He waved, shook hands with Carrie, then trundled away—closely followed by Jasper, who hurried, bowing and scraping, to open the cafeteria door for his cousin.

Carrie slammed her gavel on the podium. "Order! Order! Please, everyone, sit down!"

And so began the important part of the meeting—the decision over what kind of fund-raiser to hold (because there was no doubt we'd do it; it had been two whole months since our last one), and the intricate politics involved in nominating committee chairs. (We PTA members are not above a little payola, it must be known. You'd be surprised at how far a little carpool duty can get a person.) And through it all I sat, trying to look interested, although I was really trying to get Carl to look at me. When he proved resistant to my long-distance powers of subtle persuasion (consisting of a series of blinks and nods that made me look like I suffered from a neurological disorder), I gave up. And sulked, paging through the *National Enquirer* hidden on my lap.

MAN DIES OF A BROKEN HEART—IT LITERALLY CRACKED IN TWO, ACCORDING TO STUNNED DOCTORS
by Jimmy Nelson

I smiled, recognizing my old friend's name—the ace reporter who had helped me break my first superhero case. Then I continued reading.

> DOCTORS PERFORMING an autopsy on Stanley Weatherby reveal that the thirty-five-year-old telemarketer and iguana breeder died of a broken heart. "I've never seen it before—the heart muscle was in two parts, literally broken in two," Dr. Fred Bentley said. Friends say that Stanley had recently broken up with his longtime girlfriend, Stacy DuPont. "They're all saying I killed him, but it wasn't my

fault," Ms. DuPont sobbed. "He was standing in the way of my film career!" Ms. DuPont has starred in several adult films, the most recent being *Around the World with Eighty Lays*. But Dickie Newton, Stanley's best friend, disagrees. "He loved that tramp, man. When she left him, he just sat in his chair and stared at the walls. He didn't shave, he didn't eat, he didn't even change clothes. And then, one day, he fell out of the chair, flat on his face. He broke his nose, man. We couldn't even have an open casket."

Doctors say this may prove conclusively that certain people—particularly out-of-shape, middle-aged men—can truly die of a broken heart.

I looked again at Carl. He was sitting at a back table, his head on his hand, staring into space. His sweater was a little worn at the elbows, he hadn't shaved in a couple of days, and it looked to me like his socks didn't match.

"Fashion shows are so nineties," Marge Miller was saying with a determined nod. "I think we should have a mother-daughter Botox party!"

I bit my lip, looked up at Carrie, who was now a violent shade of purple, and tried to follow the debate (I think it was about the possibility of getting Kelly Clarkson to perform the national anthem at the opening-day ceremony, backed up by the high school show choir). But I couldn't keep it up; my gaze was pulled toward Carl like he was a magnet and I was a helpless paper clip. This time he met my eyes for a second before turning away, his face flushing red, and my heart did a slow flip inside my chest. He was so handsome. Every time I saw him like this—in a crowd of ordinary PTA parents—I discovered it again, and felt once more that first stir of giddiness and disbelief that he was mine. He had always noticed me, he'd said that first night. And always wondered why other people did not.

He raised his head again and smiled—picking me out from the crowd once more. My heart started to beat a little faster, and I smiled back.

Then I dropped my head and turned another page.

GENETICALLY ENGINEERED GIGANTIC MUTATED TURNIP SWALLOWS NEBRASKA FARMER

"WE WAS working in the fields, just like usual. Just the two of us, side by side. I turned my back for a second, heard some kind of rustle and a shout, and then poor Solomon was gone. Just like that! The only thing left of him was this hat," sobbed his widow, Caroline. "Those durned turnips! I didn't want to mess with all those chemicals but Solomon insisted. Said he wanted to make some money for a change, buy me some pretty new things. That old fool! He should have known I didn't want anything but him. . . ."

I burst into tears. Carrie turned to me, tugging on her bangs. "Birdie, for heaven's sake! No one's saying you can't be committee chair, but honestly, you chaired last year's Casino Night—"

"No— I mean, I know—but—never mind." I took a big breath and hiccupped, waving my hand at Gail Tinley, who apparently had just been nominated. (Or more likely, bought her way into the nomination by promising free Mary Kay makeovers.) I studied the picture of poor Caroline, standing all alone in a field of turnips holding a weathered ball cap. What if Carl got eaten by a giant vegetable? My heart seemed to crumple in on itself; I couldn't breathe right.

"All right then." Carrie banged her gavel down on the table so forcefully I jumped, dropped the *National Enquirer,* then ducked under the table to retrieve it. "The PTA has voted to hold a gala Silent Auction and Dinner Dance, proceeds to go directly to Astro Park-O-Dome Field. Although I would like it noted that the president does not approve of all proceeds going toward what is, after all, a commercial venture devoted only to athletics when the marching band can't afford the royalties on any song written after nineteen-eighty."

"If I have to hear 'Love Will Keep Us Together' one more time, I'm going to puncture my own eardrum," Gloria Tubwell—mother of five, all of whom played tenor sax—muttered.

"Who will we get to emcee?" Mary Denton wondered. "A celebrity would be nice!"

"Remember what a good job Jim Nabors did last time?" Gloria asked.

"But isn't he dead?"

"I don't know. Maybe," Gloria mused.

"Well, actually . . ." One of our newer members stood up, with a cute, apologetic little wave of the hand. "My cousin happens to be Ryan Seacrest. . . ."

Everyone screamed and bestowed the startled newcomer with the title of Talent Coordinator. For life.

"All right then, Ryan Seacrest is emcee. Any other new business before we adjourn?"

Sweet little Lois stirred in her chair, almost raised her hand—I could see her shoulder muscles tense—but then shook her head and hid behind her hair again.

"All right, meeting adjourned. Don't forget to talk to Marge about donations." Carrie rapped her gavel and whirred over to me. I was pretending to put my tape recorder away, but in truth I was looking at Carl. He was still seated, studying his hands. Was he waiting for me? I thought he was. I hoped he was.

"So are you going to donate anything?" Carrie hit me on the shoulder; I jumped and almost dropped my recorder.

"Huh?"

"You. I mean, Super Mom. You should donate something—like a free housecleaning or something."

"Carrie! I'm not a maid service, you know. I'm a superhero. We don't hire ourselves out."

"I thought you said Superman does birthday parties."

"Only for members of the JLA." I watched as Carl leaned down and picked up his jacket off the floor. "Oh! I've got to go. I'll talk to you tomorrow."

"But, Birdie, you've got to donate something. I may not like this whole thing, but we're not going to have a dud of a fundraiser. Not on my watch. . . ."

"Later!" I grabbed my tote bag and started to run toward Carl. But the closer I got, the slower I ran. I didn't know what was going to happen next. I only knew that I had to begin it.

"Carl—I—"

He looked up at me. Brown eyes, adorable dimple, thick brown hair—naked hope, written all over his face. "Follow me," I whispered, reaching up to touch his cheek. He placed his hand over mine, holding me there, just for a moment—and time stood still. Then he nodded, starting the world back up again; he followed me out of the building, and we got in our respective cars. And we drove.

It didn't look like much. Just a neglected park with some rusty playground equipment, a small pond, a couple of picnic tables.

But it was where Carl and I had found each other. Where

we'd first discovered how nicely we fit together, bone to bone, flesh to flesh. Sheltered beneath an old pine tree, on cold, hard ground sprinkled with maple leaves and pinecones. It was our place, our beginning. I drove there because I needed to touch it, like a good-luck charm, before we took the next step together.

We parked our cars, got out, walking toward one particular picnic table without saying a word. We both climbed up on top of the table, our feet resting on the bench so that we faced the small pond, water softly lapping the white boulders along the shore.

"So, you didn't call the other day," I began.

Carl turned toward me; his face looked white in the moonlight and I couldn't tell if he was happy to be here or not.

"I know. I'm sorry. I didn't know what to say—you're all right, though? Your head?"

I showed him the little scratch on my forehead that was almost gone. He nodded, then surveyed the pond again.

"I'm sorry, too, about the whole thing—I don't know what happened, I just got kind of dizzy, and . . . you took me by surprise, you know."

"I did? I thought—I thought it was what you've been thinking, too."

"I have . . . it's just . . ." I thought about Doctor Dan, the other day at his office. "I made mistakes. In my first marriage. It wasn't just Dan, it was me, too, and I'd forgotten about that. And I don't want to make mistakes again."

"I'm not Dan" was all that Carl said, as he balled up his fists and shoved them in his jacket pockets.

"No, you aren't. Which is why I don't want to mess this up. Aren't you afraid, just a little?"

"I'm only afraid of one thing," he said, his voice suddenly husky. "I'm afraid of a life without you."

"Me, too," I said, knowing that, at last. When I thought of

everything there was about marriage—the good, the bad, the indifferent—it all came down to this. I couldn't stand to wake up every day and know he was alive in the world, somewhere. Somewhere I couldn't be.

"Do you still mean it?" I whispered.

He didn't say anything, and all of a sudden I was afraid; I felt an actual body blow of cold, crippling terror.

"Carl?" I started to cry, softly; my shoulders shook and the tears rolled down but I didn't sob. The air was so still, as if the sky, the stars, the moon, were all holding their collective breath. But in spite of my terror, I didn't want to force anything; I didn't want him to feel sorry for me.

Carl still didn't turn toward me. He didn't take his eyes off that pond. But he did reach for my hand.

"Yes, I still mean it."

And somehow there wasn't any room between us at all. I was in his arms and he was in mine; I had a mouth full of corduroy and his face was tangled in my hair and we both, finally, breathed. And so did the sky, the stars, the moon; the air was vibrant, dancing, alive.

"I'm such an idiot," I sniffed. Carl's great booming laugh skipped across the pond.

"Yes, you are, but I love you anyway."

"Me, too. Oh, me, too!" And it was the truest thing I had ever said.

We sat together, laughing, crying, for such a long time. We babbled and talked but the words made no sense; I can't remember most of what we said. I can only remember this—the absolute perfection of the moment when he stopped laughing, took my hand, got down on one (slightly creaking) knee, and asked if he could have that hand. In marriage, in love, in life.

And this time I just concentrated on his eyes. His kind,

brown, honest eyes that reflected back to me my truest self of all—not a superhero, not a mother, but a woman loved. This time I didn't pass out. This time I said yes.

And we began to live happily ever after, sitting side by side on a picnic table. I could see us there in thirty years, old, arthritic, slightly smaller. But together, clasping hands, watching this same pond, the same moon, the same stars. And I was happy.

"So when?" my fiancé asked.

"When what?" I sighed, too full of contentment to lift my head from his shoulder.

"When do you want to get married? When do you want the wedding?"

"The wedding . . ."

"Yes, you know, the ceremony with the cake and the guests and the presents. When should we tell the kids?"

"The kids . . ." I lifted my head off his shoulder. Kelly, Martin. *Greg*. His name seemed like an unwelcome visitor, an uninvited party guest.

"And we should probably think about where we'll live— your house or mine? Do you own yours, or is it in Doctor Dan's name?"

"Name?"

"Your house. Do you think it's big enough for all of us? I only have three bedrooms, I'm not sure that will work. What do you think? And what about our beds? Which one do you like best? I have a queen, but isn't yours a king?"

"Toenails," I said.

"Birdie?"

"Gah foo."

"Put your head down," I heard him say from a very long distance away. "Take deep breaths, now, sweetheart. Don't worry. I'm here, I'll always be here. Don't worry about a thing."

"Geee," I said woozily. Carl patted me on the back and waited, patient as ever, for me to come back to my senses, for me to come back to him. I had to reach out and take his strong, capable hand, holding on to it like a lifeline. And he told me, his voice tender with happiness, what would happen next. The part that follows *Happily Ever After.* A fable about dates and plans and children; whose vacuum we would keep, which lawnmower was the most fuel-efficient. And I realized that we weren't just combining hearts. We were combining households—which was much harder work, if you really thought about it.

"Can we—maybe talk about this later?" I swallowed, my throat constricted.

"But, sweetheart, we need to decide some of this. . . ."

"Later? I'd like to pretend. . . ." I didn't finish, because it seemed silly. I wanted to pretend that I was twenty and he was twenty-one. That we both lived in cheap apartments with no furniture, paintings, appliances—or pasts.

"Pretend what?"

"Pretend that we can celebrate our fiftieth wedding anniversary. You know we can't, can we? We'll be dead by then."

"Well, that's a cheerful thought. But so what?"

"So, well—I just want to pretend that we're young and—Oh, never mind. It's stupid. Never mind."

Carl whistled for a minute, thinking. I could tell by the way his hair seemed to stand up on end, as if he'd run his hand through it.

"So . . . how many kids do you want to have?"

I almost fell off the picnic table.

"Are you out of your mi—"

"I think a boy and a girl. Twins. Maybe triplets. The more the merrier!"

"Carl Sayers, you cannot be serious!" But then I saw that his brown eyes were twinkling in the moonlight.

"And someday we'll build a house, way up on a hill. With a picket fence and rosebushes so I can bring you a flower every morning, I'll put it on your pillow so that the first thing you see is one perfect red rose, every day." He pulled me close.

"And we'll go to Hawaii on our twenty-fifth anniversary, and Europe on our fiftieth . . ."

"And everyone will say what a young couple. What a sweet young couple—look at how much time they have. Look at how in love they are . . . don't they know that love will change? Don't they know that time runs out?"

"No, no, they don't. They don't know it, because it's just beginning—they're just beginning." I nodded, understanding, finally. "It's all new, to them."

"That's right. And it always will be—I promise you that, Birdie. I'll make mistakes, I'm sure—all young newlyweds do—but I'll never take you for granted. This isn't just my second marriage, do you understand that? It's my first real marriage. The one I used to dream about."

"Mine, too." I blew my nose on the sleeve of his shirt, because I knew he wouldn't mind. And he didn't. He just laughed and wiped it off on the sleeve of *my* shirt. "Now what?"

"Well, I don't know about you, but I'm starving. Want to celebrate by grabbing a hamburger?"

"You're so romantic!" He slid off the picnic table and grabbed me around the waist, lifting me off and plunking me down—a bit too hard—next to him.

"You know what the best thing about being engaged is going to be?" he asked as we walked toward our cars, hand in hand, kicking at the grass like two ten-year-olds.

"No. What?"

"I can finally eat onions! I haven't had onions on my hamburgers in six months!"

"No, you can't. Onions make me sick to my stomach."

"Well, then, I can stop shaving on weekends."

"Deal. That way I can stop shaving my legs every day!"

"And I can wear my favorite pair of sweats when I watch football—the ones with the holes in them."

"And I can wear my fat clothes when I've got PMS!"

"Fat clothes?" He stopped, a stricken look on his face.

"It's just a—euphemism. That's right, a euphemism." I smiled and fluttered my eyelashes.

"All right . . . so I assume there will be feminine products in my medicine cabinet?"

"Afraid so. Oh—and where do you cut your toenails?"

"In the sink. Why?"

"No reason. The sink? Ew. Ever hear of a wastebasket, buddy?"

"No, but I suppose you'll tell me about it." My fiancé shoved me—a little unceremoniously—into the passenger side of his car. Then he started to walk around to the driver's side—but stopped. He spun around and planted one on me—a big, luscious, endless, tongue-numbing kiss that left me weak in the knees and moist in all sorts of places.

"I'm gettin' onions," he said with a manly set of his shoulders.

"Okay." I sighed, my heart all aflutter, a goofy smile on my face, as I shut the door.

And really, what else could I have said?

CHAPTER 6

Carrie took the news solemnly, letting it process for a moment before she finally smiled, nodding once as if bestowing her blessing. "It's about time. And as your matron of honor, it's my duty to inform you that *pink* is a four-letter word."

Howard, her husband, hugged me so tightly I couldn't breathe. "Our little girl is growing up! Have you had *the talk* with her?"

Carrie snorted.

"It's a little late for that, I'm afraid." I grinned, then took the beer he offered me, and we all clunked bottles in a toast.

Kelly squealed at first, then got quiet and a little teary. "Are you all right, sweetheart?" I asked, afraid of the answer.

She hesitated, blowing her nose. Finally, she nodded. "But of course, you know that there's no way I'm sharing a bathroom with Greg and Martin."

"Of course," I said, smoothing her hair—even the part with the pink streak. I watched her leave the room, and I wanted to follow her. Why, I had no idea. It wasn't like I could do or say anything else, really. I just wanted her to know I was still there.

Martin shook Carl's hand like a gentleman. "I wish you much happiness," he said, so formally I would have laughed, had I not been on the verge of tears instead. Then he didn't say another word about it; he went off to play a video game, just like nothing had happened. Or—just like he was determined that nothing had happened.

But in the days after that, he did spend a lot of time up on top of the garden shed. And I spent a lot of time watching him, hiding behind the curtain in my bedroom so he wouldn't see.

Greg was the last person we told. Carl stood with his arm wrapped around my waist so tightly he left an imprint of a thumb just below my rib cage. "Greg, I don't think this will come as a surprise, but we're getting married. Her"—Carl jerked his head toward me—"and me."

"She and I," I whispered. Carl looked at me blankly.

"That's nice." Greg shrugged. Then he calmly produced an impressive collection of boarding school brochures. "I'll really miss you guys, but after all, there's always Christmas break."

Carl's face got very tight, and his jaw worked back and forth. Then he laughed and hugged Greg. "That was a good one, buddy. You almost had me!"

Greg, I noticed, did not return the laughter. Or the hug. He just stared at me over his father's shoulders, his eyes big and black and expressionless. I shivered, but kept smiling that deranged preschool teacher smile. I wondered if it would leave my face, ever again.

Kelly appeared one evening before I went to bed, slightly hysterical. "Mommy? Who's going to walk me down the aisle when I get married? I mean, who? Daddy or Carl?" She flung herself down on my bed and sobbed and sobbed until I thought she was going to make herself sick.

"Oh, sweetheart, don't worry about that right now! Whoever you want to, that's who. Daddy will always be Daddy. Carl will be—"

And I stopped. Because I didn't know. I just hugged her until she was breathing like a normal person again, and when she went back to her room I spent ten minutes picking up the phone to call Doctor Dan, then changing my mind and putting it back in place again. Over and over. And that night, I slept on the floor, curled up in my comforter, once more.

"Mom?" Martin sank down into his seat at the kitchen table the next morning at breakfast. I stared at him, my eyes puffy and heavy with all the sleep I didn't get the night before. "I just want you to know that I'm not going to change my last name."

I froze, my spoon hovering over a pan of oatmeal.

"Oh," I said. "That's all right." I guessed. I hoped.

"Yeah, there's no way I want people to know that I'm semi-related to that dorkwad."

"Why don't you like him, Martin?"

"Because. He's so lame. Such a geek."

I opened my mouth—about to point out that he and Greg were both in cartooning club, both devoted to video games, and both comic book savants. But then I shut my mouth, realizing, finally, that this was probably the problem. Because they each recognized in the other their worst fears about themselves.

But I was too sleepy and raw to try to psychoanalyze anyone just now, so I switched off the burner and spooned out Martin's oatmeal, giving him a quick, swooping kiss on the temple. Then I threw the saucepan in the sink without even rinsing it out,

even though I knew perfectly well that oatmeal dries to the con-
sistency of cement if you just let it sit there, which I did, which
shows how messed up I was—and shuffled, like a zombie, up to
my bathroom. Massaging my temples, I pulled out my secret stash
of sexy single-women magazines—*Cosmopolitan*, *Glamour*, *ELLE*.
I hadn't read those kinds of magazines in years.

But suddenly, for some reason, I couldn't stop buying them.

"Are you sure this is a good idea?" I whispered to Carl as we got
out of my minivan.

"Absolutely," he said, plopping his ball cap on his head with
a defiant tug.

"I'm not so sure. . . ." I watched as three teenagers slid out of
the minivan. Three very different teenagers, two against one—
Martin and Kelly tumbled out of one side of the van; Greg the
other. Then they stood, more alike than they would have
dreamed—arms folded, heads averted, eyes trained to the ground.

"Isn't this fun?" Carl asked as we walked through the vast,
empty parking lot of the half-finished Astro Park-O-Dome Field.
He had decided this was to be our first official family outing—
watching the boys in their first Little League game, an exhibition
game to raise funds for the new stadium. "Well, isn't it?"

Martin grunted. Kelly sighed. Greg snorted.

"Isn't the new stadium going to be awesome?" I asked as we
entered the concourse, where, unfortunately, the new Starbucks
wasn't yet open. Although lots of pierced young people in black
were lined up to fill out applications.

Martin rolled his eyes. Kelly flipped her hair. Greg snorted.

"Doesn't that popcorn smell good?" Carl wondered.

"Anyone up for a Coke?" I queried.

"When are we going to stop talking in questions?" Carl's
mouth was pulled tight in a forced smile.

"When someone answers." I sighed, defeated.

We stopped in the middle of the concourse. Martin and Greg looked so different in their identical outfits—Greg rather doughy and lumpy, yet somehow managing to wear his pinstripes with ease, with comfortable-looking creases and slouches. Martin, however, looked uncertain and stiff, his costume far too pressed and new, I realized with a sinking sensation in the pit of my stomach.

"Birdie, did you iron Martin's uniform?" Carl looked at me in dismay.

"Um, maybe. . . ."

"Is that *starch* in his shirt?"

"Could be. . . ."

Carl shook his head, while Greg tittered and Martin turned red.

"I told you, Mom!"

"I'm sorry. I just wanted you to look nice for your first game!"

"Look, I gotta go." Greg sauntered off toward the locker rooms, expertly tossing a baseball up in the air and catching it with the same hand. "Don't wait around for me after the game. I can catch a ride with somebody."

"Nonsense—I thought we'd all go out for some ice cream!" Carl called after him.

Martin groaned. Kelly stamped her foot. This time, *I* snorted.

"Sweetheart, don't try so hard. We made it this far, don't go for the gold right away."

Carl's forehead wrinkled like a sleepy puppy's, his eyes all big and brown and sad. But he nodded in agreement.

"I guess I'd better go, too. . . ." Martin followed Greg—but not too closely. And when he tossed his baseball in the air, he missed.

I bit my lip. I didn't have a good feeling about this game. Not at all.

"Birdie!"

Carrie was sitting at a table festooned with bunting and balloons. PTA GALA DINNER/SILENT AUCTION!!! declared a big, hand-lettered sign. (Decorated by Mrs. Peterson's second-grade class. The PTA never underestimated the selling power of children's artwork. Stick some crooked hearts and flowers and a few stick figures on anything and you can increase the value by at least fifty percent.)

"How's the fund-raising going?" I strolled over.

"Well, we have a problem."

"What?"

"Them." She nodded across the room to another table, guarded by two old men in funny red hats.

"Who?"

"Shriners." Carrie's nostrils flared in disgust.

"Oh."

"They're raising funds for the stadium, too. Remember the Great Newspaper Drive of oh-two? For the Children's Hospital? They kicked our butt. I *hate* them."

"Well, it was for charity—"

"I mean, how can we compete with men in tiny cars? How, I ask you?"

As if to prove her point, at that moment two chubby men in miniature cars roared through the concourse. The tiny police car had "Smokey" painted on each door, the tiny Firebird was christened "The Bandit." The gathering crowd clapped and cheered.

"Shriners," Carrie hissed.

"Try not to let it get to you. And for heaven's sake, don't let the air out of their tires this time!" I squeezed her shoulder in PTA solidarity, then rejoined Carl and Kelly as we walked through the rest of the unfinished concourse. It was enormous, unpainted, made of dull, hard surfaces like brick and concrete and steel beams. None of the food vendors was open yet—there were a lot of empty rooms with counters—no machinery was in place, only a couple of portable popcorn stands and a vending machine. Finally we made it out into the stadium itself, blinking up at the sun. It was vast, overwhelming; I felt like we were gladiators walking out into the Colosseum. Although there were only about ten rows of seats finished, the skeleton of the structure rose endlessly up in the air, dotted with cranes and construction equipment dangling between steel beams. The grass on the field wasn't all the way in yet; it was just a green haze on brown dirt.

But Mayor Linseed stood on the pitcher's mound, waving at parents, his chins jiggling in greeting.

"Welcome, welcome!" he boomed into his handheld microphone. He was dressed in a huge, tentlike baseball shirt, which he didn't even try to tuck into his black-blue jeans (nicely ironed so that there was a neat, crisp crease running down each leg—which I refrained from pointing out to Carl). He wore his usual shiny black Italian loafers, and even though he was wearing a baseball cap, he still looked as if he needed a top hat.

"Welcome to the future Astro Park-O-Dome Field!"

"Do you think this is safe?" I asked Carl as we shuffled into the stands. One of the cranes dangled directly overhead.

"Do you really think he'd have a game here if it wasn't?"

"I don't know." I held myself still and waited for something to tingle—the back of my neck, the hair on my head—some sign that my Super Mom Sense was kicking into gear, which it always did when a child was in danger. But nothing tingled. Except my thigh, where Carl had parked his hand. "Stop it!" I slapped it away before Kelly could see.

"Sorry." He smiled sheepishly. "Habit."

"Well, get over it. We're getting married—no more sex!"

"What?"

"I mean—well, you know what I mean. Not in front of the kids."

Suddenly the Astro Park Jetpacks ran out of the dugout in their bright new blue uniforms, arms and legs winter-pale in contrast. "Oh, look, they're going out on the baseball emerald!"

"Diamond," Carl moaned.

"Martin! Yoo-hoo! Martin, over here!" I stood and waved; Martin turned his head away from me, pretending not to hear.

"Birdie!" Carl yanked me back down. "What are you doing?"

"Waving! Oh, look at that smudge on his costume—he's going to look just awful before the game even starts!"

"Birdie! Jesus Christ!"

I stared at Carl, shocked. He'd never spoken that way to me before. "What?"

"You have got to get a grip. This is baseball—a sport. Martin will get dirty. He might even get scraped and bruised. But you can't act like . . . like . . . such a mother! He's almost fourteen. And this is baseball!"

"So you keep saying." I kicked my sneakered foot against the seat in front of me. "All right, I'll try to behave. But honestly, I don't understand what all the fuss is about. . . ."

"Oh, I see Vienna!" Kelly waved at a girl in a tank top—even though it was only sixty degrees out—and low-rider jeans with black hair (complete with purple streak).

"What's she doing here?" I watched as Vienna waved at Kelly and started toward us, trying in vain to tug her tank top over her belly.

"Oh, her brother's on the team, and even though her dad totally ignores her, he makes her come to the games. He's such a jerk." Kelly shook her head.

"Kelly! I do not want you talking about other people's fathers like that! You don't know what goes on in anyone's home. You only hear one side of the story, and it's Vienna's."

"Well, trust me. If you'd ever met him you'd agree."

"That doesn't matter."

"Sorry," Kelly grumbled. Then she and Vienna squealed and hugged and admired each other's hair.

"Hello, Vienna," I said with a tight smile. "How are you?"

Vienna's pierced nostrils flared. She shrugged. I pursed my lips.

"We're going to go over to the concession stand, okay, Mom?"

I consulted Carl, who had planned the outing—and who had been watching the squealing and the hugging and the piercing and the streaks with a stricken look on his face, as if he had just discovered a rare and dangerous animal. Which he had, in a way— the teenaged girl. I patted his knee in sympathy; he had a lot to learn, too.

"I think it's all right, don't you?"

All he could do was nod. Kelly and Vienna squealed, then sauntered, oh-so-cool, over to the stand, where they parked, hands on hips, looking as if they weren't trying to be looked at. Carl shook his head, and I gave him a sympathetic hug.

Mary Denton was waving at us, two rows down. "We're going to have a championship team this year!" she squealed.

"I hope so!" I shouted back. "Did you see Martin? Doesn't he look adorable in his costume? I took him out the other night to buy him a cup—I hope we got the right size, and— Hey!" I glared at Carl, who had punched me in the arm. "What did you do that for?"

"Oy vey," is all he said, dropping his head in his hands.

"That hurt!"

"Birdie, for God's sake, stop shouting about Martin's cup. And stop saying that he looks adorable in his costume—which is a uniform, by the way. I should have known better than to bring a girl to a baseball game."

"Well, now that was uncalled for!" I turned away from him.

We sat in silence, watching the boys. Greg moved with surprising grace on the field—scooping up the ball, throwing it in one fluid motion. While Martin—didn't. He lunged and ran and tried to catch, but always a step behind, like the worst dancer in the chorus line. I still had no idea who the peachy brunette was, but her allure had to be considerable to make him put himself through this. Because even I could see, from way up in the stands, that his teammates weren't exactly throwing or hitting the ball in his direction. At least not on purpose. And it made my mother's heart ache— that familiar ache, the one I always get when I know my child is going to get hurt and there's nothing I can do to prevent it.

"Martin doesn't look bad out there," Carl said just then, and I forgave him for whatever he had just done—and for whatever he might do in the foreseeable future.

"You think?"

"I think. In fact, I think they all look pretty good. Maybe we will have a championship team—which will make the mayor happy, since he'll have a lot easier time raising money."

"Well, they look good to me . . . oh, my!" Another group of baseball players emerged, blinking, into the bright sunlight. "Who's that?"

"That can't be Smallville! Did they send the wrong team?" Carl sat up straight; Mary Denton clutched her ample bosom and gasped. There was a frenzied buzz among the parents in the stands.

For trotting around the bases was a team—of what looked like thirty-year-olds. Masquerading as Little Leaguers, the word "Smallville" on their massive chests, and "Li'l Giants" on their broad backs.

"That kid has a beard!" I pointed. "There's no way he's a seventh-grader!"

"They must have sent the wrong team," Carl repeated, as if he could make it come true.

One of the "seventh-graders" paused, looked up in the stands, bared his teeth, and growled. Then he continued to lap the field, barely breaking a sweat.

"They're ringers. They have to be!" Carl jumped up and ran toward Coach Henderson, who was clutching a post in the dugout and pouring Pepto-Bismol down his throat. Mayor Linseed, meanwhile, stood in the middle of the field, microphone dangling at his side, apparently, for the first time in his illustrious career, speechless. He simply stared, his mouth open, his rimless glasses falling down upon his shiny nose, as the Smallville Li'l Giants grunted and growled through a series of warm-ups—including one-handed push-ups—while the Astro Park Jetpacks huddled together, whimpering in fear.

"Move your butt, Brian! Hustle, hustle, hustle, what'd I tell you? What did I say?" An undersized man with a sharp face ran behind the dugout. I recognized him as the man in the grocery store—Mr. Derringer. And Brian was out there on the field, a frail, pale figure trotting diligently past one of the bases.

"Not him," Carl groaned, returning to his seat.

"Do you know him?"

"Everybody knows him. He's been warned and warned about his behavior."

"What do you mean?"

"Oh, just wait." Carl took his baseball cap off and folded it in two, then put it back on his head.

"What did Coach say about the other team?"

"He didn't. He just kept clutching his stomach and moaning. But I saw the paperwork—that's the seventh-grade team, all right."

"What, were they all held back a few years?"

"No, but . . . well, I hope it's not what I'm thinking."

"What?"

"Ever hear of José Canseco?"

"Is he one of the Three Tenors?"

Carl groaned. "I have so much to teach you, grasshopper."

"Before we sing the national anthem," Mayor Linseed boomed from the field, recovering his composure, "I'd like to point out some of the construction going on here at the Astro Park-O-Dome Field. As you can see we still have a lot of work to do, but I'm happy to announce that the school board met last night and agreed to donate funds as long as the schools can use the facility. To which I say, of course! Anything to complete this wonderful venue for the youth of our town. Right, kids?" He beckoned to the Jetpacks, who shuffled over to him in a clearly rehearsed move. Mayor Linseed spread his arms wide, as if to embrace the entire team.

"Aren't they worth it, folks? Aren't they? Let's hear it for our valiant ball team—the best Astro Park has to offer. . . ." He broke off, looked over at the Smallville dugout, full of lounging mini Arnold Schwarzeneggers, and gulped. Then he leaned down to Jimmy Denton. "Better eat your Wheaties, son. Er, as I was saying, let's hear it for the future of our beloved hometown!" His Honor flashed his "V" for Victory sign, then couldn't resist a quick "Vote for Linseed!" as he herded the team back to the dugout amid wild applause from the forty or so parents in the stands.

"I wonder if he says that all the time," I whispered to Carl. "Like, say, after . . ."

"You'd probably have to ask Mrs. Linseed about that."

The umpire took his place behind home plate. "Play ball!" he shouted with a theatrical flourish of his arms.

Carl gripped my arm as the first humongous Li'l Giant walked up to the plate, swinging a bat. I looked at the field—Martin wasn't there. He was in the dugout, seated next to three other boys whose costumes—I mean uniforms—looked shiny and pressed, too.

Greg, however, was crouched down at third base, swaying side to side, punching his glove. Cute little Johnny Twelvehawks from down the street, whose face was always hidden by his baseball cap yet was the ace pitcher for the Jetpacks—threw the ball.

The Astro Park parents leaned forward, holding their collective breath. "Strike!" the umpire whooped, and then we all relaxed, chattering nervously. *Well, let's play some ball!" "Those kids don't look so tough to me!" "I think it's going to be a great season!"* The Li'l Giant slugger took a step away from the plate with a snort. Johnny beamed. Coach Henderson put down his Pepto-Bismol bottle. Johnny threw again.

Crack!!!! The meeting of bat and ball was thunderous; the ball sailed over the heads of all the Astro Park Jetpacks, who simply stood, staring at it with their mouths open. It flew over the back fence. It looked as if it could keep flying for days.

The not-so-Li'l Giant rounded the bases, returning to home plate without breaking a sweat. Mayor Linseed, sitting in the dugout next to the Jetpacks, wiped his brow with a sparkling white handkerchief—handed to him, naturally, by the omnipresent Jasper, whose greasy hair kept hiding his face so that I could never get a good look at his expression. For some reason, I was dying to know how he felt about being kept on such a short leash. But with his curved body, almost in an S shape so that his head was always hanging low between his shoulder blades, and that hair, he was a cipher.

"Here we go," groaned Carl, hitting his knee with his ball cap. And so it went, inning after agonizing inning. Jetpacks tossed, stumbled, swung, dropped; Li'l Giants threw, leaped, hit, and caught. By the seventh inning the score was 17–0. (And Mayor Linseed had gone through twelve handkerchiefs.)

Parents started grumbling in the stands.

"Coach needs to get tougher on those kids."

"When's the weight room going to open? The entire outfield needs upper-body strength training."

"I say we add an extra practice. They don't need to sleep in on Sunday mornings."

"They're just kids!" I couldn't help it; the words burst out of me. "It's just a game!"

One mother sitting behind me gasped and covered her young son's ears with her hands.

"She doesn't know what she's saying, folks. She's new." Carl stood up and put his arm, protectively, around my waist. I threw it off and glared at him, plopping down in my seat and staring at the field as the teams switched places. Martin remained on the bench, which broke my heart. Particularly when I saw him sit straight up, twist around to look in the stands, and turn such a bright shade of red that it provided a very nice contrast to the crisp blue and white of his uniform.

I could also see, out of the corner of my eye, a cascade of hair making its way toward the seats behind the dugout. Brunette hair. Hair that, even from way up here, looked as if it could smell of peaches.

"Oh!" I plopped down, my legs suddenly unable to hold my heavy mother's heart.

"What's wrong, Birdie?"

"Nothing." Which was the biggest lie I'd ever told in my life. Because Martin turned around, looked at the brunette, whose face I still couldn't see, and smiled. A smile that shattered my heart in two; a beatific, openmouthed, helpless smile.

The smile of a man willing to go into debt in order to provide a lifetime supply of *gum*.

"Oh, please—" I crossed my fingers and prayed that Coach would put Martin in so he could show off in front of his paramour—even as I was still making sense of a world in which my son was so obviously in love.

"Mother, this is stupid. Do we have to stay any longer?" Kelly and Vienna had returned.

"Hmm, sure, no, I guess, whatever. . . ." I hardly looked at them, intent as I was upon the spectacle of Martin leaning, elbow cocked, casually against a pole in the dugout—James Bond in pinstripes—while talking to Coach Henderson, obviously lobbying to get in the game. In order to impress this gold-digging, gum-chewing hussy.

Kelly mumbled and held out her hand; I reached into my pocket, grabbed something, and handed it to her without thinking. "Bye!" And she evaporated, like blond smoke, tugging Vienna after her.

"What did you just do?" Carl turned to me.

"Huh?" I blinked, shook my head, pulling my gaze away from Martin.

"You gave Kelly the keys to the van."

"I *what*?"

"You just gave Kelly the car keys, and she and Vienna left."

"Where were they going? When will they be back? Is anyone going with them? Does she have her cell phone?"

"I don't know."

"Well, why not? You don't give car keys to teenagers without asking these questions!"

"You just did," Carl pointed out.

"Damn." I kicked the seat in front of me. "I'm off my game, and it's all Martin's fault. How are we going to get home?"

"Beats me."

"Oh—look!" I pointed; Martin was running out to third base—the base previously guarded by Greg.

"Well," Carl said, pulling on his chin thoughtfully. "I guess they are down by seventeen so it shouldn't matter. . . ."

"What's that supposed to mean?"

"Nothing, it's just that Greg is the starter, but since they're down by so much nothing can really hurt them at this point. . . ."

"I can't believe you said that! Martin should play, too—it's not fair for Greg to be the third base hog!"

"He's not a hog! He's the starting player—and he's played third base for ten years. How long has Martin played?"

"That's not the point!"

"Oh, yes, it is!"

"I think," I said, licking my lips, "we'd better not discuss this any further."

Carl took several deep breaths and stared intently at his hands. Then finally he nodded. "You're right. I'm sorry. It's very— nice—that Martin gets to play."

"Thank you." We both turned to watch the game, already in play—just as a ball rolled through Martin's legs. "Oh," I said, my heart breaking all over again.

Carl took his hat off and hit his knee. Then he smashed it back on top of his head and patted my shoulder.

"That Smallville team is tough."

"Yeah."

"Nobody's having any luck against them."

"Yeah."

"It'll all be over soon."

"Yeah."

Although he was wrong about that. It was, I later discovered, the longest inning ever recorded in Little League history. Fourteen more Smallville runs were scored, twelve of them a direct result of Martin making what I thought were perfectly understandable mistakes. Like, you know, having the ball bounce off the top of his head as he was running back to catch a pop fly.

Finally, mercifully, the inning was over, and Astro Park was up to bat.

"Pinch-hitting for Martin Lee is Greg Sayers," the announcer said over the loudspeaker.

"What does that mean?" I turned to Carl, who was grinning.

"Nothing. Just that Greg's going to take Martin's place at bat."

"That hardly seems fair—"

But before he could answer, we both turned and stared at home plate, where Brian Derringer was huddled, bat trembling in his hands.

"Brian! Look at me! What was that? Why did you swing at that, you idiot?" His father paced behind the home plate fence, his face pinched, his tiny eyes pinpricks of disgust.

The Smallville Li'l Giant pitched again. This time Brian didn't swing, but the ump called out, "Stee-rike!"

"*What?!!*" Mr. Derringer turned purple. "What? Are you stupid, ump? Are you blind? What the hell kind of call was that?"

"And you!" The little weasel trained his wrath on his son once more. "Just standing there. Like a lump. If it had been a strike you weren't ready to swing at it! What were you thinking? What were you—"

A huge hand clamped itself on Derringer's shoulder. Coach Henderson leaned in and spoke into his ear.

"What?" Mr. Derringer sputtered.

Coach leaned in again, apparently not wanting anyone else to hear.

"What did you say?" Derringer shook his hand off.

"I said," Coach Henderson boomed, "you are being ejected

from this game. From all our games. Your son is welcome to stay but you are not."

All eyes were pinned on the wiry man standing behind home plate, fairly vibrating with rage.

"You can't—you can't—"

"Yes, I can."

"Try it." Derringer drew a line in the sand. Coach Henderson pushed his huge hands—the size of oven mitts—into his pockets with admirable self-control.

"Excuse me," I said to Carl, who just looked at me and nodded. And then I ran toward the ladies' room, my Jolly Green Giant tote bag, which never left my side, clutched to my chest, the top of my head singing, every nerve quivering—

Super Mom Sense propelling me toward an empty bathroom stall, where I changed into my costume in record time, before the stall door had even stopped swinging. I pushed through it, tying my apron, tugging my mask, hopping on one foot as I pulled on the other high-heeled pump—pausing only to zap up a patch of mud by the door.

"Oops!" I ran smack into Janitor Bingo, who was coming into the ladies' room pushing a mop and roller bucket.

"You!" He dropped his mop and stared.

"Oh, hello, Janitor Bingo!"

"Wait—did you just clean that—?" Janitor Bingo pointed to the sparkling spot on the floor, his one eye gleaming, his shoulders shaking.

"You bet! Thanks aren't necessary, really—it's my job!"

"But—but—"

"Gotta run!" I waved and ran back outside.

Coach Henderson and Derringer hadn't moved; Coach was standing with his arms across his big chest, a vein on his neck throbbing. Derringer was still screaming, his ferret face pinched and purple. "You can't make me. It's my right! No one can make me leave!"

Meanwhile, Brian had appeared to shrink; his little arms and legs, so spindly already, seemed to fold into his uniform so that it hung on him like a pin-striped potato sack.

"What's going on, Coach?" I stepped smoothly between the two men; Greg, who was standing on deck, swinging his bat, caught my eye and swallowed.

"Hello there, Super Mom. I was just asking this gentleman to leave the premises," Coach growled.

"Well then, I'd be happy to escort him out." I turned to Derringer.

"I'm not going anywhere!"

"Daddy?"

We all turned and looked at Brian, who had walked around the fence to tug on his father's sleeve. "Daddy, let's just go. It's all right, let's just go."

"You would say that, wouldn't you? You want to quit? Fine. Then quit." And Derringer grabbed the bat out of his son's hand and threw it with all his might—over the fence, heading in a line drive straight at Greg. Everyone gasped; out of the corner of my eye I saw Carl begin to leap over seats, his arms outstretched, as if he could catch the bat himself. I turned my head and saw the bat tumbling, end over end, in slow motion—Greg stood still, unable to move—

But I could. I streaked around the fence and somehow, before I could tell it to, my right hand flung a steady stream of cleaning fluid right in the path of the bat, forming a liquid force field in front of Greg. The bat hit it and bounced back, falling to the ground, where it rolled away harmlessly. I turned around just as Mr. Derringer, Brian in his clutches, was trying to back away.

"You!" I thundered with my Mighty Roar, striding over to them. "Leave the boy alone!"

Derringer blinked, not moving. Brian whimpered, "Daddy?"

"Let him go!" I raised my right hand, prepared to fling the most powerful cleaning fluid known to man right in his beady little eyes.

"No!" Brian stepped in front of his father.

"What?" I lowered my hand, surprised. And just a little disappointed.

"Don't hurt my daddy!"

"But, sweetie, I'm just worried about you."

"You don't have to be." Brian's voice dropped, as did his gaze.

"Brian, look at me." I lifted his chin. "Has your father ever hurt you?"

"No." He shook his head, his big brown eyes never leaving mine. And I looked way down into his soul, his heart; I saw everything. I saw a child. A gentle, timid child, wanting desperately to please; a child capable of so much love, so much laughter. A child withering without being the recipient of the same. But I didn't see a child who had ever been abused—at least, not physically.

"You're telling the truth," I said, surprised to hear myself say it.

Brian nodded, his pointed chin quivering.

"Of course he's telling the truth!" Brian's father grabbed his arm again, too roughly for my tastes, but not rough enough for me to do anything about it. "Now if you don't mind . . ."

"Oh, but I do. I don't ever want to see you around here again. Do you hear me?"

"How are you going to stop me?" He leaned his face into mine, his yellowish teeth bared; I recoiled from his sneer. (Not to mention his bad breath.)

"Oh, I have—"

All of a sudden a crash of organ music broke over the PA system, playing the first few bars of "Take Me Out to the Ballgame." Then it segued into "The Hokey-Pokey." Then it stopped, mid-chord, and a deep, raspy voice came on over the loudspeakers. "Testing . . . testing . . ." A throat cleared. *"Super Mom! Stop interfering in the town of Astro Park!"*

"Excuse me? I'm in the middle of something here. . . ."

A crazy, maniacal cackle echoed throughout the empty seats in the half-finished stadium. Heads craned this way and that, looking for the source.

"Super Mom, go away! We don't need you anymore! Not after what you did to New Cosmos Industries!"

"Oh, for Pete's sake! Move on, people! It was for your own good!" I spun around, looking up, down, sideways, looking for a glimpse of—

Way up high, up on one of the cranes hovering over the dugouts, I saw something move. I jumped away from the crowd near home plate and ran toward the pitcher's mound, my high heels sinking into the turf. "Not the Bermuda grass!" I heard the mayor yell.

"Who are you? What are you talking about?" I called up to the sky. Then I realized I was taunting an evil villain while surrounded by Little Leaguers, and I came to my senses, shooing all the kids back toward their dugouts (while reaching into the pockets of my Apron of Anticipation and passing out apple juice and animal crackers).

"Here you go, guys, I'm sure you're a little hungry!"

"Thanks, Super Mom!" Jimmy Denton piped up. One of the Li'l Giants drank his juice in one huge gulp, crushed the box against his forehead, and grunted.

I stopped, perched atop the pitcher's mound, my hands on my hips (Classic Superhero Pose #1), and shouted at the swaying crane.

"You want a piece of me? Do ya, punk? Well, show your face!"

Another maniacal cackle filled the stadium.

"Never! But I'll haunt your dreams forever, you second-rate cleaning lady!"

"I am not a cleaning lady! I am a *superhero!*"

More laughter. Then more organ music—*"Na na na na, na na na na, hey hey hey, good-bye!"*

"Go away, or else!"

"Make me!" I shouted up at the crane. Which started to sway as a dot, dangling on the end of a chain, swung down toward the field, getting bigger and bigger. The crowd gasped, ducking, as a figure flew out over the stands. I stood my ground, every muscle tensed, coiled, waiting to jump into superhero action.

The figure got nearer and nearer, until I could make it out. I blinked, not quite believing my eyes. For hurtling toward me was a slight figure with a bucket on his head, wearing a gray jumpsuit, a makeshift suit of armor fashioned out of trash can lids, and thick-soled industrial work boots. He wielded a mop with one hand while holding on to the chain with the other. And tucked under that arm—I couldn't quite believe my eyes—was a Swiffer WetJet.

"What the heck?" I ducked as he swung over me, cackling. "You can't be seri— Ouch!"

For the figure bopped me on the head with the mop.

"Hey! That hurts! Watch it!"

"Leave now, or I'll bop you again!" he boomed in a raspy voice, still resonating over the PA. I spied a wire dangling from underneath the bucket; he must have had a cordless microphone

in there. He spun around in midair and twirled the mop like a
nunchuck.

"Come down from that thing right now, young man. You
might hurt yourse— Hey!" For he bopped me again, this time
getting a little too close to my eyes.

"Fear the wrath! Fear the wrath of the Phantom of the Bullpen!"

I laughed. So did the crowd, which had come out of hiding
to watch. I felt like this strange, comical figure and I were part of
some surreal halftime show.

"That's it? The Phantom of the Bullpen? That's all you've
got? How cute!"

"I am not cute. *Prepare to die!*" And the Phantom of the
Bullpen aimed his Swiffer, pulled the trigger, and fired.

Only whatever was in it wasn't just cleaning fluid. Whatever
was in it *burned*. It burned a hole through my Apron of Anticipation, through my dress, and scorched my tender upper-thigh
region. I bent over in pain, gasping, my flesh branded.

The Phantom of the Bullpen cackled again, his laugh reverberating in the metal bucket upon his head. He swung back and
forth, just out of reach.

"Do you fear me now, you second-rate cleaning woman?"

"I . . . you . . ." I struggled upright, my hand on my leg.
When I pulled it away, a little bit of skin came with it, and I
swallowed a wave of nausea.

"Listen to me, Super Mom." The Phantom of the Bullpen
stopped swinging. *"Never show your face here again, or I'll see to it that
this stadium never opens. I'll tear it down, brick by brick. I'll blow it up if
I have to. I'll make sure that Astro Park never again forgets about me!"*

"What? What do you mean, forgets about you?"

In answer, the Phantom of the Bullpen cackled. He swooped
toward me, Swiffer raised—

But this time I was ready. I raised my right hand, pointed,

and the twin arcs of fluid collided in the air, forming one mighty—

Jolt. Of something. Something that sent an electric shock up my arms so powerful that we both screamed, hurtling in opposite directions, the Phantom flying up toward space, me toward the ground. I fell with a thud, twitching and jumping and inhaling a brain-freezing blast of ammonia, bleach, Swiffer, and a lot of other things I couldn't name. My lungs burned, my eyes; the stadium grew fuzzy and I grew weak. I rolled around on the dirt gasping, wheezing, singing along to the organ music, which suddenly began to play . . .

"*He flies through the air, with the greatest of ease . . .*"

The song. That stupid song, always popping into my head at my weakest moments.

"*That daring young man on the flying trapeze . . .*"

The nursery song I'd sung to Kelly and Martin when they were little. The song that had called to me across my dearest memories on the morning of my Origin, the first time I did something stupid with a Swiffer. . . .

The song I was singing, softly now; a crowd gathered around me, murmuring and buzzing. Coach Henderson had great big tears in his eyes; Mayor Linseed—unaccompanied, for once, by Jasper—was wringing his hands and saying something about how this couldn't be good publicity for the new stadium. Mr. Derringer and Brian seemed to have disappeared.

As had two other people. I tried to lift my head but it was too heavy . . . I tried to find Kelly and Martin, tried to tell them I'd be all right, that they shouldn't worry, I'd be just fine . . . but then I remembered that Kelly was gone, she'd driven herself away. And Martin—where was Martin?

Oh yes. I remembered a cascade of brunette hair, smelled peaches—peaches everywhere, peaches in the soft breeze that fanned over me, cooling my fevered brow—and started to sob, pitifully, at the memory of my son's love-struck smile.

My head lolled over to the other side . . . Carl . . . where was Carl? I heard his voice call out my name, but when I looked up the face I saw wasn't his.

It was that of a pasty, puffy boy with sweaty black hair plastered on his forehead, terror in his eyes, a trembling lip. . . .

And warm, steady hands that reached out to me, grasping my own, as I mumbled, "Greg?" He nodded, started to say something, but what it was, I'll never know.

Because just then I looked up. The Phantom had vanished into thin air, leaving an empty chain dangling from the crane. However. A tiny dot was coming toward me—a dot that got bigger and bigger, blotting out the sky . . . all I could do was lie there, watching it, as a plastic bottle of Mr. Clean came hurtling toward me. I gasped, unable to move as the bald genie's head got bigger and bigger, seeming to suspend itself for one final moment as he winked at me, a bold, lascivious wink.

Right before the bottle hit me on the head and knocked me out cold, capping off the series of events leading to my Second Horrible Swiffer Accident.

CHAPTER 7

heard their voices before I saw them. Like the sound of water rippling over polished river stones, it was a musical babble, teasing, beckoning. I tried to find the source; I parted tall grass and brushed cobwebs out of my eyes, searching, searching. I turned left; the babbling faded. I turned right; louder now, louder still. The sun emerged from a cloud and I had to shield my eyes as I plowed ahead, getting ever closer. Finally I could make out what they were saying—

"And then I turned around to see who was shooting at me, and it was a giant Elmer Fudd!" Martin's voice sounded odd; light, happy, like a baby bird's.

"That's silly!" Kelly laughed. "A giant Elmer Fudd!"

"And then in front of me there was Bugs Bunny! And I ducked 'cause then I knew that Elmer wasn't aiming at me. And then I fell down. And then I woke up."

"That's the silliest dream!" Kelly laughed again; silver tinkling, like jingle bells.

"What's this about a giant Elmer Fudd?" I joined them on a faded picnic blanket, that old comforter my mother had given me as a wedding present. Someone had packed a picnic lunch with real fried chicken, carrots, apples, and brownies. I picked up a carrot but I didn't eat it.

"Martin! He had a silly dream!" Kelly fell backward and looked up at the sky. The clouds drew shadows across her freckled face, her jaw padded with that softness of childhood.

"Silly Billy." I tickled Martin, who giggled and squirmed, all sharp bones, despite the soft curve of his chubby cheeks.

"Who wants to go fishing?" I smiled as I heard the deep voice, familiar, yet—not. I hadn't heard it for such a long time. Or had I? Wasn't it just this morning that he asked me to make him poached eggs, not scrambled? "Kids? Birdie? Anybody?"

I turned, a smile on my face. I reached out my arms, and Dan pulled me to my feet.

"Look, I brought the fishing poles. I told you I wouldn't forget them!" The sun bleached his blond hair, thinning a little (although I'd never tell him that, ever), almost white. I couldn't see his eyes, though—the sun was too bright. It was funny how the sun could highlight some things and obscure others. I never could figure out how. Or why.

"Not me. But you three go ahead. I'll clean up here." I leaned up for a kiss, but he had turned to run after Martin, who was scampering down to the creek bed.

"Martin, wait up—don't go down there without me!"

I watched as Kelly and Dan caught up with Martin, each reaching out to grab a hand. They walked down the narrow path toward the creek, and I smiled. I looked at them, my perfect family, and waited for that familiar glow of contentment to radiate across my chest, which contained my heart, which belonged to the three of them. . . .

But it didn't come. There was an impatient itch instead. A funny little catch, as if something was wrong, something was out of place. It was like when you reach for a puzzle piece that you know will fit, but it doesn't, and you can't figure out where else it goes. Or what else could possibly fit in the empty place instead.

I looked again at the three of them. Dan turned and yelled something; I couldn't hear so I just stood there and shook my head. He yelled again. I took a couple of steps toward him.

"Birdie?" It was so faint, it didn't make sense. My own name didn't make sense.

"Birdie?" Louder now, stunning me into some sense of awareness. . . .

"Birdie?" A hand was shaking me, gently; I reached out to grab it and suddenly that puzzle piece clicked into place, and I smiled.

"I knew if I waited long enough, you'd come back," I whispered, feeling his knuckles, the soft hairs on the back of his hand, the long fingers.

"Birdie? What are you talking about?" Now his lips were on my forehead, so gentle. I wanted to go to sleep, but I also wanted to look at him, make sure he was real.

"What?" I opened my eyes, not sure I'd heard correctly. "What did you—?" Someone was looking down at me—someone with big brown eyes that glittered with fear, a weary, puzzled crease in his forehead, and a patient smile on his lips. I blinked, confused. "*Carl?* What are you doing here? Where's—?"

"Shhh . . . it's all right." Carl smiled down at me. "I think you were dreaming."

"What?" I wanted to rub my eyes, but my arm felt like it weighed fifty pounds. "I don't . . . I don't dream."

"But I think you were, sweetheart."

"What?" It seemed as if that was the only thing I could say; my mind felt too stupid and thick for anything to penetrate it.

"You passed out. You're at the Astro Park-O-Dome Field, remember?"

"Sort of." Whatever I was lying on wasn't very comfortable; I pushed myself up, head suddenly throbbing, and saw that I was on a bench. In an unfinished locker room.

"We had to put you in here until everybody left."

"Where's . . . ?" I looked around; Martin and Kelly were standing against the wall, their faces pale and pinched—the teenagers that they were, not the little children in my dream. I smiled—even as my heart lurched in disappointment—and they ran over.

"Mom, it was just like that day we found you in the bathroom!" Martin patted my arm.

"How did you get here?" I asked Kelly, who was frowning.

"I think you should be in a hospital." She didn't direct this at me; she folded her arms and threw it over her shoulders, toward Carl.

"I'm all right. But how did you get here? I thought you went shopping with Vienna."

"The miracle of modern technology," Carl said. "Cell phones."

Kelly glowered. "Why did he have my cell phone number?"

"I don't know, sweetheart, I suppose I gave it to him at some point . . . aren't you glad he did?"

"Well, I suppose . . . although I'm not entirely comfortable with the situation." She shook her head and stomped off toward the other side of me. She stood, her arms folded, glaring at Carl. While I sat there, tentatively feeling a growing lump in the middle of my forehead, a searing pain on my upper thigh, caught in the middle.

I heard a soft cough from a corner of the room, and

(painfully) turned. Greg was standing there. I smiled at him; he smiled back, and it was, I realized with another jolt to my system, the first time he'd ever done that. And that smile changed his whole person. It warmed his pasty skin, it made him seem taller, less hunched. It made him seem like a boy, a boy I could maybe get to like someday.

"I caught you. Before you fell down." He blushed, suddenly mortified, and looked down at his big black baseball cleats.

"I know." I smiled again, hoping to catch his eye. I reached out my hand to him—

But Martin grabbed it instead.

"So, we should probably go home," he said, rising. "To our house. The three of us."

"I'm not sure you should go anywhere yet, Birdie." Carl sat down beside me. "How do you feel?"

"Like I got run over by a truck."

"Last time we put her in bed and took care of her ourselves," Martin said, although like Kelly, he wouldn't look at Carl directly. "We took good care of her."

It was a testament to my loyalty as a mother that I could nod in agreement and pretend that they had. Because if memory served, they'd stuck me up there like an unwelcome great-aunt and forgot about me the rest of the night.

"I'm sure you did, but I'm here now." Carl kept smiling, but it was a tight, forced smile.

"Tell you what," I said. "Maybe we can all—"

"We really don't need your help, but thanks anyway." Kelly's voice had icicles hanging from it.

"Kelly!" I didn't know what had gotten into her; she'd always been so nice to Carl in the past.

"I know you did a good job before, but now that I'm here things can be a little different. Easier for you kids." Carl's voice was *extremely* pleasant; almost patronizing, actually, if you asked me. (Although nobody thought to.)

"Really, I don't think this is necessary, we can all work together—" I tried to stand up, but both Kelly and Carl pushed me back down.

"Sit down, you're not yourself, Mother."

"Birdie, please, just take it easy, I can handle this."

"Stop it, just let me up." I pushed my way to my feet, stood, took two wobbly steps, and ran smack into a brick wall of— something. Something that sent me reeling, stumbling backward, reaching for hands that helped me back to that bench. My eyes watered, my nostrils burned, and my sinuses felt like they were being yanked out through my eyeballs.

"Oh . . . oh . . ." So much, so much—*fragrance*. A nauseating, overwhelming patchwork of odors—grass, paint, Kelly's perfume, Martin's deodorant, recycled onions (courtesy of Carl's earlier hot dog), perspiration, the sticky-sweet smell of hairspray, soap, vanilla, wood smoke—and Swiffer cleaning fluid.

"What is it, Birdie? What?"

"I don't know—it just smells, all of a sudden. Do you notice it? It's making me sick to my stomach." I hung my head between my knees.

"Smells?" Martin sniffed. So did Kelly. So did Carl. So did Greg.

"I don't smell anything." Kelly wrinkled her nose.

"Me either," Carl said. Kelly glared at him.

Greg looked at me, sorrowfully, his dark eyes wide and sympathetic. But he, too, shook his head.

"Well, I smell—everything. Everything that can possibly be smelled, I'm smelling now." I closed my eyes; my senses were so assaulted I couldn't see straight. It was as if the very air around me was pulsating with scent.

"It must be from the accident," Martin said. "An aftershock or something."

"I guess. . . ." I opened my eyes; Martin was frowning, as if he were trying to work out a long math problem.

"I mean, when you think about it . . ." Carl's eyes took on that wild, absentminded-professor look, his hair standing up straight. "Who knows what else happened to you? There's precedence, you know—"

"Superman and red Kryptonite!" Martin snapped his fingers at Carl. Greg nodded. Then they all three started pacing, arms behind their backs, paths crossing.

"Superman and what?" I looked at Kelly, who shrugged, her freckled nose turned up, superior in her comic book ignorance.

"Red Kryptonite," Carl explained with a patient smile. "It gave him all sorts of strange side effects."

"Like what?"

"Well, I think he turned into a giant ant once, didn't he?" Martin asked Carl, who nodded with authority.

"A giant ant?" I felt faint.

"And he turned into a baby, don't forget that," Greg chimed in.

"Remember when he grew a third eye?" Martin asked.

"Where's a mirror—I need a mirror—"

"Birdie, you don't have a third eye," Carl said, whirling around to stare at me. "But who knows what else you might have? You might . . . I don't know . . . maybe you're flammable or something. . . ." He backed away a couple of steps. The kids all jumped behind him, afraid to take their eyes off me.

I stared back, holding myself perfectly still, too terrified to even scratch my nose, which was starting to itch from all the odors. I couldn't move; I was afraid I might zoom off the bench, turn invisible, or spontaneously self-combust.

"What do I do now?" I spoke as quietly as I could, careful not to disturb whatever new superpowers were bubbling up beneath my skin.

"I don't know," Carl said, pulling on his chin, thinking. "Try not to move too much."

"I am!"

"Don't get mad—remember the Incredible Hulk?" Martin asked, a wild gleam in his eyes.

"I don't want to turn green!" I started to cry.

"I don't want you to either!" Carl ran his fingers through his hair and started to pace again. "Okay, okay, let's just calm down. You look normal. Why don't you try to zap something up?"

"Do you think it's safe?" I flexed my hand and pointed it at the terrified group in front of me. They all four ducked.

"Wait a minute!" Martin ran to a closet; he rummaged around and emerged with a fire extinguisher. "Okay, go ahead!"

"Martin!"

"Just in case?"

"Thanks for the vote of confidence." I glared at him. Then I swallowed and tried to steady my trembling hands. "Okay." I took a big breath and aimed my right hand. A quick, hot jolt surged through my veins, and fluid came shooting out with much more force than usual—enough force to bore a hole through the concrete floor, barely missing Carl's feet.

"All right then." Carl looked down at the smoking hole.

"Wow." I gulped, impressed.

"I'd say you can clean with the power of twenty thousand Swiffers now," Martin said with a low, froggy whistle.

"Cool." My eyes watered from the ammonia, bleach, orange, and Swiffer fragrances—more concentrated than before, especially the ammonia—but other than that I suddenly felt fine. A little eager to find some really big mess to clean up, maybe. But fine.

"Okay?" Carl took a tentative step back toward me.

"Okay." I nodded, studying my hand.

Carl smiled and took that hand, very gently at first, as if afraid one of us might break, but then he snorted and wrapped me up in a big hug. And because he wasn't afraid of me anymore, neither was I. I relaxed, let out my breath, kicked my legs back and forth, sending blood and extra-strength cleaning fluid coursing through my veins. I felt alive, more alive than ever. I was *more.* I looked again at my hands, which were crisscrossed with tiny indentations and soft ridges—unlike the bottom of any Swiffer pad I had ever seen.

"Look at this." I held my palm up; Martin and Greg both oohed and ahhed, then abruptly stopped and glared at each other.

"Lame-o," Martin hissed.

"Loser." Greg sneered.

"Boys!" I poked at my new, spongier palms. "What do you make of this?"

Carl shook his head. "I don't know. It must have something to do with the stronger cleaning fluid."

"Cool." I grinned. I was Super Mom Version 2.0—who knew what else I could do? I stood, bounced up and down on the balls of my feet, ready to go do—something—and then stopped. Because no one else in the room was smiling. In fact, it was a little bit like being in the middle of the Gunfight at the O.K. Corral, except bullets weren't flying; dirty looks were, bouncing from Kelly to Carl to Martin to Greg. And I plopped down again, too tired, all of a sudden, to try to figure out how to make them all stop.

Without warning, I remembered my dream. And the family it had represented—and how easy and familiar it had been to imagine myself back in that place. I glanced at Carl, who was taking my regular clothes—jeans and a T-shirt—and laying them out on the bench beside me, like a little flat person. That worried little pucker was between his eyes, even though he was smiling, and my heart gave a guilty little twinge. Why hadn't the first dream I'd had in my entire life been about him? It wasn't fair; I felt cheated, somehow. And worse—

I felt that Carl had been, too.

"Thanks," I said, putting my hand on Carl's arm.

"For what?"

"For just . . . for being here."

"Where else would I be?" He swooped down and planted a kiss on my forehead; all three kids stifled groans.

"Okay," I said, rising to my feet, brushing my hands—as if I were brushing the memory of that dream away. My thigh still burned, so I reached into my Apron of Anticipation and pulled out antibacterial lotion and a big Band-Aid. "Let's go. I think we could do with some ice cream after all, don't you?"

Nobody agreed. But nobody objected, either.

"All right, just let me change back into my regular clothes. Meet me outside, and try not to kill each other."

Carl, Kelly and Martin left—Kelly and Martin stomping ahead while Carl shook his head and sighed—but Greg hung back.

"I thought you might need this." He reached down and picked something up off the floor—a bottle of Mr. Clean. "This is what hit you on the head."

"Thanks." I took the half-empty plastic bottle and glared at Mr. Clean. This time, he didn't wink at me. He just stood in his usual pose, arms folded, bad-boy earring glistening.

"And, you know, thank you. Thanks for saving me from that bat. And, well, sorry."

"Sorry about what?" I looked at Greg, trying hard not to

smile, because I knew that for a fourteen-year-old boy apologies were as difficult as eating chocolate chip cookies without milk. Both left a dry taste in your mouth.

"You know, for being kind of a dickwad about you. I mean, my dad—well, I can see that he's happy and stuff, so that's good, and I guess you're not so bad."

"You're not so bad, either." And it was true; we both realized it at the same time and smiled at each other, surprised and maybe a little bit happy. Then his pasty face turned brick red and he ran from the room.

I sniffed the air behind him—he must use Old Spice deodorant, too. Another thing he had in common with Martin. Then I shook my head, trying to clear my nasal passages of all the fragrance—that Mr. Clean ammonia was *strong*—but it didn't work. So I made a mental note to stop at the drugstore on the way home and buy nose plugs.

Just then I heard a scurrying noise in the hallway. I froze, tiptoed to the door, pulled it open and peered out.

The hallway was empty. Except for a piece of notebook paper—college-ruled, not wide—fluttering to the ground, where I snatched it up and brought it up to my nose like I was a bird dog. It smelled of chewing gum—spearmint, or maybe wintergreen. Oh, and one other thing. It smelled like peaches.

"Martin? Did you—?"

But I didn't get to finish my sentence; a brain-freezing blast of something foul—something like rotten eggs, something salty and organic and musty, almost like flesh decaying—assaulted my sinuses, knocking me against a wall.

"Martin!" My voice echoed in the empty corridor. "Are you wearing your old gym socks?"

The only reply was an indignant yelp, somewhere up ahead.

"Well, you'd better change them when you get home, buddy,

or el—" As I turned to reenter the locker room, I screamed like a little girl.

Because standing in the doorway to the locker room was a great big bald genie with an earring.

And a naughty twinkle in his eye.

CHAPTER 8

Imagine your wildest fantasies come true.

Imagine the itch you can't stop scratching, the thing that drives you, pushes you, haunts you—maybe even propels you into superherodom.

Imagine that Mr. Clean is real. Imagine that he is pretty hunky, almost as hunky as you dreamed he was back when you were thirteen and all the other girls had crushes on Leif Garrett. Imagine that your girlhood crush is carrying you in his totally ripped arms, with biceps the size of frozen hams straining through his tight, white T-shirt, your superhero costume riding up so that your bare thighs are resting on his steel-like wrists, and you're trying not to blush, but even if you did he couldn't see it because of your mask and the blindfold that's tied a little too tightly around your head, and you're reminding yourself that even if you weren't engaged, it really wouldn't be appropriate to indulge in a little S&M fantasy about a hot genie who is, presumably, magically and gigantically endowed. Because, after all, you're a superhero, a card-carrying member of the Justice League of America. And that messy business with Hawkman and the Dora the Explorer balloon from the Macy's Thanksgiving Day Parade just got cleared up.

But also imagine that you have the maturity of a fifteen-year-old.

"So," I purred, batting my eyelashes even though the gentle giant couldn't see. "Is that a mop handle in your pocket, or are you just happy to see me?"

Mr. Clean grunted. Then shifted me, a little unceremoniously, so that I was now hanging over his shoulder like a sack of potatoes. My chin bumped against his solid back as he continued walking down what seemed to be a very long staircase.

"You know, you smell very good," I said, just to make conversation. "Ammonia, lemon, spring water, a little musk. Old Spice?"

He grunted again, then suddenly stopped moving. I found myself deposited onto something cold and hard, my blindfold untied and ripped away—along with several rather important strands of my brown hair.

I blinked, even though the light was dim. I was sprawled on the ground; I shifted a bit and tugged my skirt over my thighs. I seemed to be on the floor of some gigantic—underground tree house, if that made any sense. But it was the first thing that came to mind as I took in my surroundings: an enormous warren of rooms and stairs and hallways, stuck here and there and everywhere, not built, apparently, according to any plan, save for the huge expanse of white linoleum in the very center. Upon which I had been so recently dumped, by Mr. Clean.

Some of the rooms glowed with soft, yellow light; others were shot through with the cold, white-blue light of a scientific laboratory. There was a steady hum of activity in the air; the sound of many people at work at something busy, something productive, something important. Swooshes and swipes and the bright, happy zip of brushes over hard surfaces. Above my head there was a muffled sound, like a train engine. Down a hall I heard the tinny, echoing sound of liquid sloshing in a metal bucket. And the air was—pure. Scrubbed. Full of scent, yes—scent so crystalline and determined that it parted the hairs in my nostrils and brought tears to my eyes. But it was good. Clean. Familiar—orange and bleach and ammonia and lemon and pine and mountain flowers.

Something tickled my feet; I looked down and yelped, leaping into Mr. Clean's arms once more. A little—Scrubbing Bubble?—was purring on the ground in front of me, eyes all adorably big and liquid, little bristles making a chirping, happy sound.

"Aw, how cute!" I slid out of Mr. Clean's arms and patted the little guy on the head; he rubbed against my leg and scooted off, joining a bunch of other, more bashful Scrubbing Bubbles hovering over in a corner of the enormous ground floor.

"Welcome, Super Mom! Welcome to our humble home."

A tiny gnome of a man in a crisp white lab coat was hurrying toward me, old-fashioned black-framed spectacles gleaming even in the dim light.

"We're so glad to finally have you visit. We've heard so much about you!"

"We?" I turned around; other than the shy Scrubbing Bubbles and Mr. Clean, I didn't see anyone. Until suddenly a small band of similarly clad, similarly geeky (to judge from the plethora of pocket protectors) little men popped out from behind him, tittering.

"I'm Dr. Septavius. The head scientist here at New Improved You. Now, I'm sure you're wondering—"

I raised my hand. "Hold on there. New Improved Me?"

"No, You. As in University. New Improved University. New Improved 'U' for short. It's an institute devoted entirely to the betterment of society through the development of new and improved household cleansers and tools. Martha Stewart is our main donor, as you might imagine." Dr. Septavius chuckled, his bald head bobbing like a flesh-colored balloon.

"Really? Is she here? Can I meet her? I've been dying to be a guest on her show."

"No, I'm afraid she's not. Actually . . ." Dr. Septavius looked at his little band of fellow scientists; they ducked their heads and made little snorting noises. "She's at the Betty."

"The Betty? Ohhh . . ." I nodded. "You mean the Betty Ford Clinic?"

"No, the Betty Crocker Clinic. For those with an addiction to household cleansers."

"Really?" I giggled. "Well, there but for the grace of God— and Swiffer—go I. I totally understand." And I made a mental note to send Martha a Get Well Soon card. "So, could someone tell me why I'm here? And how I got here? And why the labels of some of our finest cleaning products have been messing with my mind? And one more thing . . ."

"What?" Dr. Septavius took a step toward me as I swayed woozily.

"Where can I get an aspirin, because my head is pounding?" I sagged a little, Mr. Clean catching me by my armpits and helping me to a chair.

"Ah, first things first." Dr. Septavius clapped his hands; a big lumberjack materialized, holding a bottle of aspirin and a glass of water.

"You're— Wait. Don't tell me. . . ." I closed my eyes for a second, then snapped my fingers. "You're the Brawny guy, aren't you?" I stared, picturing his face on a roll of paper towels.

He nodded, swung an axe over his shoulder, and left. I swallowed the aspirin and smiled at the row of nerdy scientists beaming down on me.

"We don't let just anyone in, you know," Dr. Septavius said with an eager grin. "We've had our eye on you for several months. As I'm sure you've noticed."

"Yeah, well, you kind of freaked me out with all that wink-ing and stuff on the labels. I mean, try telling your best friend that Mr. Clean is flirting with you. . . ."

"My sincere apologies. It was our way of communicating with you—a secret handshake, if you will. As to where you are—well, all I can say is that you're safely underground. And that all the former radiation has been one hundred percent con-tained. That might tell you something."

"Silos?" I looked up, gaping at the vast emptiness above my head.

"I can neither confirm nor deny."

"How will I get back home?"

"You'll see, when it's time. Right now, we need to discuss what happened to you today."

"What do you mean?"

"You were attacked by a rogue Swiffer WetJet."

"Excuse me?"

"A special WetJet—one that only a very few people in the world have access to."

"Really?" A little thrill raced up and down my spine. "A se-cret WetJet? Can I see it?"

"Well . . ." Dr. Septavius took out a comb and carefully parted the one thin strand of hair that was trying valiantly to cover his entire head. He looked at his fellow scientists, who all nodded eagerly. "Come with me."

I followed him—that little band of scientists trailing at a respectful distance behind me—up some stairs, down a hall, around a corner, up more stairs. I peeked into some of the rooms I passed along the way—all either kitchens or bathrooms, constructed of every imaginable material. Some kitchens had cherry cabinets and granite countertops, others had maple cabinets and Silestone counters, while others still had laminate cabinets and Formica tops. Some bathrooms had stone floors, others wood, still others linoleum. Small bands of adorable Scrubbing Bubbles were giggling and chirping and swarming around the bathrooms, like kindergartners on a playground. They were so happy—I had to laugh, watching them.

In every room, there were people scrubbing. Bright, happy people with determined looks on their faces, intent upon their task—bringing order to the world. I smiled, recognizing myself in them, right down to that corner of the tongue sticking out of their mouths as they tried to eradicate one last scuff mark.

"What's that?" I stopped in front of a room full of toddlers in high chairs. They were babbling and gurgling and flinging food about; two scientists ran back and forth with tape measures, measuring from toddler to the glob of food he had just flung, making notes.

"The Baby Room. The toughest of all. No one's yet figured out how to get strained peas out of silk."

"I can," I said with a superior smirk.

"Yes, well, thank goodness for us there's only one of you. We'd be out of business if everyone could clean with the power of ten thousand Swiffers!"

"Twenty thousand, actually." The little band of scientists clucked their tongues in admiration, and we continued down the twisting hall. That distant sound, like a small train roaring, got louder and louder until finally we were upon it. A small white tornado—it only came up to about my shoulder—spun lazy circles around a retro 1960s kitchen with turquoise floors and harvest gold appliances. He was accompanied by a sad fellow in a white turtleneck, blue blazer, and captain's hat, halfheartedly rowing a rowboat in a small children's wading pool.

"Who are they?"

"Shhhh . . . move along. It's the White Tornado and the Ty-D-Bol man. They've been like that ever since their corporate sponsors retired them." Dr. Septavius shut the door to the kitchen and shooed me along.

"Oh, that's so sad." I shook my head as Dr. Septavius continued on his way.

Finally we reached a huge kitchen. A bright, modern twenty-first-century kitchen with wood floors, oak cabinets stained white, a dark green granite countertop. And in all the shelves, all the cabinets behind glass doors, were Swiffer products. Row upon row of green and orange and purple boxes and bottles.

"Ooh!" I clapped my hands and jumped up and down. "I had a dream like this—you were there. . . ." I grabbed a box of Swiffer cloths. "And you were there. . . ." I clutched an orange CarpetFlick. "And you. . . ." I twirled an extendable duster.

Dr. Septavius scratched his nose with a bony, pale scientist finger and smiled, showing even, blindingly white teeth. "Well, of course you're a fan. As we are of you."

"So it really is true, isn't it? There really are cleaning elves?"

One of the scientists behind me made a strangling sound. Dr. Septavius frowned.

"We don't have elves around here," he said with a prissy sneer. "Elves are messy. If you want elves, go to the Keebler Institute. An institute with much lower standards than New Improved U."

Another scientist hissed. "They don't even require a master's degree." His cohorts snickered.

"Sorry." I shrugged. "I didn't know."

"That's all right. It's an honest mistake. Now, just wait right here." Dr. Septavius vanished into a little room off the kitchen.

I looked around at the other scientists, who were gaping at me like I was Miss America. I smiled. They smiled. I waved. They waved. I giggled. They giggled.

Which was a little disturbing.

"Here we are." Dr. Septavius emerged with a Swiffer WetJet in his hand. Only it wasn't the old Swiffer WetJet. It was exactly like the one I'd seen in the Phantom of the Bullpen's hands; larger, with a wider reservoir and cleaning head.

"This is the new Super Secret Super Duper Swiffer. That's just the working title; marketing will come up with something better. This is what you encountered, I presume?"

"Yep." I grabbed it and turned it cleaning-pad-side up.

"We're very excited about this new model. See, Super Mom, the pad is more rigid, better at removing those stubborn scuff marks." Dr. Septavius took it from me, demonstrating how to put the pad on. I touched the pad, then looked at my hands, which were spongy, rigid, just like the new Super Secret Super Duper Swiffer. So I *was* new and improved, after all.

"The pad stays in place better, too." He tried to pull it off, but it remained impressively intact. "And this new fiber has a strength rating of three point five." His merry band of fellow scientists, standing back at a respectful distance, murmured excitedly.

"What kind of scuff marks will it remove?" I asked, giving it a professional squint.

"All kinds."

"Black ones? Like from work boots?"

"Not a problem."

"What about tar?"

"It doesn't stand a chance against this mop." Dr. Septavius smiled and crossed his arms, his eyes glinting behind his glasses.

"Magic Marker on wood floors?"

"Gone."

"Glitter glue?"

"Gone."

"Canola oi—"

"Gone."

I thought for a moment while Dr. Septavius twirled the Swiffer with a superior smile. Finally I spoke.

"Cheerios ground up in peanut butter and molasses," I said, drawing it out triumphantly.

"Go— shoot." He hung his bald little head. "I don't think we tested that." The other scientists groaned.

"Well, that's a tough one to get out." I shook my head sympathetically. "But I'm sure it'll be wonderful. I mean, a strength rating of three point five!"

Dr. Septavius jumped up and down, wringing his hands. "Oh, yes, we're very excited about it!" Then his face darkened. "But how someone on the outside laid hands on one of them, I have no idea."

"Other than you guys, who else would possibly know about this?"

Dr. Septavius scratched his forehead with the Swiffer handle. "Yes, that's what we were trying to figure out. This Swiffer is special, you see. Not necessarily manufactured for the general public."

"What do you mean?"

"I'm afraid I'm not at liberty to say. Not even to you, Super Mom."

"Really?" Frankly, I was a little hurt. I thought we had so much in common—united in our determination to rid the world of stubborn soap scum. "What about all the people I see down here, in the rooms? Who are they?"

"People who have devoted their lives to cleaning. People who have a talent, many say a mania. This is how Martha herself started out—she took an aptitude test at a shopping mall, tested a few products, and we recognized her genius almost immediately."

"Do they ever leave?"

"No, why would they? It's so clean down here, and it's so messy up there!"

"Well, yes. . . ." Nobody knew that like I did. Which was why I belonged *up there.*

Yet—

There was something so safe about this place. Everyone had a job to do, with a common goal—cleanliness and order. Everything knew its place. Unlike my world, where adorable children turned into sullen, smelly creatures overnight, and ex-husbands popped up when you least expected it.

"But somebody has to clean up all those messes," I said, more to myself than to the scientists. "It's part of my job description, after all. So, can I try out this Swiffer?" I grabbed the mop and started to squeeze the trigger. Suddenly Dr. Septavius's pale scientist hand reached down and grabbed my arm with surprising strength.

"Oh, no, Super Mom! Don't do that. That's the experimental cleaning fluid."

"Yes, that's what I assumed." I lifted my skirt—the scientists giggled and blushed—but I ignored them, concentrating on pulling away the Band-Aid without pulling away more flesh. I winced, as I didn't quite succeed. "Whatever was in that Super Secret Super Duper Swiffer did this to me. I'd like very much to be able to bring a sample back to Carl—I mean, to my, um, test laboratory—to analyze it."

"No, you don't understand. What is in this has not been tested yet. Not thoroughly. We cannot allow it to leave this laboratory."

"Obviously it already has."

"Yes, and that's very troubling, but I simply cannot allow any more of this cleaning fluid to leave these premises."

"But you have to believe me, it's a matter of extreme importance. Superhero importance. I just need a sample—"

"Super Mom!" Dr. Septavius scolded, grabbing the Super Secret Super Duper Swiffer from me. "I would have thought that you, of all people, would understand!"

"But I just—"

"Excuse me." Clutching the Swiffer WetJet to his chest, he trotted back to wherever he'd come from, shaking his head and muttering.

I sighed, put the Band-Aid back in place, and bit my lip. Then I looked at the other scientists. We went through our usual routine—me smiling, them smiling; me sighing, them sighing. Finally one of them scuffed his feet and inched toward me.

"Hi, Super Mom," he said with a shy grin.

"Hello." I took a step back, just a little freaked out by the adoring—almost evangelical—light in his eye.

"We think you're just great!" another scientist blurted out. His friends gasped, but nodded.

"Why, thank you!" I giggled. I had my first groupies! I couldn't wait to tell Wonder Woman.

"Do you— Oh, never mind. I couldn't be so forward as to ask for— Oh, never mind."

"No, that's all right. What do you want to ask me?"

"Could we—that is, do you—do you think we could get a sample of your fluid sometime?" one asked.

"Only for scientific purposes, of course!" another said with a blush.

"I'm honored, naturally, but it hardly seems fair for me to give you my fluid when you won't give me— Oh! Oh, boys!" I had an idea; I crooked my finger at them and beckoned, winking flirta-tiously. "I need you to do a little favor for me, too."

"Anything, Super Mom!" the first one said with that shy grin. "Anything you say!"

"Well, here's the thing. . . ." My voice dropping to a whisper, I put my arms around their puny, pale little scientist shoulders as we huddled together. They giggled, gasped, looked over their shoulders in case Dr. Septavius reappeared. But in the end, they did it. I knew they would.

Because they were men, after all. And what man can resist a woman so free and easy with her fluids?

CHAPTER 9

"Let me get this straight," Carrie said, tugging on her bangs. She switched her register light off—it was our slow time, ten a.m. on Tuesday—and joined me at my register. Her little blue eyes blinked worriedly, but she kept a calm, professional smile on her face. "You say Mr. Clean jumped off the label of a bottle and whisked you away to some underground cleaning laboratory."

"Uh-huh." I nodded, straightening my cash drawer, dusting my change (you have no idea how dirty money can get!).

"And the Brawny Lumberjack gave you an aspirin?"

"Yep."

"And the Scrubbing Bubbles tickled your feet."

"That's right."

"And there were unicorns and winged horses flying through the air, and George Clooney himself offered to give you a foot massage?"

"I *wish*! Don't be ridiculous."

"It doesn't sound any more ridiculous than anything else you've just said!"

"But it really happened!" I shut my drawer and turned to face my friend. Who frowned, pulled a notebook from her pocket, and scribbled in it. And I remembered that she wasn't just my friend anymore. She was the official psychiatrist for the Justice League of America, and as such had a sworn duty to report any sudden changes in the mental state of its superheroes.

Of which I was one. And wanted to remain. (If only to make it to the Fourth of July picnic—I'd heard the Flash made a mean potato salad.)

"Well . . . I mean . . . that is . . . what are you writing?"

"Nothing." She continued to scribble, her nose all wrinkled up.

"It sure looks like something." I tried to laugh, but it came out more like a dry heave.

"Why?" She suddenly swung her head up and narrowed her eyes at me. "Are you worried that I'm writing something about you? Are you a little paranoid?"

"No, no, that's not it. . . ."

"Hmmm . . . ," she said again. Then scribbled something else down.

"Carrie, the thing is—I only told you this because you're my friend, you know? So why don't we keep it between the two of us? Just a little girl talk, okay?"

"So you have something to hide?"

"No, I didn't say that—oh, for Pete's sake!" I tried to grab the notebook out of her hand but she was too quick; she shoved it in the pocket of her smock and took a giant step away from me.

"Birdie, please! I must say I'm shocked at your aggression."

"Carrie, cut the psychobabble. There's nothing wrong with me and I am telling you the truth, but I'd prefer that you not tell anyone else—anyone at headquarters—until we get to the bottom of this."

"The bottom of what?"

"The Super Secret Super Duper Swiffer mystery."

"Ah, right, I forgot that part. . . ." And she whipped out her notebook and started writing again.

"Oh, forget it." I shoved her back toward her register. "Just remember that we're friends, okay? And that we can trust each other? Just remember that."

"Hmmm mmmm. . . ."

I shook my head, switched off my light, and went over to the service desk, where Monty handed me a stack of new *Car and Driver* magazines. I stalked over to the magazine section—passing a display of bathroom cleaners. I picked up a can, smiled at the cute little Scrubbing Bubbles on the front, and waited to hear that familiar little purr.

But the can remained silent.

"C'mon, it's okay. It's me," I whispered.

Nothing happened.

"No, really, it's fine. I won't get all freaked out now and—"

A discreet cough caused me to look up. Carrie was standing in front of me, hands on hips, head cocked to one side.

"Birdie, honestly!"

"What?"

"You're whispering to a can of bathroom cleaner!"

"I am not!" I shoved the can back on the shelf, turned and continued toward the magazines. But I could feel Carrie's penetrating gaze trying to burn holes in the back of my head. "Stupid Scrubbing Bubbles. I don't care what she says, it happened, and I'm new and improved." Looking at my hands—my stronger, grippier hands—I flexed them, admiring.

"I think you are, too," a deep male voice interrupted, startling me so that I dropped an armload of magazines, scattering them all over the floor.

"Dan?" I spun around, red-faced, as if I'd been caught doing something naughty. "What are you doing here?" For after I caught my breath and reminded myself that I was only doing my job, I realized that I was looking at Doctor Dan. In a grocery store. A building I was fairly sure he'd never entered before.

And not just any grocery store, either. Marvel Food and Fine Beverages—the place where I toiled, to his utter and everlasting humiliation, bagging his patients' Tater Tots and Cheerios. Implying that he wasn't the provider, the great father and doting ex-husband he wanted people to think he was. The thing he never understood was—I liked working here. I would have done it no matter what; I got a kick out of getting to know people through the contents of their grocery carts.

"What am I doing here?" Doctor Dan shrugged. "Buying groceries. Obviously."

"Really?" His cart was nearly empty—except for a handful of frozen dinners, a bottle of wine, a box of powdered donuts, and two rolls of toilet paper. The cheap kind, which he'd grown up with; I remembered fighting about that when we were married. My tushy required a much softer brand than he was willing to pay for.

From what I knew about Dixie, I suspected that hers did, too.

"Dan, is Dixie out of town?"

"Yes." He brushed his thin, floppy hair out of his eyes and shuffled his feet—encased in perfectly polished black oxfords, size nine and a half, I remembered with a sudden pang, wondering why that was one of the things I'd chosen not to forget about him.

"Oh."

"Actually, Birdie, I'm glad to see you here. I've been—"

"You're glad? To see me? *Here?*" I stared at the magazine in my hand, as if the buxom blonde posing next to a Corvette could provide some kind of verification that I was, in fact, hallucinating. (Again.)

"Yes, here. Because I've been meaning to tell you something."

"I've been meaning to talk to you, too, Doc— Dan." Had he noticed the engagement ring—a perfectly set diamond solitaire— that Carl had picked out all by himself, with only a little help from Carrie? I couldn't tell, so I hid my left hand behind my back. Just—because.

"You go first." Dan nodded regally.

"No—you can go ahead."

"No, you—"

"No, I insist—"

Then we both spoke at the same time—

"Dixie and I are getting a divorce."

"Carl and I are getting married."

We shook our heads, did a double-take, and each blurted, *"What?"*

"You're getting a divorce?" I felt like I needed to sit down.

"You're getting married?" He evidently felt that way, too. Because he did sit down, right on a pile of *Cooking Light* magazines, neatly stacked alongside a special display of Calphalon skillets (buy a skillet, get a year's subscription free).

"What happened, Dan?" While I waited for his answer— which seemed to be a long time coming—I tried to analyze my own jumble of emotions upon hearing the news I thought I'd waited for, for years. Was I happy? Joyous? Hopeful?

Not exactly. More like numb, weary. To feel any of those other emotions would have been to go back to the beginning of a crushing marathon, a race I felt I'd only recently finished. And I just didn't have the energy to start down that road again.

Dan finally looked up at me, his fine, slender hands dangling between his knees. His thinning hair flopped over into his eyes, but he didn't push it back; he let it hang there. The resemblance to Martin was staggering; since I didn't get to see them together on a daily basis, I was always knocked breathless whenever I was reminded how much they looked alike.

"What do you want me to say, Birdie? It's over. I failed. Is that what you want to hear? Does that make you happy?"

"No, it doesn't. Even though . . ." And I couldn't finish that thought, although we both knew what it was. *Even though he'd left me for her.*

But I always understood, even way back then, that she wasn't the reason our marriage ended. Even in my worst moments, I understood that.

"Well, that's very generous of you, considering the circumstances." Dan shook his head ruefully. "I didn't expect any sympathy from you, of course. I don't deserve that."

I didn't contradict him.

"So you're engaged?"

I nodded.

"Congratulations." Ice, masquerading as words; I shivered as his blue eyes turned glacial. "I hope you'll be very happy with Cal."

"Carl."

"Whatever."

I watched him in silence as he hung his head, dangled his wrists, and sighed—a great, wronged, disappointed sigh. And slowly a little flame of anger started to thaw some of the ice heaped my way. How dare he? How dare he act hurt? Doctor Dan—the man who had left me with two small children in the most humiliating way imaginable, telling the entire world (or at least Astro Park), in effect, that I wasn't good enough for him?

He had done those things. Yes, I had made mistakes, too. But I hadn't done what he'd done. I hadn't wounded him so deeply that he wondered if he could ever look at the world in the same way again; I hadn't kicked him so hard he started to believe that he had deserved it all. And didn't deserve anything else, ever again.

But now I knew I was deserving of love. Carl—not *Cal*—had reminded me. Carl had healed me.

"I think your dinner is melting," I finally said, looking into the pathetic little grocery cart—and willing myself not to worry about the nutritional value of a Hungry-Man frozen turkey dinner.

Dan rose, groaning—everything about him seemed to say "Pity me, for I am in despair." He looked into his grocery cart and sighed. But when he spoke, his voice was surprisingly soft and sincere. "Birdie, I want you to know I'm sorry. I'm sorry for everything. Maybe I never told you that before—"

"No, you didn't, Dan. You never, ever said you were sorry."

His face, which had looked oddly flat under the harsh fluorescent lights, suddenly pinched up, like the Doctor Dan I'd known for so long. But then he sighed again, ironing out his features once more.

"Then I was a gigantic ass."

"Well, yes."

To my surprise, he laughed, the edges of his eyes crinkling up, softening his face in a way I hadn't seen before. The last time I'd seen him laugh like that, he didn't have crow's-feet. It was amazing what a difference they made.

"Tell me, Birdie, do you ever think of me? Of us, the way we used to be?" He stopped laughing but his eyes still looked kind.

"Only when I'm under the influence of mind-altering chemicals," I answered truthfully, remembering the dream I'd had after my Second Horrible Swiffer Accident.

He stiffened for a moment, his gaze freezing over; then apparently he decided that this was a joke, too, and he laughed again. A little less heartily.

"I'll be seeing you, Birdie. Soon, I hope. And tell Cal that I think he's a lucky man." Dan put a hand on my shoulder, gave me a quick, fond squeeze, then pushed his cart down the aisle—noiselessly. Leave it to Doctor Dan to have found the only cart in the entire store that didn't have squeaky wheels.

"Carl," I muttered, watching him until he rounded the corner and disappeared. So Dan was getting divorced. Dan would be all alone. Dan would be sad. Dan would be hurting.

And I—wasn't. Any of those things. I was loved, taken care of, about to start all over. It was good. Wasn't it? It was all good?

But why did I feel like it was too hard? Why did I feel, just for a minute, that it would be easier to go backward, not forward?

"Some Super Mom you are." I started to gather up more magazines. "Afraid of a little thing like being a stepmother."

"Birdie?" Carrie came whirring around the corner, clawing at her bangs. "I just saw Doctor Dan! What on earth is he doing here? I thought he'd die rather than set foot in this place!"

I looked at her, notepad at the ready. I wanted her to be my friend, not my psychiatrist.

"Nothing," I finally said with a sad grin, patting her on the top of her head. "He was just doing a little grocery shopping."

"Really? That doesn't seem like him!"

"Maybe he's changed, Carrie." I looked past her, in the direction that Dan had gone. "Maybe he's different now."

"Yeah. Like that will ever happen!"

"I guess you're right." I sighed and went back to the magazines. "I guess it's too late."

I didn't look up when Carrie gave me a quick squeeze—unexpected, but not unappreciated. But I did smile. And allowed her to help me restack all the *Cooking Light* magazines Dan had knocked over.

CHAPTER 10

"So, what is it?"

Carl didn't reply. He just fiddled with his microscope and furrowed his forehead until there were four little scraggly lines running across it.

"Is it bleachier?"

Five scraggly lines.

"Ammonier?"

Six.

"Swiffier?"

He finally lifted his head from the microscope and blinked at me. "Birdie. You're not even talking English now."

"But what is it?" I jumped up and down, impatient as my kids on Christmas morning.

"You'll just have to wait." He bent down toward the microscope once more. I sighed and looked around. We were in Carl's secret laboratory—or la-*bore*-a-tory, as I liked to call it, when I was feeling neglected—surrounded by vials and machines and Bunsen burners and test tubes, little Pyrex measuring cups full of mysterious liquids and powders. You'd almost expect a crack of lightning to flash across the sky. Except we were in his basement, and all his cool scientist stuff was spread out over the top of his old pool table. Oh, and the St. Pauli Girl poster was hanging on the wall next to us, adjacent to an old dartboard.

This was where Carl had first analyzed my fluids—those same fluids I was now giving out freely to any scientist who looked my way. It was also where he'd first kissed me, first tasted me—first held me until I was limp with desire. I smiled, remembering. That had been a great night. And down here, watching him be all adorably nerdy scientist-like, I fell, with a thud, more deeply in love with him than ever. Deep enough, I hoped, to drown out the noise of everything else—the kids, the mortgages, the ex-spouses. If only we could remain down here, just the two of us. (Minus Miss St. Pauli Girl, whom I might have to "accidentally" destroy with a rogue flick of a cleaning-fluid-filled finger.)

"So go over the whole thing again." Carl raised his head and peered at me, a little red V above his eyes from the microscope. "You were kidnapped by Mr. Clean?"

"I am so tired of repeating this story! Honestly, who among us hasn't been kidnapped by an advertising icon?"

"Uh-huh." Carl rubbed his eyes tiredly.

"You believe me, don't you?"

"Well . . ."

"I'm not sure that Carrie does—she started trying to analyze me. But you do, don't you?"

"I don't know where you disappeared to that day, that's for sure. We looked all over the stadium and couldn't find you, and just when we were going to call the police you showed back up. And remember, you did hit your head pretty hard when you suffered your Second Horrible Swiffer Accident. . . ."

"What's that supposed to mean?"

"Only that something happened to you that the rest of us can't explain. That's all."

"So do you believe me?"

He took a big breath, fiddled with the microscope, and asked, "So what happened next?"

"Mr. Clean took me to a secret subterranean cleaning laboratory, where the Dow Scrubbing Bubbles were so cute I almost wanted to adopt them. And the Ajax White Tornado was all sad in his own little room. And where this doctor guy is testing all the latest Swiffer stuff."

"And you were able to steal this so-called experimental fluid by—?"

"Using my feminine wiles." I hung my head modestly.

"On a group of Swiffer scientists?"

"You still sound like you don't believe me!"

"Well—even if I don't begin to address the fact that you were lusting over a giant fictional bald genie, which I know you were because you conveniently omitted any mention of how, exactly, he bundled you up and brought you to this place—the fact is, I know scientists. And—present company excepted—you're not exactly their type. You know the whole Marilyn Monroe–Albert Einstein thing? That's the type they usually fall for."

"I am hurt that you doubt my word. And what's worse, I'm more hurt that you don't give nearly enough credit to my feminine wiles." I reached around and grabbed his cute butt, pinching it until he gave a little yelp.

"Of course I do. I just don't believe that a group of scientists would be willing to risk their careers in order to smuggle out a vial of a super-secret cleaning fluid. That's all."

"They don't get out much. Apparently, I looked very good to them."

"And?" Carl raised an eyebrow.

"And—I gave them each a little squirt of my cleaning fluid in exchange."

"Aha!" Carl smirked and went back to fiddling with the microscope.

I twisted my lips in a pathetic pout—which he didn't notice. So then I started picking up vials and pinchers and clamps, shaking them, holding them up to the light—trying not to inhale the toxic fumes, which involved holding my breath until I was almost blue in the face, letting it out, taking a big breath while hiding my nose in my shirtsleeve, then holding it again.

"Don't touch that!" Carl grabbed my hand, which was holding a small container that looked like a pillbox. I couldn't avoid smelling this beauty—it reminded me of the bottom of Martin's clothes hamper. Rotten eggs, mildewed socks, earth, matter, refuse all emanated from this curious little box made of the heaviest steel imaginable, sealed with clamps and locks and some thick plastic-looking glue.

"What?" I started to toss it back, but Carl winced and caught it before it could fall to the table.

"Don't—just—don't—just—go stand over there." Arms waving, hands fluttering, he bustled me away from the pool table and pointed to the other side of the basement, where a rough wooden workbench leaned up against the cement block wall.

"But—"

"Go."

"But—"

"Birdie, please. This is very dangerous—I shouldn't have brought you down here, now that I think about it. . . ."

"Why not? I've been down here tons of times before."

"Yes, but it's different now. I'm in the middle of some experiments."

"For the pharmaceutical company?"

"No, not really . . . just a little something I'm doing on my own time. . . ."

"What?"

Carl turned, leaning back against the table. He rubbed his eyes, like a cranky toddler, and sighed.

"I can't tell you."

"Sure you can. I'm a superhero!"

"Very funny. It's just something I've been thinking about for a while, and I don't really want to talk about it. Yet. Sometime, I promise. But not yet."

"Why, Carl Sayers!" I grinned, surprised—and tickled. "You've got a secret!"

"Well, sort of. . . ." He bent his head and kicked his tennis shoe against a pool table leg.

"Hmmm. I love a man of mystery!"

"Really?" He raised his eyebrows up and down—like Groucho Marx.

"Growwwl. . . ."

He laughed—I giggled, leaned up to rub my face against his sweatshirt—but he took my arm and marched me over to the workbench instead, shoving me down with a pat on my head before walking back to the microscope to resume his fiddling.

"But why does it smell so bad?"

"What?"

"That thing you won't let me touch. It smells terrible."

"No, it doesn't. It can't." Carl raised his head and stared at me.

"Well, I'm sorry to break it to you, but yes, it does."

"Birdie, it can't. It's natural gas. But I haven't added mercaptan—that chemical that's added to make it smell. Because natural gas is completely odorless."

"Well, I'm telling you it's not. I can smell that thing over here."

"Birdie, I think your super smeller's a little mixed up. That is one of the absolutes in science—natural gas is completely odorless. Which makes it so deadly."

"Whatever." I shrugged. "So what's in the fluid?"

"Acid," he said finally, flipping off the microscope light. "Hydrochloric acid, trace amounts. Which will certainly remove dirt—and layers of skin, too. Although why anyone would put this in a Swiffer WetJet—if in fact they did—" He studied me for a minute, and I knew he was still deciding whether or not to believe me—"is a total mystery. This stuff will burn right through linoleum."

"Not to mention flesh." I winced, gingerly patting my thigh. "Well, that explains it. But it doesn't explain how it got out of New Improved U—or who the Phantom of the Bullpen is, or how he got it in the first place."

"Or why he was at the ballpark when you were, and threatened to blow it up if you didn't disappear. Why the ballpark? That's the part I can't figure out. The entire town is crazy about that thing."

"The entire town is crazy. Period. Even Carrie! They've decided not to buy new band uniforms this year—everything's going to the Astro Park-O-Dome Field and Carrie approved it. She's obsessed with beating the Shriners."

"Speaking of . . . wanna be my date for the Silent Auction Dinner Dance?" Carl sat down next to me, his long leg twisting around so that our ankles hooked beneath the bench.

"I thought you'd never ask!" I nuzzled his shoulder, inhaled his vanilla-and-wood-smoke smell—and onion and soy sauce and curry and garlic and bean sprouts.

"Thai for lunch?"

"Yes, but I brushed my teeth."

"Nothing is safe from the Super Sniffer." I sighed.

"Oh, speaking of—Greg bought you a present." Carl started climbing the rickety wooden basement stairs; I followed him up to his kitchen, where I smiled, for the thousandth time, at the periodic chart on his refrigerator door.

"He didn't need to do that."

"No, but he wanted to. Look!" And Carl turned around, holding a giant bottle of—Febreze.

"Oh, how sweet! For all the smells!"

"He thought it might help." Carl stood tall and proud, a fatherly gleam in his eyes.

"Well, tell him I said thank you. That was very thoughtful." I sprayed a mist of Febreze in the air and walked right into it, eyes closed; I sniffed, and sure enough, the smells—my constant companions ever since the Second Horrible Swiffer Accident— seemed to fade a bit. I could still recognize them; they just didn't bore holes into my sinuses anymore. "I'm never going anywhere without this!" And I spritzed some behind my ears and on my wrists, like perfume.

"So, how are Kelly and Martin?" Carl asked, looking down, using his finger to trace imaginary lines on his kitchen counter. "I mean, are they—?"

"Any better? About us?"

He nodded.

"Not really." The way his eyes clouded over with hurt almost broke my heart.

"I just don't understand—I thought everything was fine and then—"

"And then we told them we were getting married. I know. I guess it was okay as long as it didn't seem so permanent. But now—I wonder . . . huh." I sat down in a kitchen chair, struck by a realization.

"And now what?"

"Doctor Dan is getting a divorce." I watched his reaction, curious. His eyes got wide, his face a little dark, but other than that, he seemed okay. "Anyway, now I wonder if he told the kids. Before he told me. I wonder if that's why they're acting so hostile."

"But why?"

"Hasn't Greg ever wanted you to get back with his mother?"

Carl shook his head. "He didn't know her, not really. She's not in our lives at all."

"That's not the case with Doctor Dan. He is in their lives. We live in the same town. And now the idea of us getting back together isn't so ridiculous."

"It isn't?" Carl turned away from me and looked out the window above his sink.

"I mean, it's not to the kids. Of course it's ridiculous to me."

He spun around, a big goofy smile on his face.

"You nerd," I said, running over and wrapping my arms around him. "You can't get rid of me, you know."

"That's convenient. Because I don't want to."

We stood, wrapped together like two ends of a pretzel. As long as we could stay like this—as long as it was just the two of us—everything was fine. But even as I was resting in his arms, eyes shut against the real world, I knew I couldn't avoid it forever. It was no longer this simple; it was no longer just us.

"I have to go," I said, even as I couldn't let go of him. I tilted my head up and looked into his eyes—those sweet, befuddled, kind eyes. "I'll talk to the kids—we have a family movie night planned. The first one in months."

"VCR or DVD?" Carl's forehead wrinkled thoughtfully.

"DVD, I guess, could be VCR, though. The kids are choosing."

"I only have a VCR player. So I guess I can get rid of that, then, right? We don't need two VCRs."

"No, sweetie, I guess we don't. You go right ahead and get rid of it."

"Maybe we should have a gigantic garage sale," my fiancé said, his voice light and happy again.

"Maybe," I agreed. And wrapped my arms around him once more, nice and tight. Maybe he didn't have Mr. Clean's muscles. And just imagining him with an earring made me giggle.

But he was still the sexiest man I knew.

"Kelly?" I walked into the dark house, switching on lights, stepping over the discarded shoes.

No answer.

"Martin?" I closed assorted kitchen cabinets and zapped up a puddle of milk on the kitchen table.

No answer.

"Guys? Where are you? I have pizza!" I held up the cardboard box in front of me, an offering (because I had omitted green olives just for the kids, even though they were my favorite). Eyes watering from the onions and sage and sausage and basil and oregano, I reached into my Jolly Green Giant tote bag and pulled out the bottle of Febreze.

Still no answer. Although I did hear voices in the family room.

"Kids?" I walked to the top of the stairs and peered down. The room was dark, except for the blue glow of the TV. The voices were louder—and familiar. Doctor Dan's voice, for one. And for the other—

My own.

I sat the pizza box on the table and followed the voices down the stairs.

"Aren't you going to kiss the bride, Dan?" It was my father's voice, younger and heartier than I remembered. That's because it was his voice nearly twenty years ago—coming from the television. Which was showing images—ghostly images, from my past. Me in a frothy white wedding dress, about two sizes smaller than my current self—and hair two shades darker, too—smiling at the camera. My uncle Bob had been the one holding it, I remembered, a sudden stab of pain to my heart. Uncle Bob had died ten years ago. But all of a sudden I heard his voice on the tape.

"Kiss 'er, Dan. Kiss 'er!"

And the younger version of Dan—the happy, smiling, Viking Groom—obliged, leaning down to kiss me while I giggled and protested and pretended to try to squirm away, but of course I didn't try too hard. Because my thin, pale arms reached up around Dan's neck, a blissful, perfect O, as my face met his. We both closed our eyes, and in that moment looked exactly like the ideal couple—the plastic bride and groom, forever happy, on the top of every wedding cake you've ever seen. Was he in love with me, even then? Watching his face, it was impossible to tell.

Watching my face, it wasn't. I wanted to shout at the television screen, warn that young girl of the heartache ahead.

I plopped down on the couch, my legs unable to bear the weight of my suddenly heavy heart.

"Say cheese," Uncle Bob's hearty voice called out, and I blinked away tears.

"Cheese!" The young couple on the screen beamed at the camera, as her face was crushed against his chest—his young, narrow chest, so boyish, I saw now. Not much more developed than Martin's. But back then I thought he was so mature, so *big*—and not in a fat way. But in a solid, unyielding, protector—man—way.

Not the unsure youth I saw now, waving at the video camera, his equally childish bride hanging on for dear life, unable to let him go. I noticed that, as the tape played on and I sank back in the cushions, unable to stop the memories—as we cut the cake, walked among the guests, took our place on the dance floor.

I never let go of him, or at least a part of him. I was always reaching, clutching, grabbing—an elbow or a wrist or even the tails of his tux.

Why was I holding on so tight? What was I afraid of, even then?

Finally I'd had enough; I couldn't stand to watch it anymore. I dried my moist eyes with my sleeve, reached for the remote, and turned off the VCR. And that's when I saw the note on the coffee table.

Hi Mom,

Something came up—Kel had to go to Vienna's to work on a project, and Coach called an extra practice. Sorry we couldn't do pizza night. But we found this tape and we thought you might like it.

Martin and Kelly.

P.S.: Dad called, and said that he wanted to take us all out to dinner Friday night. Okay?

Was it? Okay? That exhaustion, which I'd tried to avoid in the grocery store with Dan the other day, started to steal away my resolve. When was the last time we'd all eaten dinner together? I couldn't remember; it had to have been before the divorce, when the kids were still small enough to command all the attention— all the energy. Which had always been something Dan hated; he wanted to carry on intellectual conversations even when the kids were toddlers. And I just couldn't do it—not while I was simultaneously trying to remove spaghetti from Martin's hair, or cut

Kelly's steak into perfect one-inch squares, which for a long time was the only way she would eat anything—cubed.

I admit, I was curious. What would it be like to sit around a table as a complete family—no empty chair; someone else to argue Martin out of ordering extra fries because his eyes were always too big for his stomach?

I wadded up the paper and threw it in the trash basket, walked over to the phone, and punched in the numbers.

"Hello?"

"Dan?"

"Birdie?"

"What are you trying to do?"

"What do you mean?"

"Calling the kids, telling them you'll take us all out to dinner. They left me a note—they sound so excited. But didn't you hear me the other day? I'm engaged now. I don't think this is appropriate—"

"I don't know what you're talking about. I merely suggested we all go to Wally's Pizza Station." He sounded so reasonable, so smooth. He never got upset—so he never looked like the bad guy with the kids. I hated that about him.

"You don't like Wally's Pizza Station," I reminded him. "You think the little train that brings the pizza to the table is cheesy."

"But you like it. Plus they have free breadsticks."

"True, but that's not the point. You're filling up the kids' minds with a ridiculous hope, and you'll only end up hurting them. Is that what you really want to do, Dan? Hurt your own children?"

"Birdie, I don't understand. You always wanted me to spend more time with them, didn't you?"

"Yes, but—"

"And now I am, and you're complaining?"

"No, but—"

"Make up your mind—do you want me to be a better father to my children or not?"

"Of course I do, but—"

"Then let me take them out to dinner Friday. Let me take you all out—I think you deserve a night off, too."

"I— but—really?" I sat down on the arm of our ratty old recliner, not sure what to think.

"Really. I know you're going to marry Carl, Birdie. Believe it or not, I'm happy for you."

"You are?"

"Yes, I am."

"Oh." Now who was being ridiculous? (Not to mention vain and pathetic?) "I don't know—let me think about it. I'll see you on Friday." And I hung up the phone, picked up the remote, and turned the VCR back on. Videotapes, pictures—we choose the moments we want to be remembered in this way. But what about the fights, the tears, the silences that Dan and I could maintain for days? Where were the mementos of those?

What if they'd never happened? I didn't have any proof that they did. Except in my own memory, my own bruised heart. And my own tears, as I relived our hopeful beginning.

But when Friday came, that weariness overwhelmed me again, and I greeted Dan at the door in old sweats and a T-shirt. His face fell when he saw me.

"Are you—are you going out like that?"

I shook my head.

"But I thought—"

"You three go on ahead. You'll have a nice time. I'm a little tired. I thought I'd order in Chinese and watch a movie."

"But—"

"Hi, Daddy." Kelly brushed past me with hardly a glance. Martin followed, less surly, but still not looking me in the eye. I hadn't mentioned the videotape to either of them. I hadn't had the courage.

"Hello, Kelly, I thought we might be able to persuade your mother to come along with us."

"No, you go on ahead. You said you wanted to spend more time with the kids, remember?" I tried to read his face, wishing I could make him tell me the truth—and momentarily forgetting that I actually had the power to do so. My superpowers—which I used to such great effect with everyone else in the world— completely failed me when it came to my ex-husband.

Dan blinked, brushed his floppy hair out of his eyes, then smiled politely. Pleasantly, even. There was no hint that he was angry or disappointed.

"You're absolutely right. We'll have a great time, right, sport?" He clapped Martin on the back and ushered the kids down the sidewalk. I stood there in the doorway, watching them drive away. Then I went back inside, ordered Chinese (moo goo gai pan) and flipped through the TV channels, looking for a good movie to watch, somebody else's story. Not mine.

The only requirement was it couldn't be *The Parent Trap*.

CHAPTER 11

Squeals of excitement bounced off the walls, echoing through the vast, crowded space. I jumped up and down, trying to see over people's heads (because I'm only five feet three inches), but I couldn't. However, I sensed a ripple in the eager crowd in front of me so I stood still, knowing that, eventually, it would have to get to me.

And so it did. The sea parted and lo—a tiny man appeared.

"Wow, is he a shrimp," I whispered to Carl, who nodded.

"And tanned. Very, very tanned."

"Did you see those teeth? I needed sunglasses, they were so white!"

"And that hair—what kind of man has blond tips?"

"Isn't he dreamy?" Marge Miller grabbed my arm and sighed. I shrugged.

Ryan Seacrest didn't seem all that dreamy to me.

"But it is nice that he's emceeing the Silent Auction Dinner Dance," I said, because standing behind me was the woman who had said she was his cousin.

We—the PTA, local dignitaries, Mayor Linseed, Ryan Seacrest, and anyone else who had ponied up the seventy-five dollars per couple—were all packed into the still-unfinished concourse of the Astro Park-O-Dome Field, clad in unaccustomed finery. (Well, except for Ryan Seacrest. He wore ragged jeans, black T-shirt, and a blazer. Which might have been fine in Hollywood, but was a little informal for a PTA function.) Mary Denton had had so much Botox for the occasion that her eyebrows were frozen halfway between her eyes and her hairline. And she couldn't blink.

But it was for a good cause, as Mayor Linseed, standing up on a temporary stage decorated with giant papier-mâché baseball bats (courtesy of Mr. Sunderland's eighth-grade art class), kept booming out to us. For the kids. Those adorable li'l sluggers.

The decorating committee had done a fantastic job as usual— I recognized the disco ball hanging from the ceiling as a remnant of the Disco Daze fund-raiser five years ago. The tablecloths— linen, with only a few Kool-Aid stains visible—were from last year's Madrigal Dinner. And the huge chandelier hanging over the concourse was earmarked for this year's second-grade production of *Phantom of the Opera*.

"You look nice, Birdie!" The lower half of Mary's face crinkled up in a friendly way.

"Thanks, Mary!" I twirled around in my new cocktail dress, full skirt and a flattering ballet-neck top, sleeveless. I patted my brown hair, put up in an unaccustomed chignon, a few strands softly framing my face, coaxed there at Kelly's insistence.

She'd helped me get ready, to my great surprise. Even though she hadn't been talking to me that much lately, she'd actually shown up in my bathroom right at that moment when I was staring at my naked face in the mirror and wondering if there was any way that new shade of blush would suddenly transform me into Jennifer Aniston. "Mom?" Kelly had asked, clearing her throat. "Want some help getting ready?"

And even though I really didn't—the last time she'd offered

to "help" I'd ended up looking like I'd been attacked by a gang of glitter-glue-wielding preschoolers—I hugged her and sat down on the toilet (after first closing the lid), and obeyed when she instructed me to close my eyes, purse my lips, and hold still. And somehow she was able to work around my fidgeting and itching and runny nose (because every single item of makeup had its own artificial smell, sickening sweet) and "do what she could," as she put it.

And the results were smashing, if I did say so myself. I could tell by the way Carl stood still, staring, when he'd picked me up. I'd had to hit him in order to jolt him out of his stupor so that we could get to the dance on time.

My only regret was that I couldn't carry one of those tiny beaded evening bags, due to the need to carry my costume around with me at all times. (Rule #3 in the JLA handbook: *A superhero must have his costume with him at all times, no matter the occasion or weather.*)

So I shifted my Jolly Green Giant tote bag on my shoulder, trying not to notice that the faded green clashed with my teal dress.

"Birdie! Birdie!" Carrie whirred up to me, tugging on her bangs for all she was worth. "Guess who's out front?"

"I know, I saw them." I patted her on the head sympathetically.

"Stupid Shriners! They are really crossing the line. Do we stand out in front of their events asking for money?"

"Well, yes, we do. And usually we stop by the kindergarten class to pick out a few of the cutest kids to stand with us."

"That's different." Carrie's eyes gleamed dangerously behind her thick lenses. "They have tiny cars!"

"I'm sorry, but they can't take away from all this. You've done a great job! This is going to raise a ton of money. Now, where do you want me?"

"I have you on the cash box for the raffle tickets. Until the live auction, then of course I'll have to bring you onstage when we auction you off."

"Okay, that'll be— Huh?" I blinked.

"When we auction you off—you're the last item—of course you'll need to be up there."

"What the hell are you talking about?"

"For the Super Mom housecleaning. Remember?" Carrie shook her head. "I swear, Birdie, sometimes you're so forgetful—" And she whipped out her notebook and scribbled something down.

"Stop that! It's really getting on my nerves!" I yanked the notebook out of her hand. "And no. No, no, no. Don't even try that on me! I did not agree to this! I'm a superhero, Carrie!" I looked around and lowered my voice. "I'm a superhero. Not a cleaning service."

"Hello, girls!" Carl interrupted. Carrie and I both turned on him, hands on hips.

"What?"

"Nothing! Nothing . . . I think I'll just . . . go grab a beer. . . ." He backed away, eyes wide. I spun around and faced Carrie again.

"My services are not to be auctioned off," I informed her.

"But it's for the kids!" Carrie switched tactics, smiling adorably, shrugging her slender shoulders. I glared at her until she stopped.

"Don't give me that crap. This is all about you and your ego! You want to raise more money than the Shriners—who, by the way, are actually very nice people, and you know what? I love those tiny little cars! Love, love, *love* 'em! I think they're hilarious! Crack me up every time!"

Carrie gasped and twitched.

"You just want to raise more money than any PTA president ever, even if it means ignoring everything else—Kelly told me that the marching band's bass drum has a hole in it, but they don't have enough money to fix it so they're covering it with Saran Wrap and hoping for the best. Because every cent is going to this stupid stadium! Well, I'm not going to be a part of it. No sirree, I'm not gonna. . . ."

"Excuse me?"

Carrie and I both turned around. Ryan Seacrest was flashing his laser smile.

"Is Super Mom here yet? I'm really eager to meet her. I told Simon—"

"Simon?" I squeaked. "Simon Cowell?"

"Yeah, he really has a crush on her, so I told him I'd get her autograph."

Carrie made a gagging sound; I stepped on her foot.

"Well, we'll certainly be on the lookout for her, and let you know. Simon Cowell, you say? He has a crush on her?"

"Well, he's British. There's no accounting for taste." Tiny little Ryan Seacrest—I didn't even have to look up to glare at him—shrugged and walked away.

Carrie snickered.

"Okay, I'll do it." I folded my arms—accidentally-on-purpose hitting her in the head with my tote bag. "But I won't like it."

"Fine."

"Fine."

"Mr. Clean groupie."

"Shriner stalker."

"Spoiled brat."

"Control freak."

"Harrumph!" We both spun around and flounced off in opposite directions. I plopped down at the raffle ticket table, opened up my cash box, and leaned my head on my hand, fuming.

"Two, please," someone said, and I tore off two red raffle tickets, took the money, and handed back some change without even looking. More people bought tickets as the line got longer and longer. The concourse was really packed now with the best and brightest of Astro Park. Naturally, Mayor Linseed was squiring Mrs. Linseed—an impressively built matron with a bosom designed to challenge even the most intricately constructed underwire bra. Jasper was there, too, following around in the mayor's trail—either that or scurrying ahead to open doors for him. He looked odd in a suit, though. It was far too big for him—his hands disappeared in the sleeves and the bottom of the trousers puddled up around his ankles. It almost looked like it was a hand-me-down from the mayor.

"Three, please." I tore off tickets, counted change. And yawned.

"Fifty, please."

I looked up, not sure if I'd heard right. "Fifty? Oh!" For staring down at me, looking extremely dapper in a black custom-tailored suit with a vibrantly blue, French-collared shirt and tasteful tie, was Dan.

"Dan," I said stupidly. And then I felt a pimple start to form on my chin.

"Hello, Birdie. My, you look lovely!"

"Um, thanks. You, too. Handsome, I mean."

"Thank you."

He gazed down at me, smiling fondly, for so long that I didn't know what to do. I patted my hair to see if it was still up. I shook my feet out of my shoes and felt my leg for pantyhose runs. I checked to make sure the clasp of my necklace hadn't somehow found its way to the middle of my chest. I felt trapped, pinned to my chair by his brilliant blue eyes. "So," I finally said with a little cough. "You wanted fifty tickets?"

"Oh, yes, that's right. Pardon me, I was so taken by how you look that I forgot what I was here for."

"Thank you. I guess."

"You're welcome." Dan laughed, very, very merry for a man who was in the middle of his second divorce. "Don't act so surprised."

"I'm not surprised. I'm just—never mind." I concentrated on counting fifty raffle tickets off, messed up twice, then finally tore a hunk off and handed it to him.

"Keep the change." Dan handed me a hundred-dollar bill, which I held, reverently, before tucking it under the change tray.

"That's very nice of you, Dan."

"No, no, it's for the kids, isn't it? And besides, how can I resist such a beautiful salesperson?" He took his pile of raffle tickets, folded them neatly into his wallet, and started to walk away. But then he turned around and reached his hand toward my breasts . . . where the clasp of my necklace *had* ended up, dangling between my not-so-perky-anymore bosoms. He pulled it up toward the back of my neck, a perfect gentleman, except for the naughty wink he bestowed upon me.

"Thank you," I croaked, a little shiver running up and down my spine as his hand lingered, just for a minute, on the nape of my neck.

"My pleasure."

I watched him walk away with a sure, confident bounce in his step. He looked different from everyone here; like an actor in a soap opera. Handsome, tanned, tailored—almost airbrushed, in a way. No other man here wore a suit nearly as well.

Not even, I noted with a tender sigh, Carl. Who was coming toward me with two glasses of wine, his tie askew, his suit coat

flapping behind him, his brown hair, normally so sexy and un-
ruly, carefully parted and combed, just like a six-year-old about
to have his first school picture taken.

"Hi." I smiled up at him. He was still much more handsome
than Dan—that ruddy complexion, those intriguing little lines
that bracketed his mouth, the myopic softness of his brown eyes.

"Thought you might like a glass of wine. Business been
good?"

"Oh," I said, remembering the hundred-dollar bill. "So-so.
Guess what? Carrie had the nerve to offer up a free housecleaning courtesy of Super Mom for the final auction item. Will
you bid on me?"

"Depends." Carl sat down on the folding chair next to me.
"What comes with the cleaning?"

"What do you mean?"

"You know. Sexual favors, scantily clad costumes, that sort
of thing."

"Pervert." But I grinned and leaned back against his arm,
which had automatically reached out to embrace my shoulders.
It was like a Pavlovian thing for Carl. He simply couldn't keep
his arms from reaching out for me, all the time. Very different, I
reminded myself sternly, from the way Doctor Dan had treated
me when we were married.

"Oh, for the love of—look who's here." Carl's muscles
tensed as he pointed across the crowded room. I followed his
gesture, which led right to Mr. Derringer. He was marching
through the crowd, his pinched face grim, determined—a man
on a mission. "Let's hope he doesn't make any trouble."

I nodded. And sold three more raffle tickets.

"Speaking of trouble, do you think that Phantom guy will
be here?"

Carl's arm grasped my shoulder in a protective vise. "He'd

better not be. Dammit, Birdie, I'm still not used to this superhero thing!"

"I'll always have enemies intent on destroying me, you know. It goes with the territory."

Carl didn't say anything; he just pulled me closer, as if for that moment, at least, he could keep me safe.

"All right," I said as the lights dimmed and the high school jazz band started tuning up. "I'm all done here. Let me turn this in and we can mingle a bit."

"I'll wait here." Carl waved as I locked up the cash box and made my way through the crowd, heading to the locker rooms, which, I assumed, the PTA had taken over as Command Central.

"Excuse me." I brushed against someone lingering outside a closed door, her ear flattened against it. She jumped, emitting a little peep, and blushed. "Oh, Lois! Lois Blane! I didn't mean to startle you. I was just going—" But I stopped, watching as she furiously chewed some gum. I sniffed. And inhaled—wintergreen. And *peaches.*

I almost dropped my cash box as images tumbled through my mind, out of order—Martin in the dugout, smiling at her; the piece of notebook paper fluttering to the ground in the hallway, after I suffered my Second Horrible Swiffer Accident; Martin in the dugout. Smiling at her.

I stared at her—wide green eyes, trembling hands clutching the college-ruled notebook to her chest, thin shoulder blades poking out of a dress that looked like she'd worn it for her First Communion.

"Lois, you—"

"Shhh!" She put her finger up to her lips, whispering. "I'm investigating. The mayor's in there. And Jasper. And also the head of the construction company building the stadium. . . ."

"You seem to hang around here a lot, don't you?"

Her eyes darted quickly to me, narrow, suspicious. Then she blinked and they were wide and innocent once more. "I don't know what you mean."

"Like the other day, at the baseball game—"

"I cover sports, too."

"Ahh." Well, that answered the question as to why Martin suddenly decided to impersonate Babe Ruth.

"Have you heard anything interesting?"

"Nothing yet, but I'm pretty sure I'm on to something big—so big it's going to blow this town wide open!" Then she stopped, fiddled in a pocket, and replaced one of the rubber bands on her braces. "Corruption in the mayor's office!"

I laughed. "I don't think that's going to stop the presses." I continued down the hall.

"Not like, say, disclosing the true identity of Super Mom?"

I whirled around. Lois was consulting her notebook, seemingly innocent—she even popped a gum bubble.

"Don't do that—it'll get all over your braces."

She shrugged, eyes wide and pure.

"You come with me, young lady," I said, pulling her away from the door.

"What? What'd I do?" Lois struggled. "You don't understand—there's something important going on back there—"

"It can wait. We need to have a little talk." And I opened up a door to an empty weight room, turned the light on, and threw her in, slamming the door behind us.

"What?" Her big green eyes started to fill with tears. "What do we have to talk about, Mrs. Lee?"

"Well . . ." Now that we were alone, I didn't really know. I watched her, all junior Nancy Drew innocence. "I was wondering . . . you mentioned Super Mom's true identity. Have you ever met her?"

"Ooh, no, but I'm dying to!"

"Weren't you at the baseball game the other day?"

"Yes, but it got so crazy when she passed out. I hung around a while after, to . . . well . . . to try to see someone on the team. . . ." She blushed and blinked her green eyes innocently. Very innocently. *Extremely* innocently—almost as if she was trying to convince me that she was very innocent. Of—just what, exactly?

I dropped the money box and tote bag on a bench, put my hands on my hips and marched over to her, looking into her puppy-dog eyes with my Merciless Gaze. I looked, and looked, and saw clouds and curtains and veils and shades—there were a million stories in this girl's eyes, and she wasn't going to give up any of them freely.

"I don't believe you," I finally said, standing down.

She rubbed her eyes like a sleepy child. Then all of a sudden she grinned. "I guess that Merciless Gaze really does the trick, doesn't it?"

"Why—you! You—"

"Yes, I know. I saw you the other day in the locker room, after your accident. I'm sorry, Mrs. Lee. Really I am." And she did look it—her eyes big and sorry and a little bit fearful.

"Well, why haven't you broken the story yet?" I sat down on the bench, shoulders sagging. I was *so* going to be kicked out of the Justice League of America for this!

"I was going to, honest." Lois sat down beside me. "But then I realized I was on to something bigger, and a good journalist has to follow the trail while it's warm."

"What's bigger than me? Super Mom? Don't you think that's a pretty good scoop?" I pouted, hurt.

"Not bigger than corruption in the mayor's office!"

I laughed.

"What? Isn't that exciting?"

"Oh, sweetheart, that's adorable! You honestly think that a corrupt politician is news?"

"But this is about the town! And the future! And civic responsibility, and voters' trust, and . . ."

"And it happens all the time, and you haven't done your homework because everyone knows Mayor Linseed isn't exactly a Boy Scout. Look at all the family he has on his payroll! Look at Jasper, for heaven's sake."

"Right!" Lois opened up her notebook and started flipping through pages, looking for something. Her braces gleamed in the overhead light. "Jasper! I have a lot of questions about *him*. . . ."

"I can't believe you'd think a corrupt politician was a bigger scoop than me."

"And if I could just find my research about those abandoned salt mines, I'm sure you'd understand how important this might be." She fumbled in her backpack for some notes, pulling out old scraps of chewing gum wrappers and crumpled napkins.

"All right, all right. I get it. What, exactly, were you listening to back there?"

"I'm not sure I should tell you. I really want this scoop for myself!"

"Well, you obviously don't read comic books, or else you'd know that every good journalist has a superhero who feeds her information. We can help each other out—I can get into places you can't, especially since you have a curfew and I don't. And obviously if there's some danger to the community, Super Mom needs to know about it."

"But how do I know I can trust you?"

"Lois, I used to be snack mother for your soccer team. My daughter used to babysit you. My son . . . well . . . Besides—I have to trust you with my identity. Why can't you trust me?"

"I don't know . . ."

"Also, I have an idea. If you promise not to reveal my secret identity—assuming it was ever a big enough story for you, anyway—" I snorted.

"I'm sorry. I didn't mean to hurt your feelings." She patted me on the back.

"So if you promise not to reveal that, I promise not to scoop you. I also promise to get you an internship at one of the finest newspapers in the country—one of the best examples of journalistic integrity, and a place where I think you'll fit right in."

"Really?" Her green eyes threw out sparks of excitement.

"Really. I have a trusted source, and he owes me one. So—how about it?"

She hesitated, hugging her notebook to her chest. Finally she let out a big breath, stuck out her hand, and nodded. I shook her hand.

"Great. Now, I have my first mission for you."

"What?" Her eyes got huge.

"What time is it?"

"Ten o'clock."

"Go home."

"What?"

"Go home, Lois, it's past your bedtime and you need at least eight hours of sleep—many studies show teenagers need ten."

"But—"

"Don't make me put you in a Super Time-Out, young lady. Are you going to call your parents for a ride, or should I?"

"I will." She got to her feet, replaced one of the rubber bands on her braces, and followed me back out to the dance. "But don't you want to know what's going on with the mayor?"

"Some other time, Lois. I'd like to get some punch before it's all gone."

"But—"

"Later, I promise." I patted the shoulder of the teenaged temptress who was ruining my son's life, but who actually was cute little Lois Blane, whom I'd known forever. But who, even more actually, could do me great harm if she ever revealed my secret identity, but at least for now I knew I was safe.

Because she had a curfew, and I didn't.

"Did you know that this is our first dance?"

"It is?" I smiled up at Carl. "I didn't realize!"

"I think it's going well, don't you?"

"Very."

I closed my eyes and let him spin me around in a very impressive twirl—which I ruined by stepping on his feet.

"Wow!" I giggled. "I had no idea you could dance like this!"

"Just one of my many secrets," he said, raising his eyebrows. "Although I wish I could say the same about you."

"Sorry, I've never been much of a dancer."

Carl twirled me around a couple more times, admirably ignoring my two left feet.

"So do you think we'll dance at our wedding?"

"What do you mean?" I leaned my head on his chest.

"Have you thought much about it? The wedding, and the reception, and, well, the wedding . . . ?"

"What are you trying to say?" I lifted my head and looked at him. There were little beads of perspiration on his forehead.

"It's just that we haven't really talked about the details yet, and I haven't wanted to push you, but don't you think it's time?"

Did I think it was time? To worry about a million details like invitations and dresses and colors and napkins and matchbooks and flowers and . . . and . . . shoes? Right now, with that Phantom guy lurking in the back of my mind, and Doctor Dan pounding in the front, and this horrible smell, like rotten eggs and dirty gym socks and fermenting leaves, that had been getting stronger and stronger as the evening progressed, threatening to bring on a headache the size of New Hampshire before the evening was out. . . .

Did I think it was time for all that?

"Carl, I have to be honest. I'm not sure I'm up to planning something big right now. Can't we—can't we think about it a little later? And maybe do something a bit smaller? I just think that with the kids and all, it might be best to, I don't know. Elope, maybe?"

Carl laughed, despite a little pucker that appeared between his eyes.

"Maybe you're right," he said, holding me close. "Maybe something smaller would be better."

"But you know what?"

"What?"

"I promise I'll dance with you. I promise I'll dance with you at our wedding, no matter where, when, or how."

"That's a coincidence." Another male voice broke in. All of a sudden Carl was no longer holding me close; he stood still, his eyes glinting like brown steel, as Doctor Dan poked him on the shoulder.

"What is?" I tried to control my voice, keeping it low and pleasant.

"You danced with me at *our* wedding. And for old time's sake, I'd like the privilege again."

"What?"

"Could I—would you mind, Cal? I'd like to dance with the mother of my children."

And Dan steered me away before Carl had a chance to say anything, which was probably good because his face turned purple and his eyes got darker than I'd ever seen them. I think steam started to puff out of his ears.

"Don't worry!" I called out to him. "This will only take a second! And boy, does that bring back a lot of memories." I glared at Dan.

To my surprise, he laughed. "Very funny, Birdie. When did you get to be so witty?"

I scowled at his shoulder, determined not to look him in the face.

"This is nice." Dan pressed his cheek to my hair and guided me across the floor as the Jerome Siegel Junior High and High School Jazz Band played "Close to You." "Do you remember what was playing at our wedding?"

"No," I lied, not about to tell him I'd just been watching the videotape of that occasion.

"I do. That song from *Top Gun* . . . what was it called?"

I didn't answer.

"Now, Birdie, what was it? I can hear it, but I can't remember the name. . . ."

Still I kept my mouth shut.

"If you don't tell me, I'm going to start singing it right now. Only I don't know the words, and I can't sing very well, and it will be extremely embarrassing—"

" 'Take My Breath Away,' " I relented.

"Yes, that was it." Dan spun me around so tightly that my head fell back and I couldn't help but look up; he was smiling, his crow's-feet crinkling so that he looked almost kind. Handsome, of course—I'd never been able to take that away from him. But almost kind. "Remember? We had the DJ play 'Simply Irresistible'? And all the bridesmaids stood behind me, like those models in the video, and I borrowed somebody's sunglasses and pretended I was Robert Palmer?"

"They were my cousin's sunglasses." I couldn't help it; I had to giggle at the memory. He'd looked so ridiculous—and so adorable—standing up there lip-synching while all my bridesmaids gyrated behind him.

"That was a great day," Dan said simply.

I nodded, looked away, and continued to allow myself to be spun across the dance floor, once more thrown into a tizzy of conflicting memories and emotions. Yes, it had been a great day. But what came after hadn't been, and the man so carefully guiding me around the dance floor as if I were a delicate flower was the one responsible for that, yet why was I the only one who remembered that part?

But then I had to wonder, why was I the only one who *wanted* to remember that part?

Carrie, who was barreling her way across the crowded concourse with a pair of pliers in her hands (which didn't bode well for the Shriners), saw us, stopped, and gaped. Howard—his bald head reflecting back all the tiny little lights from the chandelier—stopped right behind her and gaped, too. I smiled and shrugged, which didn't seem to do any good at all, as they continued to stare, two disapproving middle-aged vandals.

"Dan, what are you up to?" The jazz band swung—or rather, lurched—into a rendition of "Smoke Gets in Your Eyes."

"What do you mean?" His voice was too smooth, too pleasant. My Super Ex-Wife Sense started in, the tiny little hairs on the back of my neck standing at attention.

"You're up to something. For eight years you've ignored me. Now you're getting divorced. And I'm getting married. And you're suddenly turning on the charm. You can't possibly be jealous—not after all this time."

"No? I can't? Tell me why I can't be jealous that the mother of my children—a wonderful, beautiful woman who I wronged deeply—says she's going to marry another man? Tell me why I can't all of a sudden realize what a terrible mistake I made when I let you go, when I behaved like a complete asshole and embarrassed you and hurt you and did a lot of stupid things that I now regret with all my heart?" Dan stopped dancing, dropped my hand, let go of my waist, and stood before me, seemingly stripped bare of everything I used to attribute to him—pride, attitude, smugness, superiority. He seemed almost naked without them.

"Because it's too late. You have no idea how much I ached to hear you say those things, even just a couple of years ago. But not anymore. I've grown—oh, in so many ways that you can't even begin to imagine. I've changed. I'm sorry."

"You shouldn't be apologizing to me, Birdie. Not for anything. It's I who should spend the rest of my life apologizing to you."

"Yes, well, I won't argue about that. But do you really believe that, Dan?"

"Yes, I really believe it. I made a terrible mistake, and I hate the way that I treated you."

I looked at him, and I couldn't read what was in his eyes. Maybe because it had been so long since I'd looked there for the answers to my questions. "The only thing I know, right now, is that if you're telling the truth, then I'm sorry for you."

"Is that all you feel for me?" He took my hand again and held it against his chest. I could feel his heart, beating so steadily; was I imagining it, or did it begin to speed up at the touch of my hand?

Before I could answer, Carl was looming over Dan's shoulder, poking at him.

"So listen, bub." I almost laughed, but caught myself just in time; I'd never heard him say the word "bub" before. Sniffing, I realized he'd had a couple of glasses of Marge Miller's famous

Nuclear Option Punch—my Super Smelling Sense put him at a blood alcohol content of approximately .05. "I think you'd better skedaddle."

"It's all right, Carl, I've got it under control." I patted his arm, alarmed to find his muscles tensed and his fists clenched. "Really, it's all right. Dan was just about to leave. . . ."

"No, actually, I wasn't. What I didn't finish saying, Birdie, is that I'm not prepared to give up so easily. Not without a fight."

"Dan, what is this about? Why now? Why after all this time?" Hot, frustrated tears pricked at my eyelids. I just wanted him to go away—go away and take all these false memories of our marriage, and how it ended, and whose fault it was, with him.

"Birdie, stay out of this." Carl continued to poke at Dan's shoulder.

"What? Carl, now come on. This is between Dan and me. There's no need to—"

"Listen to her, Cal. She's smarter than either of us gives her credit for."

"Now that's ridiculous. Just stop it, Dan!" I stomped my foot, surprising us all. "There is nothing to talk about. I don't know what's going on with you, but one thing I do know is that it's over. And it has been for a long time, and I'd appreciate it if you'd leave the kids out of this little fantasy of yours. Because it's too late for—"

All of a sudden the jazz band squealed to a stop. A spotlight picked out Mayor Linseed—wearing his top hat, so that he looked appropriately formal—and followed him as he waddled up to the stage, where Ryan Seacrest was hanging out, eating a sandwich and talking to the cute kindergarten teacher, Miss Kyle.

"It's time we get down to some serious fund-raising! Allow me to introduce our special guest, Ryan Seacrest, as he begins the live auction portion of the evening!"

"Oh, crap," I said. "I have to go."

Both Carl and Dan grabbed an arm and started to walk off in different directions.

"Ow! No, I have to go. I have to, um, go make sure Carrie isn't torturing the Shriners, so I'll see you two a little later. Don't . . . don't kill each other, okay?" And I shook off their hands and sped away, running down a hallway until I found an empty bathroom.

Then I changed into my Super Mom costume, preparing to be auctioned off to the highest bidder.

"Super Mom, this is a surprise." Mayor Linseed bowed as we stood side by side under hot stage lights. Rivers of sweat poured out from under his top hat, running down his jowly face.

"I'm being auctioned off. I mean, my services are. Someone will win a free housecleaning from me."

"I admit, I was hoping you'd stay away after the last— incident. I'm dismayed that you'd want to jeopardize the future of this fine town, after what happened last time."

"Mayor, relax, that was just an isolated incident, I'm sure—"

"Let's hope so. For both of our sakes."

I flashed a quick Merciless Gaze his way, but Ryan Seacrest's blinding white smile must have deflected it, because the mayor's eyes blinked back at me, wide and innocent.

"And we're back!" Ryan Seacrest bounded down to the end of the stage, as if we'd just been to a commercial. "Now, our final item for the evening—and my personal favorite. A special housecleaning by that maternal dynamo herself, Super Mom!"

I waved at the crowd, acknowledging the applause—pausing to wrinkle my nose at Carrie, who folded her arms and glared.

"Now let's start the bidding at fifty dollars! Which is a bargain, if you ask me. I wish I could bid myself!"

Someone raised a hand, and I let out a sigh of relief. I *so* didn't want to tank.

"Great! Do I hear sixty? Seventy? Eighty?" The bidding climbed and climbed, and I couldn't stop myself from giggling. I was going to fetch the highest price for the evening, leaving Barbara Murray's free piano lessons in the dust. But then I started to worry, because the higher the bidding rose, the more wealthy the bidders. Which meant—really big houses with lots and lots of rooms to clean.

I was rescued from such a fate, however, by a knight in shining armor.

"One hundred!" Carl shouted, smiling. "A gift to my lovely fiancée!"

I beamed at him.

"One fifty!" Doctor Dan materialized next to him, raising an aristocratic finger. "A gift to the mother of my children!"

The crowd—heavily populated as it was with PTA members—gasped. Carrie staggered a little, then looked at me, one eyebrow raised as high as it could go.

"One seventy-five," Carl said, the muscles in his neck popping.

"Two hundred," Doctor Dan countered smoothly.

"Whoa!" Ryan Seacrest broke in. "Let me do my job—don't go all Paula Abdul on me, boys!"

The crowd roared while Carl and Dan glared at each other. I stood, helpless, silently pleading with Carl to sell his car, sell his blood, sell anything in order to keep me from having to figure out how to explain to Doctor Dan that I—Super Mom—couldn't be a gift to me—Birdie—because . . . I was me. And her. Both.

Then that headache, caused by overwhelming fumes of rotten eggs and compost, attacked with a vengeance, shooting arrows at the backs of my eyeballs.

"Two twenty-five." Carl raised his hand, sounding very un-sure of himself. I knew he was mentally calculating how much that garage sale might bring in.

"Two fifty," countered Doctor Dan, still as confident—and as condescending—as ever.

"Two fifty-five?"

"Two seventy-five."

"Two eighty." And the way Carl said this—flat, emotion-less, his arms dangling lifelessly by his side, told me the end was at hand.

"Three hundred." Dan folded his arms, his blue eyes glinting flecks of steel.

"Going once . . . going twice . . . sold!" Ryan Seacrest raised his arm. "Seacrest . . . out!"

There were wild cheers at first—exuberance over the money raised. Then the crowd started to murmur sympatheti-cally, and I saw lots of people make their way toward Carl to clap him on the shoulders.

Meanwhile I had to remain onstage while Doctor Dan was brought up to claim his prize.

"Hello." I glared at him from the safety of my masked iden-tity. "Nice to meet you. Your name is?"

"Doctor Dan Lee, Dermatologist." His nose turned up, bored, as if he talked to superheroes every day. Doctor Dan wasn't a fan of Super Mom. She'd made rather a fool of him a few months back. (A little thing involving a lost bet and a forced, very public apology from Dan for past sins.)

"I suppose we should set up a date for this cleaning. Next Saturday okay for you?"

"I'll have to check with my ex-wife. You're—this—is a present for her."

"She must be quite a woman." All of a sudden an

unexpected—yet interesting—thought formed itself in my pounding head.

Dan shrugged. I narrowed my eyes, that interesting thought taking an interesting shape.

"Here's my card, with my e-mail address." I reached into one of the pockets of my Apron of Anticipation and pulled out my JLA business card. (Everything goes through their server, so our secret identities are well protected.) "Let me know when you want this done."

"All right. I'll have to check with her—speaking of which . . ." Dan broke off and looked out at the crowd. "Birdie? Where is she, anyway? Birdie?"

"Gotta go!" Backing away, I prepared to make a quick exit. But then I heard a scream, at the exact same time the hair on top of my head started to tickle, and my neck began to tingle—my Super Mom Sense was kicking in.

"Look! Up there!"

I looked up, along with everyone else in the room. Crawling along a beam in the unfinished ceiling was a wiry figure wearing a bucket and carrying a Swiffer. A Super Secret Super Duper Swiffer. Suddenly organ music began to blare; this time the song was "We Are the Champions."

"See?" Mayor Linseed materialized, pulling at the ties of my apron. "What did I tell you? Why can't you stay away?"

"Because it looks like someone is trying to make sure that I do. Which can only mean that *someone* is trying to hide something. You wouldn't know anything about that, would you, Mr. Mayor?"

"I don't know what you're talking about—I just want that thing to go away!"

"Leave it to me!" I ran to the edge of the stage. "Get down from there! Are you crazy?"

"I am the Phantom of the Bullpen. . . ." That disembodied voice echoed again, this time without any benefit of wireless technology, so that it was a little muffled and faint.

"Get down! Do you hear me? You'll break your neck!"

"But . . . but . . . other evil villains swoop down on their prey. . . ."

"If other evil villains jumped off a bridge, would you? Now get down from there. You'll hurt yourself." I strode out onto the dance floor, which was packed with PTA members craning their necks up at this weird, bucket-headed figure.

"No . . . but . . . Super Mom! I told you to stay away from here! You didn't pay attention. And now someone has to die!"

There was a dramatic scream—I think it came from Mary Denton, although with all that Botox it was hard to tell.

"This is ridiculous! You have a trash can lid for a shield and a Swiffer for a weapon. And speaking of—I'm really interested in learning how you got that particular Swiffer in the first place. So why don't you come down here and—"

He replied by aiming that Swiffer—with the acid cleaning fluid—right at my head. But this time I wasn't afraid; I knew I could safely cross streams with it without suffering yet another Horrible Swiffer Accident. (Which, by the way, was getting a little old.)

I responded by shoving people out of my immediate vicinity (including Ryan Seacrest, who was light as a feather and flew about twenty feet before he was caught, somewhat awkwardly, by Mayor Linseed); I crouched down, graceful as a panther, my hands poised, ready to rumble.

But the Phantom didn't fire at me after all. Instead, he jumped off the beam—the crowd gasped—and hung from the huge chandelier. Only he didn't know—as I did—that the chandelier was just a stage prop; it started to groan and creak and shudder.

"Get off the floor!" I started shoving people this way and that; the chandelier creaked more ominously so I braced myself—glancing over at Carl, who was pale and wide-eyed—and flung my cleaning fluid, more powerful than before, up at the chandelier. Just as it tore from the chain the Phantom reached out and grabbed a beam, saving himself as it started to fall—in slow motion. Or so it seemed as I strained, firing my cleaning fluid with enough force to catch and sustain it, this giant light fixture made up of thousands and thousands of prisms. I grunted, muscles aching and trembling from the force, until finally I was able to cradle the thing gently to the ground, my knees buckling, yelling at everyone to stand back. And then I let go, wincing as it settled safely to the ground; I shook my arm, every muscle in my body—particularly in my neck and upper arms—kinking up, pinching all my nerves.

The crowd burst into applause; I smiled, exhausted, content just to stand there and bask in the glow. Until somebody shouted—

"Look! There goes the Phantom!"

Then I sprinted off, running beneath the little man on the beam high above, tensed and ready to catch him if he fell. But he didn't. He scrambled like a monkey along the beam, handling the Swiffer like a pro. I couldn't help but admire him. Even as I was shouting up to him, "I'm going to get you! You can't run away from me!"

"Wanna bet?" He never once lost his footing.

"Can I help?" All of a sudden someone was panting beside me; Lois Blane was trotting along, clutching her notebook to her chest.

"No! Go back! This is no place for children!"

"I'm not a child, I'm a journalist!"

"You're fourteen. Go back. Tomorrow's a school day—don't you have any tests to study for?"

"I'm not leaving! And no, I don't have any tests."

I glared at her, but I didn't have time for a Super Time-Out because I had to follow the Phantom. He was scrambling so fast I couldn't keep up, so I fired cleaning fluid on the floor before me, ran, and slid on it, surfing like Gidget.

"Oh, man!" I heard Lois yell, way behind me. "That is so cool!"

"I learned it at JLA Boot Camp!" I looked up—the Phantom was gone.

"Wait—there—over in the corner!" Lois called out. I looked; there was a vast ironworks above us, the base of the domed part of the stadium. And over in a corner, up a far wall, climbed a bucket-headed figure.

"Damn! I mean, darn—don't put that in your article!" I looked around for a way to reach the Phantom; spying a stairwell down at the end of the hall, past all the locker rooms and training rooms and weight rooms, I surfed toward it. From far behind me I heard Carl's voice calling, "Super Mom! Be careful!" I sort of waved, then ran into the stairwell, looked around, and found a closed door. I pulled it; it didn't budge. I pushed and shoved and heaved and pulled, but still it remained closed. Finally I fired my super-duper cleaning fluid at it, and cut a Birdie-sized hole in the steel, slicing like a knife through butter.

"Cool!" I chirped. Then I saw a ladder, like that on a fire escape, reaching toward infinity; far up ahead of me, on the same ladder, climbed a wiry, scrabbling figure. I said a quick prayer, hoped that Lois wouldn't need to write an obituary so early in her career, and started climbing.

"You stay down there, young lady," I tossed over my shoulder. To my surprise, she did.

" 'Kay," she called up with a wave.

I turned and looked at the steel rungs in front of me, and

I climbed. I climbed and climbed and once I thought I was going to break off one of my heels, but I didn't, and I kept climbing, never looking down, only focusing on the steel rungs, approximately eight inches apart, shiny and new—aware, always, of the figure scrambling ahead of me. And I knew there was no way I was going to catch him. Especially not in high heels.

"Stop! In the name of the Justice League of America! Stop!"

"Make me!"

"All right, you asked for it." I stopped climbing, clung to the ladder with one shaking hand, while with the other I fired cleaning fluid up at him. He screamed.

"Stop that!"

"You stop climbing and let me take you into custody!"

"Never!"

All of a sudden something hit me on the head, hard. I bit my tongue, tasted metallic blood. It was a brown work boot, falling toward the ground. "Look out below!" I yelled; Lois screeched.

"All right, that's it!" I fired again. This time the Phantom wavered; I saw his body flap, like a flag in the wind, and falter. So I fired again, trying to aim at his hands. And it worked; he let go. I watched him, had a split second to smile in triumph before I realized that he was falling, falling, like a little doll, to his certain death, and that was a bad thing.

My arm shot out before I could even think; I caught him as he fell and the force of it pulled me off the ladder, too, and I screamed, he screamed, there were screams echoing all around the stadium—my ears were torn with the sounds of our terror. The ladder was rushing past me and I reached out with my left hand, clawing at it, but knowing that I was going to end up flat as a pancake on the floor somewhere below, and the only thing I could think of was that I hoped Lois was out of the way. I didn't have time to think of Kelly and Martin and Carl and everything else you're supposed to think of when you're hurtling toward a messy death. I didn't have time—because all of a sudden I strained upward with one giant, last-ditch effort, reaching for the ladder, the sky, the stars—

And I felt suspended. Suspended on the breath of a prayer, a hope. A dream. I looked at the ladder, no longer rushing past me; waiting for me to reach out and step back on, light as a feather despite the person dangling from my right arm.

"Oh!" I gasped, my ears beating with the throb of my heart. I looked at the person whom I was holding up—his bucket had fallen off, one of his eyes was gray and terrified and puzzled and angry and grateful, all at once. And I gasped again, shocked. Because the other eye—was glass. The person I was holding, as I clung to the ladder, saving us both with the power of my own dreams—

Was Janitor Bingo.

CHAPTER 12

There are certain words and phrases that strike fear into every parent's heart. "My tummy hurts," uttered by a toddler, for example, signals impending bouts of vomiting, diarrhea, or more likely a messy combination of both. Just when you've run out of clean towels.

"Mom, you know that really expensive vase in the dining room?" asked by a twelve-year-old boy nervously tossing a baseball means that that really expensive vase—usually a rare heirloom passed down from your great-grandmother—is no more.

"We have a situation" written or spoken by any school administrator means that you'd better start looking into private schools. As soon as possible.

And for parents of teenagers, the words "prom night" are sure to conjure up nightmarish visions of empty beer bottles, mangled cars, and blood-spattered gowns. We can't help it. It's part of our pop culture, from countless horror movies to classic episodes of *Death on the Highway*. It's no wonder, then, that when a parent hears the words "prom night" she drops to her knees, pulls out her hair, and screams with terror. (And that's even before she's presented with the bill for the dress.)

In an effort to further scare our children out of their minds regarding just about every aspect of their teenaged years, I—as a special guest of the PTA—was standing in front of an assembly at Jerome Siegel Junior High and High School on a chilly day in mid-April, the beginning of prom season, about to deliver a stern Super Mom lecture.

"All right, listen up," Coach Henderson—who was also the driver's ed teacher and so the first line of defense in the school's campaign to save teenagers from themselves—barked. "I want you all to welcome Super Mom, who has a few words to say about prom night."

Nobody clapped. The only sound was the ancient creaking of the gym bleachers as teenagers shifted in boredom—and the whisperings and flutterings of a hundred prom invitations being proffered, declined, recycled, and accepted.

"Thanks, Coach." I stepped up to the mike, scanning the crowd for Kelly. I spotted her in a third-row bleacher, next to Vienna, her hair hiding her face, which was probably a picture of mortification. Vienna was scratching her head with a pencil, when she wasn't adjusting the black bra straps that were peeking out from her torn white T-shirt.

"I just want to say a few words about prom night safety, and then I'll let Police Commissioner Borden tell you about an exciting new program we have planned. First of all, the most important thing is—don't drink and drive. The life you save might be your own. Prom night should be an important night in your young lives, but remember just that—you have a lot of years ahead of you. A driver's license doesn't make you an adult. Neither does a prom ticket, or a fancy dress or a tuxedo. You're still kids, and as such, we adults are here to help you. So before I turn it over to Police Commissioner Borden, I just want to say one thing for those of you who might be feeling a little left out. You might not believe it, but I didn't go to my high school prom, and look how I turned out!" I waited for a reaction—applause, murmurs of astonishment, something. But all I got were blank, bored stares. "Um, what I'm trying to say is, it's not the end of the world if you don't go. Your life will turn out just fine. Some might say *super fine!*" Again I waited. The only reaction I got was from a group of chubby girls in the back row, who looked at one another and started to nod.

"Anyway," I said, disappointed. Man. Teenagers were a tough crowd. "Here's Police Commissioner Borden."

Borden took the microphone. "This year the police department is going to be clamping down on underage drinking. Now, in the past, we've been fairly successful, but this year we have a new ally in Super Mom. So we'll be having roadblocks stationed all around the high school, with officers equipped with Breathalyzers. In addition, Super Mom will be a floater, assisting us wherever necessary." Borden winked at me, and I winked back. Only he and I were aware of my new Super Smelling Sense, which, I'd recently discovered at the dinner dance when I was surrounded by PTA parents and an open bar, had turned me into a walking, talking Breathalyzer. Or Momalyzer, as I liked to call myself.

During Borden's lecture, I'd been watching the crowd, making mental notes of who seemed most upset. Darren Sinclair, for example, had gestured dramatically to Sean Braden. Jennifer Kendall and Ashlee Morton, too, looked particularly glum. I watched Kelly closely. While she never parted her curtain of hair so that I could see her face—clever girl!—I did notice that Vienna gave her a well-timed elbow to the ribs. I didn't know Kelly's plans yet, or if they included Vienna. But I would definitely find out. And soon.

Coach Henderson finally released the teens, who jumped up, chattering and gesturing and flipping hair. They filed out of the gymnasium, leaving us adults to huddle over the game plan.

"All right, so—Super Mom, you'll assist when necessary, and of course, vice versa. Coach Henderson, you have the PTA parents doing the post-prom party in the gym again, right?" Borden asked, mopping his chubby face with his handkerchief. All those hormones had given off their own heat; the room was stifling.

"Yep," Coach said, with less bluster than usual. His whole manner was subdued; his broad shoulders slightly hunched, all the creases in his face sagging.

"All right, we'll meet again the Wednesday before prom. Everyone got that?"

We nodded, synchronized our watches, and then I caught up with Coach Henderson on his way out the door.

"Coach, wait up!"

He turned around, patient as ever.

"I couldn't help but notice—is there something wrong? You seem a little down."

"Oh, Super Mom, nobody can hide anything from you, can they?" He sat down on a bleacher, and I joined him.

"Well, I didn't need to use my Merciless Gaze to see that something's bothering you. What's up?"

"I got fired."

"What? The school fired you?" I couldn't believe it. There wasn't a more beloved teacher than Coach Henderson. That gruff exterior hid nothing. Everyone knew he had the softest heart in town—and everyone knew how lonely he was, too. His wife had died a few years back, and they hadn't had children. So his students went out of their way to include him in their world, and his fellow teachers all fought to invite him to their homes for holidays.

"No, not the school. The mayor. I'm not coaching Little League. He wanted to get someone with more drive. He said it's only for this year; after they win the championship I can have the team back."

"Oh, that's so not fair!" I leaped to my feet, vibrating with outrage on his behalf. "I didn't know—Mar— I mean, nobody told me. What are all the parents saying? I bet they're pissed!"

"Well, that's the thing. They aren't. I counted on them to back me up, but they all want a championship team, too. They're tired of coming in last place year after year, I guess. But the kids—they're happy. I always thought that was the point. I guess not."

"Oh, Coach." I plopped back down. "I'm so sorry."

"Yeah. Hey, will you do me a favor?" He looked up, his face so creased and tired, his big blob of a nose red.

"Of course. Anything!"

"Will you stop by practice now and then, just to make sure everything's okay? I don't want to go—it'll just confuse the kids. They need to listen to their new coach. That's the way it is in the big leagues. But if you stop by, I'll feel better."

"You bet, Coach!"

"Good. They're all practicing at the new field now. The mayor says it's safe, although all that construction's going on. But he wants them to get used to it."

"Of course I'll go," I said, although I knew I wouldn't be welcome. Mayor Linseed had made that perfectly clear. But I also knew that I had a secret weapon up my sleeve. And speaking of . . .

"I've got to go, Coach. I have an errand to run. But don't worry! I'll make sure everything's okay."

"Thanks, Super Mom." Coach Henderson rose and gave me a great big bear hug, practically crushing my ribs. When he let go, I gasped in relief. "I love those little guys. And I'm worried about them, for some reason. I guess I'm just an old softie."

"Tell me something I don't know!" I patted his arm—which was as solid as Mr. Clean's.

Then I ran to join Police Commissioner Borden, who was waiting for me by the squad car. We had a little visit to make.

"So are we going to do this the easy way, or the hard way?" Borden paced up and down the jail cell, occasionally stopping to hit his palm with his nightstick.

"Really, Commissioner." I rolled my eyes. "Don't you think you're being a little dramatic?"

Janitor Bingo, seated on his cot in the only jail cell in Astro Park, seemed to agree. Because he trembled every time that nightstick hit.

"I didn't mean no harm," he said, stroking his grizzled chin over and over. "I didn't mean to hurt anyone."

"Well, you did!" Borden spun around and leaned over his shoulder, hissing into his ear. "You did!"

"No, he didn't," I pointed out. "He only hurt me. And I'd like to ask him a few questions about that, if you don't mind. Alone."

"Alone?" Borden's shoulders drooped. His nightstick hung sadly by his side, and he pouted.

"Yes, alone. But I brought you a little treat."

His eyes lit up.

"Out on your desk—milk and cookies for you and the boys."

"Oh, boy! Thanks, Super Mom!" And Borden pushed open the cell door and ran down the hall—forgetting to turn around and lock the door again. I shook my head and wondered, for the millionth time, how this town had survived before Super Mom came along.

But I also didn't think that Janitor Bingo was in any shape to make a run for it, as he was currently curled up in a fetal position on his cot.

"All right, first of all. Why, Janitor Bingo? Why did you want to hurt me?" Sitting down next to him, I put my hand on his shoulder and shook my head sadly. "After all I've done for this town?"

"That's why," he said, his voice raspy and flat. "Because you've done so much. So much cleaning. I haven't had anything to do in months, and I felt—well, I felt like nobody appreciated me anymore."

"Oh." I removed my hand from his shoulder and stared at it. My strong, grippy hand, full of such power—and such cleaning potential. I'd thought I'd been doing the right thing; like any mother, I didn't completely trust somebody else to do my job because, of course, nobody cared as much as I did. It was just like at home—I complained that Martin and Kelly never lifted a finger. But when they did, I ran around behind them, wringing my hands, sure that they'd forget to sweep under the refrigerator or dust the tops of the pictures.

But I hadn't realized that I was making someone feel useless—as useless as my kids made me feel, at times. "Oh, I'm so sorry. I, of all people, should have known. I didn't mean to take your job away, honest, I didn't. I just like to clean!"

"Me, too," he mumbled into his pillow.

"Well, don't you think it's time we're friends? It sounds like we have more in common than most people. I mean—who else really appreciates that feeling of accomplishment you get when you finally remove a stubborn rust stain from a bathtub?"

"Or get that tile grout to sparkle like new?" He raised his head.

"Or how satisfying it is to take a messy kitchen and make it look like no one's been there—to get all the dishes cleaned and counters wiped, everything like new again?"

"I know—that's how I feel every time I clean the cafeteria at school!" He sat up and looked at me with his one good eye, his gray little head bobbing up and down, like a baby bird's. "But nobody else seems to appreciate it. The kids—they're all afraid of me, or they make fun of me. They don't know how hard I work to make that school shine."

"Tell me about it." I nodded, crossing my legs—and wincing as I felt that tender scar on my thigh. Which brought me back to the purpose of this visit. "But we have to deal with the little fact that you did, apparently, try to kill me. And also, that you almost—although accidentally—killed a bunch of PTA parents at the dance. And one more thing—that you seem to want to keep me away from the Astro-Park-O-Dome Field for some reason. So, spill it, Bingo." I rose from his cot and paced—menacingly, I hoped—in front of him.

"Someone recruited me. I been tellin' everyone how much I hate you—that wasn't no secret. So I got a note from some-body askin' me to meet him outside the school one night. But when I got there I couldn't see nobody. Just this glow from a cigarette. He told me he couldn't reveal his identity. He just said that he wanted to have some fun, that was all. And if you were out of the picture, that wouldn't be a bad thing."

"Why did he want me out of the picture?"

"I dunno. This guy really sounded like he had it in for the whole town, really."

"What happened next?"

"He gave me that Swiffer. He told me to use it like a weapon. I didn't know what was in it, I swear! I hate those things anyway—give me a good old-fashioned mop and bucket any day."

"Have you tried one?"

"No."

"Well, do. Trust me—you'll never go back to a mop and bucket again."

"Mebbe," he said, stroking his chin.

"Nobody saw you leave the stadium with me the other night." I'd taken him out the back way; Lois was the only person, besides Bingo and me, who had seen. And I'd threatened to tell her orthodontist that she'd been chewing gum if she spilled the beans. "And nobody knows you're here besides Borden, and I know I can trust him. Especially if I keep bringing him snickerdoodles."

"So?"

"So—I think I need you to meet this guy one more time. Will you do that?"

"Mebbe." Janitor Bingo looked afraid; his scrawny little bones and muscles all tensed up, and his good eye got as cloudy as his fake one. "But what if something happens to me?"

"I won't let it. You trust me, don't you? From one fellow clean freak to another?"

"I guess. But what will happen after that? What will I do? I don't have a job left, really. I don't have anything to clean. And what if he comes to get me?"

I looked at him, this gnarled gnome of a man whose whole life had been spent in pursuit of clean toilets. And I got an idea. A brilliant idea, if I did say so myself.

"Don't worry about that." I grinned. "I think I know a place where you can go. And I'm pretty sure you'll like it there."

"Is there anything to clean?" he asked, his one eye shining hopefully.

"You have no idea." I grinned—spied a bottle of Mr. Clean over by the open toilet in the cell, and trotted over to retrieve it. "Just look at this!" I brought it back to show Bingo.

I winked at Mr. Clean, and waited. And waited . . . and waited. . . . He remained, one-dimensionally crossing his arms over his chest, staring back at me.

"Look at this," I repeated, winking again—winking so violently it must have looked like I had a nervous tic. Bingo eased away from me on the cot. "Damn you, wink at me!" I shook the bottle in frustration.

"What do you mean?" Bingo whimpered. "I can't—I have this bum eye, remember?"

"Not you—him!" I thrust the bottle in his face.

"Mr. Clean?"

"Yes! Oh, forget it!" I tossed the bottle over by the toilet again and started pacing around the cell—so agitated I started tugging on my bangs, just like Carrie did. What was going on? Why weren't my cleaning friends talking to me anymore? Why had they abandoned me, just when I needed them—

Needed them to convince my friends, my family—myself— that I hadn't hallucinated the whole thing?

"You all right, Super Mom?" Bingo was standing next to me, concerned, his weathered hand upon my shoulder.

"Yes." Glaring at the bottle—as if I could make Mr. Clean flirt with me with the force of my own desperate desire not to be labeled mentally incompetent and kicked out of the Justice League—I shook off Bingo. He crept back to his cot and lay down again.

"I'm sorry." I felt bad; it wasn't his fault I wasn't seeing things or hearing voices. "Really, I am. We'll get you out of here soon, I promise."

"And you'll take me somewhere where I can clean things?"

I smiled, nodded, and promised him that, at least. Even if it wasn't in the land of Scrubbing Bubbles and White Tornadoes— we'd find him something to clean. Because, as I well knew, the only things certain in life were death, taxes—and salsa stains in unusual places, wherever two or more men gathered.

CHAPTER 13

Ever since the dance, when I'd seemed to surge upward while hanging on to a ninety-pound janitor with a bucket on his head, I'd wondered about something. I'd wondered about clouds and sky and joy and freedom and endless possibilities—

I'd wondered about *flight*.

Had I done it? Was that what had happened in that moment between falling and holding on? I didn't know. And I was afraid to find out, in some of the more traditional ways. You know— leaping off tall bridges, being tossed out of buildings. That sort of thing.

No, there was only one place where I wanted to test my wings, test my desire—test gravity. And that was on top of the old garden shed in the backyard, with my trusty sidekick cheering me on—the person who had first believed in me, before I believed in myself.

But that person had disappeared; replaced by a quiet, hungry ghost who showed his human form only at mealtimes and the occasional snack. My son was a stranger to me, and I didn't know how to approach him, afraid, as I was, of ghosts. Especially fourteen-year-old ones.

I tried the usual—baking his favorite cookies. They worked

to lure him out of his lair, but he simply folded five of them in his mouth, washed them down with half a gallon of milk, and returned to his room.

So then I took to hanging outside his room, listening for that familiar *ding!* that told me he was on his computer so I could engage in some Super Eavesdropping, courtesy of my Super Electronic Hearing. But here I made a major miscalculation. I'd forgotten one of the most annoying things about boys—they didn't talk to each other. Except in grunts and burps and other bodily functions. They talked to girls—somewhere else. Somewhere I couldn't be.

They talked to their mothers—never.

And it frustrated me, because I used to think that Martin was the easy one—that boys, as a breed, were easier than girls. Kelly and her friends had so many little squabbles growing up. Martin and his friends, well, the only social arbitrating I ever had to do with them involved making sure they didn't poke each other's eyes out with sticks. I'd loved his childhood, the simple, free way—like a litter of puppies—he and his friends interacted with each other. They either liked each other or they didn't, and they said so, and nobody acted hurt, and they always kept an open mind to the possibility that they might be friends again. Which was totally opposite of the way Kelly and her friends had scrabbled through childhood, pouting and gossiping and testing each other; grudges were held for entire years, thoughtless words were never forgotten.

So why, all of a sudden, did Martin seem the problem child, the cipher, the stranger—

The man?

One bright afternoon, when Kelly was still at band practice, I knocked on his door. He didn't open it. He just grunted.

"Can I come in?"

"Why?"

"Just open your door, Martin, please?"

"What for?"

"Just do it!"

He opened it a crack. His hair—shaggier than ever—flopped past his eyes, tickling his nose. He had a pimple on his chin. Which made me want to cry. His first pimple! For a minute I wondered if I ought to take a picture of it. His neck looked thicker to me, too; there was a faint shadow on his upper lip. This was a stranger's face; I couldn't believe how much he had grown in the last couple of weeks, but I knew that adolescent boys tended to do that. Particularly when you kept searching for the little guy you hoped was still trapped inside the growing man.

"What do you want?"

"I thought we could go outside to the garden shed. It's a nice day, and maybe I could try to—"

"No," he said. Firmly.

"Oh, but—you see, I really think that this time I could—"

"No."

"Well, what *do* you want to do?"

"Nothing." He started to shut the door.

"Martin! Wait—just a minute, we haven't talked in a while and I was wondering . . . has Lo— the gum girl—what's been going on with that?"

"I don't know."

"What?"

"I don't know."

"But—what about baseball practice, then? How are things there?"

He shrugged.

"How's the new coach?"

He rolled his eyes.

"How's school?"

He sighed, dramatically, leaning his head against the door. "I'm busy now," he told me. Not meanly, just matter-of-factly.

"But . . . I could help if you want to talk about anythi—"

But the door had closed. And locked, with a defiant click. I heard his mattress creak as he flopped down on his saggy twin bed with the faded cowboy sheets, soft as flannel after a decade of laundering. I'd tried to get him to redecorate his room many times, but he'd refused. Martin didn't like change. Martin liked things to remain as they were.

So did I. Which was why I sank down to the floor, my bones cold, my heart actually aching—I put my hand to my chest, as if I could heal it myself. But I couldn't. Only one person could, and he was gone, replaced by this brooding stranger. But I wanted my little boy back, my pal, my trusty sidekick. I wanted to tell him that he'd be okay, that broken teenaged hearts would heal, that baseball season wouldn't last forever—if indeed he was bothered by either of these things. But I was the last person who would know that, or anything else about him. Ever again.

I didn't know if I'd ever fly, now. It didn't seem to matter so much. Not if Martin wasn't there, eyes shining, to witness it—to tell me it was real. But there was a door between us now, and one thing I knew about men—

If they didn't want to let you in, there was no way you could make them. Not even if you were a superhero.

I heard footsteps clomping up the stairs, laughter. Kelly and Vienna rounded the corner but stopped, surprised to find me sitting in the hallway outside Martin's door. I shook my head, eyes watering; the hydrogen cloud of cheap, flowery perfume hovering over the girls was almost too much to bear. I wondered where I'd left my Febreze.

"Um, hi, Mom." Kelly raised her eyebrows at Vienna, who raised hers back.

"Hello, girls. What are you up to?"

"Nothing. Just studying." Vienna giggled, but Kelly pinched her to make her stop.

"Do you girls have any plans for prom?" I stood up, looked at Martin's shut door, looked at Kelly and Vienna with their purple and pink streaks, and decided it was time I did a little mothering. Appreciated or not.

"We're going with a group of people, you know—Tommy McFarland, Seth Williams, those guys."

"Hmmm. Who's driving?"

"I don't know, we haven't figured it out yet."

"Where are you going after the prom?"

"I don't know—"

"Vienna, I just realized I haven't met your parents yet, and since you and Kelly have been spending so much time together, I probably should."

"You can try," Vienna said with a bored sigh. "But my dad's not around much."

"Her dad couldn't care less about Vienna," Kelly announced, putting her arm around her friend.

"Well, that's too bad, but I think I should meet him anyway. What about your mother?"

"Oh, she split. Like, years ago."

"Oh." My mother's heart wanted to thaw a little toward this girl—this girl with the nose piercing and too-tight T-shirt that showed off rolls of puppy fat—this girl who had mesmerized my daughter so that she was ignoring her best friend since kindergarten and putting pink stripes in her hair. But I wouldn't let it. Paris Hilton probably had mother issues, too, but that didn't mean I wanted her to be best friends with my daughter.

"Well," I stalled, wondering what to do next. Kelly had

been smart about all this; she hadn't tried to hide her friendship, knowing that I could uncover it with my superpowers. Everything was out in the open, and just skating along the lines of what Kelly knew I felt was acceptable teenaged behavior. Grades hadn't suffered, curfews weren't being broken . . . oh, she was good, my daughter. Very, very good.

"I do want to meet everyone before you go to prom. Including your father, Vienna. And I want to know who's driving, and what your plans are, and I'll take you out to buy your dress, Kelly—and Vienna, you're welcome to come along." I smiled, pleased with myself.

"Fine." Kelly looked untroubled, unworried—denying me my victory. I'd been hoping for at least a small show of resistance. Counting on it, in fact, just so I could feel I was making her life miserable in some small way. There was no better validation of parental power than that.

"All right," I said, defeated. "Have you girls had anything to eat?"

"We stopped at McDonald's on the way home," Kelly chirped, leading Vienna into her room—and not closing the door. Ooooh, she was really, really good.

I stood helpless in the hallway, entirely thwarted of maternal satisfaction. My daughter cleverly not hiding anything from me, and my son refusing to communicate in any way, good, bad, or indifferent. I clenched my fists, frustrated. I wanted to nag someone. I wanted to meddle in someone's life. But there wasn't any opportunity in my own home.

So I did the next best thing. I went into my room, grabbed my tote bag, and ran to the Mom Mobile.

The children of Astro Park had better watch out. Super Mom was on a mission. And she would not be denied.

———

SUPER MOM ON WORLD RAMPAGE!!!

The article in the next day's *Astro Park Daily Bugle* read:

HOMETOWN SUPERHERO has record night, turning the town upside down looking for teenaged mischief. "Man, she just flew in here without any warning," Kyle Stratton, high school senior, recalled. "She knocked over the table, chips went flying everywhere. But we were just having a regular poker game with poker chips, no money. And no beer, either. She seemed really upset about that."

But Super Mom did manage to arrest two liquor store owners with past histories of selling alcohol to minors, as well as reduce more than a few parents to tears, berating them for not pulling seat belts tight enough through car seats and in one case for allowing a five-year-old to ride in the front seat. Mrs. Sandra Henry was so upset after Super Mom scolded her for leaving a pot turned handle-out on a stove that she had to be briefly hospitalized.

"I was only out of the room for a second," Mrs. Henry sobbed. "Just to answer the phone, and I knew the baby was in her playpen, but that wasn't good enough for Super Mom. 'Don't you know that you can't take your eyes off them for an instant?' she yelled. 'Don't you know that if you turn around, they'll be gone? Grown up? You have to take care of them now, while you can!' She just kept yelling and yelling at me; I begged her to stop, but she wouldn't."

Mayor Linseed commented on the night of terror. "Obviously Super Mom is suffering from some sort of hormonal imbalance. Perhaps it's that time of the month? At any rate, she should probably stick to what she does best, which is cleaning. Unfortunately, her concern for the children of Astro Park is starting to affect her judgment in many ways. We're taking the extraordinary step of banning her from events at the Astro Park-O-Dome Field."

On a related note, Super Mom's Memorial Trash Can has been reported as missing. Anyone knowing of its whereabouts should call Police Commissioner Borden.

"Wow." Carrie put the paper down by her register. "How are you feeling today?"

"A little hungover," I admitted, head throbbing, mouth all cottony. "I stopped by Baskin-Robbins after and had two milkshakes. Double chocolate fudge."

"Chocolate? It's not—that time of the month, is it?"

"Carrie!" I glared at her. "You, of all people, should know better. I can't believe the mayor said that, anyway. Do you think people accuse Batman of having his period when he gets angry? Noooo. It's always 'righteous anger' with him. It's so unfair."

"I'm sorry. Of course you're right. But what happened, Birdie? You can tell me." She tugged on her bangs, and I smiled. We hadn't really talked since the silent auction, and I knew this was her way of saying she was sorry for auctioning me off.

"Thanks, Carrie. Oh, you know. The kids. They're so—*teenagery*. Martin's love struck and mysterious and won't talk to me about anything—but he won't talk to anybody else, either, so how on earth can I possibly spy on him to find out what's going on? And Kelly, well, she's still friends with Vienna—"

"I know." Carrie's mouth puckered up. "Chrissie said they're not even sitting together at lunch anymore."

"Oh, I didn't know that." That was the final straw; lunch table seating was an intricate art, and once a table was established it took something major to shuffle the players around. "The problem is that there's nothing about Vienna that I can really take a stand against. Everything's out in the open—Kelly's too smart. So I can't do anything about it. All I can do is wait for something horrible to happen, which sucks. And what if it doesn't? Then Kelly and Vienna might stay friends forever, and I really don't want that. I want Chrissie and Kelly to be friends again. I want things to stay the way they were."

"I know, I know. Me, too. Chrissie really is hurt, and I hate that—because it makes me not like Kelly, and I hate that, too, because God, Birdie, she's like my own daughter."

"I know. I miss Chrissie, too. I haven't seen her in forever."

"You know, I'm sorry, Birdie, about the other night, at the auction. I'm sure part of that was because of all this with the girls, and I'm sorry."

"Me, too. And I'm also sorry I didn't tell you right away about Doctor Dan. That he's getting a divorce."

"Obviously. The way he carried on the other night!"

"I know. Exes! When Mr. Clean was carting me around that day we were talking about it—did you know there used to be a Mrs. Clean? I had no idea!"

"Birdie." Carrie shook her head sadly.

"What?"

"You don't still believe all that nonsense, do you? You're not still seeing things, hearing voices?"

I hung my pounding head. No, I wasn't hearing voices or

seeing things. But what had happened was so real—I could still feel Mr. Clean's ripped arms, picture that little band of scientists looking up at me with that scary light in their eyes. I couldn't have imagined that. Although—

My memories of my first marriage were just as real. And Dan was acting as if they weren't. So who was I to believe anymore?

"I don't know," I murmured, leaning my forehead against the cash register, which was nice and cool. "I just don't know."

"Well, I know one thing." Carrie had switched on her happy voice—all sparkly and energetic; I knew she was trying to distract me. "We are going to kick some Shriner butt this year! I have it on good authority that their Fifties Sock Hop was a bust—they didn't raise half their goal. So guess who's going to lead the opening-day parade? PTA! PTA! PTA!"

And I had to laugh at the sight of my friend—my fierce, opinionated friend—pumping her little fist in the air like a gladiator. Although I wasn't distracted from my troubles, not by any means.

Particularly knowing what lay ahead. By now I'd been fighting crime long enough to know that it was just a series of steps, sort of like a board game—the pieces assembling at the beginning, indistinguishable from one another; the roll of the dice as some surged ahead, only to prove unable to last the course while others lurked behind, waiting their turn. The final set of challenges, which would move all the leading players into the middle of the board, only one of whom would emerge victorious.

I had a feeling that soon we were heading into that last phase—dangerous, thrilling, the final outcome in suspense until the very last minute.

CHAPTER 14

"Do we need to go over it again?"

"Mebbe." Janitor Bingo scratched his chin, giving the question due consideration.

I struggled to keep my voice patient; we'd been "over it again" ten times now. "It's easy. You just talk to the man as usual. With my Super Electronic Hearing I'll be able to hear whatever you say into the microphone, without having to worry about reception. And the microphone should be able to pick up what he says, too. So just act naturally. Listen to what he says, turn to go. Leave everything else to me."

"What if he finds out I have a microphone?" Bingo's good eye widened.

"Why would he think that you do? Nobody knows about this, not even Police Commissioner Borden. There's no reason for anyone to think that you don't still want to kill me—you don't, do you?" I leaned down—trying not to be blasted by the smell of ammonia that seemed to be in Janitor Bingo's pores—and looked him in the eye with my Merciless Gaze. He pulled back a little, but I grabbed him by the overalls and held firm. His eye—watery, gray—didn't waver. I let him go, satisfied.

"All right. And don't worry. I can handle one measly little criminal myself; there's no need for backup." I brushed my hands together, tightened my Apron of Anticipation, and adjusted my mask.

"Mebbe." Janitor Bingo scratched his chin again.

"Now, go wait for him, just like he told you to." We were huddled together in the janitor's closet in the grade school; it was a close, cramped little space filled with such quaint cleaning accessories as a roller bucket on wheels, a dust mop, and wire-bristled brushes. I made a mental note to provide a special Swiffer endowment to the school system.

Janitor Bingo gave one last tug at the microphone clipped to his undershirt, which was covered by an old flannel shirt buttoned all the way to his chin. He opened the door to the closet, turned around and gave me a grizzled thumbs-up, and left, making his way, I assumed, down the hallway, out the door, and to the big trash bin behind the cafeteria, where he'd been meeting his mysterious puppet master all along.

I waited until I heard the door slam shut. Then I left the closet, crept down the hall, and flattened myself up against the wall just inside the doors. I could see Bingo standing by the trash can, his hands—which always looked so empty without a mop in them—hanging awkwardly by his side. With my Super Electronic Hearing, I could hear everything that his mike picked up: a few crickets, an owl hooting—and the hacking, juicy splat of Janitor Bingo spitting against the side of the trash can.

Finally I heard footsteps. Janitor Bingo didn't move. I could barely make out another shape—similar in size to Bingo, all in black, something, like a scarf or a mask, obscuring his face. About five feet separated the men. "So," I heard a voice say. An unfamiliar voice. "You messed up at the dinner dance."

"Yep." Janitor Bingo sounded unconcerned.

"I'm disappointed in you. I was counting on you to take care of her, once and for all."

"I tried. She's a slippery one, that Super Mom."

"She's a bitch," the mystery man hissed. "On the rag."

I stiffened, longing to run outside and fling cleaning fluid in somebody's eyes. But I couldn't. Not yet.

"Mebbe."

"So, let's talk about the next time. Opening day of the Astro-Park-O-Dome Field is in two weeks. It's going to be a day this town—and Mayor Linseed—never forgets, not if I have anything to do with it. I think we can take care of Super Mom then, don't you?"

"Sounds good to me."

"I'll be a bit busy that day. So I'm going to have to trust you to take her out before the festivities get under way. I can't have her nosing about—she's too lucky. She might find out about—well, let's just say that so far events are proceeding according to plan. So all I need is for you to take care of her, although that Swiffer thing doesn't seem to work anymore. I went to a lot of trouble to get that thing, dammit, but I'm sure you can figure something else out. Maybe you can distract her with some shoes or something. Don't all broads like shoes?"

I gasped, outraged. First hormones, now shoes? What kind of superhero did these men think I was, anyway? Nobody ever tried to distract Aquaman with a Victoria's Secret catalog, and I have it on good authority that it would work, too. "Stupid gender stereotypes," I muttered.

"I could probably bop her over the head with a really big push broom. I could make a big mess somewhere, wait for her to come clean it, then leap out and bop her," Janitor Bingo was musing—with a bit too much glee in his voice. As if he'd imagined doing this many times before.

"Do you think you could do that, Bingo?" Something was different; it was as if there was an abrupt drop in the temperature, because all of a sudden the voice sounded cool and calculating.

"What do you mean?"

"I mean, do you honestly think I can trust you?"

"I don't know what you're talking about, you dang fool—"

"Oh, I think you do."

I heard footsteps, getting closer and closer to the microphone. I heard deep, raspy breathing, like someone was standing right next to Bingo. I heard the rustle of clothing. Like someone was searching for—

A microphone.

"Hey, what're you doing?" Bingo sputtered. "Take your ding-dang paws off me— Oh, it's you!"

"Aha!" the voice cried in triumph, so loud in my ear I jumped. "Super Mom, can you hear me better?"

"Help!" Bingo cried. "Super Mom! Help!"

I bolted out the door, running as fast as I could toward the trash can.

Someone was holding on to Bingo; he turned toward me, but I couldn't make out his face. He pulled out a gun, aimed at Bingo, and said, "Sorry, old-timer." Then my ears were split with the crack, reverberating into the microphone, of a gunshot. I screamed, holding my ears, as Janitor Bingo fell to the ground.

"Noooo!" I ran toward him, pulled him over so he was faceup. His eyes were shut, his mouth open, and there was blood on his flannel shirt—but he was breathing. "Oh, God, Bingo, hang on, just hang on—"

Another crack; another gunshot; I ducked as a bullet buried itself in the trash can. I started to shake, started to wobble; the blood, the earsplitting whir of bullets flying past me, the sight of Janitor Bingo lying helpless on the ground—for a minute I was paralyzed. Then rage finally steadied my shaking limbs, propelling me after the figure that was running, gun waving in the air, around the side of the school.

I ran after him, stumbling over the ruts and anthills of the school yard. I cursed myself for not telling Borden. If I had, Janitor Bingo might not be lying on the ground with a bullet in him.

"Stop! Stop, you murderer," I called after the figure. All I got in reply was another bullet whizzing past my head.

Up ahead was the empty street in front of the school. The only car on the street was a dark sedan; I'd parked my Mom Mobile a few blocks over, so as not to tip my hand. The little figure—so closely resembling Janitor Bingo, wiry and lithe, almost simian in the way it scrambled along the ground—ran toward the sedan. I followed, gasping; when I got to the street I was able to fire two quick rounds of cleaning fluid in front of me so I could skim along the top, propelling me even faster. I almost caught up with him.

Almost, but not quite. Because the man jumped into the sedan, put it in gear, and started to roar down the street—

But not before I was able to fire another round of cleaning fluid directly at the car. It spun around and around, tires squealing as the driver tried to gain control, jerking the steering wheel this way and that. "You're supposed to steer into a spin, you idiot!" I yelled, trying to make out the license plate. But the car was spinning around too quickly for me to read it.

The car kept spinning—but somehow it remained on the street. It didn't crash into a light pole, as I'd hoped. I froze, waiting to see where it would land—when all of a sudden I saw that it was spinning right toward me.

"Shit!" I bent my shaky legs, trying to figure out which way to run, so that I wouldn't get flattened like a little Super Mom pancake. But just then the car straightened out. The driver—I could only see one eye poking up over the dashboard—chose that moment to step on the accelerator, aiming the car right at me. I didn't have time to make a decision; I only had time to say a prayer, raise my hands, look up at the moon and hope that somehow it was within my grasp as I jumped straight up, sure that I was going to land right on top of the hood that was bearing down on me, the silver grille grinning in the moonlight, like a mouth full of crooked metal teeth—

But I didn't land on the grille. I found myself hanging on to a tree limb instead. A tree limb that was—I looked below as the sedan sped away, as small as a Shriner's car beneath my feet—

Very, very high. Probably a good thirty feet off the ground. Which was good, from one perspective. I hadn't gotten flattened by the car.

However. There was one slight problem.

How would I get down?

CHAPTER 15

You know those rules we have for our kids that we neglect to follow ourselves? Like, "Don't open the door to strangers," or "Never put an open can of soda in the refrigerator door," or "Don't leave home without your cell phone"?

I really wished I'd listened to myself more often, particularly with regard to that last one, because I'll just say one thing: hanging from a tree in a dress, with a stiff wind blowing directly up your skirt, and realizing you've forgotten to bring your cell phone with you is not a pleasant predicament to be in.

I hung there, like an old shirt on a clothesline, even while I rejoiced to see fire trucks and ambulances speeding by, pulling around to the back of the school. At least someone would find Bingo, and I prayed that he was still alive.

But it took a while for the assembled paramedics, firemen, and police officers to realize that a superhero was dangling above them—and that they could get a really good look at her underpants, if they were so inclined. (Fortunately they were freshly laundered; Rule #5 in the JLA handbook states *The superhero shall have on, at all times, clean undergarments in the event of an untimely death or compromising situation in which said undergarments might ultimately end up on eBay.*)

"Cute bunnies," the fireman who rescued me said, chuckling. I blushed; it was Thursday—pink bunny rabbit underwear day.

"Who called you guys?" I asked Fire Chief Spenser when I reached the ground, smoothing my skirt with as much dignity as I could muster, under the circumstances.

"The night janitor for the school. He found Bingo outside."

"How is he?" I winced as a paramedic stitched up a gash in my knee; apparently I hadn't quite missed the hood ornament when I'd jumped over the car.

"He's in a coma. He lost some blood, and at his age, well, it's a bit dicey. But we think he'll pull through."

"Thank God," I breathed.

"Um, Super Mom, would you mind telling us how you got up in the tree in the first place?" Chief Spenser scratched his head.

"I don't know—I jumped, and I must have bounced off the car hood or something . . . where's Commissioner Borden? I need to talk to him."

"I'll get him." Spenser walked over to a crowd of bystanders being interrogated by Borden. I took a deep breath as I watched the ambulance with Janitor Bingo speed away, siren blaring. When it was gone, the whole area seemed empty, even though there were still police cars with their lights flashing, and of course the hum of excitement that's part of any crime scene.

The paramedic slapped a bandage on my knee and walked away, leaving me all alone. I looked up at the night sky, the moon, the stars, the shadows—and I started to shake. I wanted Carl. Right then. I wanted his strong arms around me; I wanted someone to take care of me. Because I realized I could have been killed. For the first time, it seemed a real possibility. All the other battles I'd fought had seemed scripted, almost. I'd felt invulnerable—the movie superhero who can't die, no matter what. Because then there couldn't be a sequel.

But tonight had felt different. Alone, with a man with a gun, I had been in real danger. Any one of those bullets could have hit me. And one of them did hit Janitor Bingo—

And I started to shake harder, bones, teeth, hitting against each other, jolting me into hysteria. Because it was my fault that it had.

"So, Super Mom, it seems like you had quite an adventure tonight." Commissioner Borden came up. He tried to look stern, but failed completely; his eyes were big and worried and he kept dropping his nightstick.

"You could say that." I tried to smile bravely. But I felt the corners of my mouth tremble.

"Why didn't you tell me about your little plan?"

"I thought I could handle it myself. It seemed so simple— this wasn't as big as . . . as . . . well, Lex Osborne trying to brainwash the entire town with a video game. This was just a little stakeout."

"Which is what we do very well," Borden said. "The police. Remember? We don't try to interfere with your superhero stuff. Why did you think you could do our job for us?"

"Because I'm a superhero." I sighed. My knee suddenly began to throb, and I wondered if it was too late to ask for a couple of Tylenol with codeine. "But also, because I didn't want anyone else to know that Bingo was working with us. But it got out anyway—the guy obviously knew Bingo was wired—and we need to find out how. It had to have been an inside job." I looked at Borden, wondering if I needed to use my Merciless Gaze on *him*. But that would have broken my heart. I wanted to know I could trust him.

"A few of my men did know, of course—it's hard to keep a prisoner a secret. Especially one as grouchy as Bingo. I can't imagine any one of them saying anything, though."

"Would Mayor Linseed have access to that information?"

The mystery man had seemed to have it in for him, too. Yet Mayor Linseed was so determined to keep me away from the stadium. There had to be some link there.

"Only if he had a reason to come looking for it. But sure, we wouldn't be able to deny him access. The computer system is all tied together; he has all the passwords he needs."

"Hmmm . . ." Maybe it wasn't Mayor Linseed, after all. Maybe it was someone who had a reason to hate him. Someone, say, who might not like having to pay kickbacks for new construction. . . .

"Well, I'll be!" I gasped. "Lois was right!"

"What?"

"Oh, nothing. Nothing a little high school journalism can't accomplish. Anyway, try to find out—discreetly—if anyone in the force might have blabbed. And now, I think I want to go to the hospital." My voice started to shake, and I squeezed the palm of my hand so I wouldn't cry.

All of a sudden I felt a hand on my shoulder. I looked up into Commissioner Borden's kind eyes.

"Don't blame yourself, Super Mom. It's part of the job. People get hurt. We've all been in this situation. Trust me."

I shook my head.

"But he's just a janitor. Just someone who likes to clean things up—that's all he wants. First I took away his job, now I might have—well, it's not right. I need to go be with him right now. And he'll have full police protection until he recovers, right?"

"Of course. But try not to blame yourself."

I smiled at him, straightened up his crooked collar, and gave him a big hug. It was sweet of him to say all this, but really.

How little he knew about mothers. All we do is blame ourselves when those we care for are hurting.

CHAPTER 16

"So basically, I have nothing," I told Carl, after I left the hospital, tired and crumpled and drained. Janitor Bingo had looked so small and gray, hooked up to noisy machines and monitors. I took the first shift, sitting sentry outside his room for five hours before Borden forcibly removed me and put his own men in place. Then somehow I drove to Carl's house, waking him up in the middle of the night but sure that he wouldn't mind. And the moment he saw me—bandaged, torn, bags under my eyes that even my mask couldn't hide—he swept me up in his arms, ran me a hot bath, clad me in a pair of his own pajamas, which I thought was the kindest, sexiest thing anyone had ever done for me, and ordered a pizza because I hadn't eaten in about sixteen hours.

"What do you mean, you have nothing?" He bit off the end of a huge piece of pepperoni (with green olives).

"I don't know who tried to kill Janitor Bingo, I don't know why someone wanted to scare me away from the stadium. The logical person would be the mayor, with the kickbacks he's getting from the construction company. But he seems to be as much of a target as I am. And then there's the whole baseball thing—the new coach, the entire stadium. This town has gone nuts." I picked a piece of sausage off my pizza and nibbled on it.

"Maybe you just don't like baseball."

"No, that's not it."

"Because, I've got to say, I don't think that you really appreciate the beauty of the game."

"What? I never said that. I just don't think that building a domed stadium complete with a Jumbotron and a Starbucks is necessary for Little Leaguers."

"But how will it harm them? How will it harm the town?"

"You mean other than costing a ton of money and shortcutting other programs?" I rolled up the sleeve of his pajamas so they wouldn't get in my pizza. "Besides that, whoever tried to kill Janitor Bingo said that opening day would be something this town never forgets."

Carl took a big gulp of soda. I'd never noticed how *loud* he drank before. He gurgled and gulped and smacked and finished the whole thing off with a loud burp, followed by a satisfied smile.

" 'Scuse me," he said happily.

"As I was saying," I said, raising an eyebrow. "There's something more sinister going on here. My Super Mom Sense is starting to kick in, I can feel it. It starts out sometimes like a little itch before it becomes a full-blown tingle."

"So what are you going to do about it?" Carl reached over and grabbed a piece of pizza from my plate. I frowned. "What? Were you going to eat that?"

"Well, no, but—really. Ever since we got engaged, you've been a little, well, lax in your eating habits. You never ate food off my plate before!"

"So?"

"Well, is this going to become a habit? And are there any other things I should know about you? Any other annoying traits or . . . or . . . secrets that a person should know about before she

decides to change her children's lives forever by marrying someone who eats food off other people's plates?" I threw my napkin
down on the table.

"What?"

"I think we should discuss this. What else don't I know
about you?"

"You know everything about me—I have nothing to hide!"

"What about that experiment in the basement?"

"I can't tell you."

"See!"

"Well, now that we're nitpicking . . ." Carl reached over and
deliberately—infuriatingly—took another piece of pizza off my
plate. "I've never been too crazy about the way you brush your
teeth. You get toothpaste all over the place."

"I do not!"

"Yes, you do. Plus I hate the way you put an almost-empty
can of soda back in the refrigerator. Why? You never go back to
finish it, you just open up a new can when you're thirsty and
then there are all these cans sitting around with about a quarter
inch of soda in them."

"I don't like to be wasteful." I glared as he bit off half of the
piece of pizza.

"It's annoying," he mumbled, his mouth full.

"Not as annoying as a grown man burping at the table!"

Carl replied by leaning over the table, about an inch away
from my face, and burping again.

"Oh!!" I stood up. "Plate eater!"

"Soda waster."

"I can see where Greg gets it."

"Gets what?" Carl stood up, facing me across the table, his
eyes getting darker by the second.

"His rudeness. Do you know what he did to Martin at practice the other day? He tripped him as he was running out to batting practice."

"I doubt he tripped him. Knowing Martin, he probably tripped over his own clumsy feet—although to be honest, he comes by that clumsiness naturally. You're not exactly Ginger Rogers."

"You leave Martin out of it!"

"You started it by mentioning Greg!"

"Dad?"

We whirled around, only to see Greg standing in the doorway to the kitchen, his black hair sticking straight up from his head, his face even puffier with sleep.

"What's going on? You woke me up."

"Nothing, son, go back to bed." Carl threw his half-eaten piece of pizza back on my plate and walked past me, toward his son. He put his arm around him and guided him out of the room.

I stood there, staring at the half-eaten pizza, and my stomach lurched, sending up a sick wave of bile and acid—appropriate symbols of how I felt about myself, and all the hurt I'd caused in just one night. I heard Carl come back in the kitchen, but I couldn't look at him.

"Did—did he hear what we were saying?"

"I don't know." Carl's voice sounded terrible—ragged and wounded.

"I'm sorry. I'm so sorry! I didn't mean that about Greg. I like him—he gave me the Febreze." A giant tear rolled down my nose and fell onto the pizza.

"And I like Martin. He's a good kid." I heard the hesitancy in his voice, and finally turned to face him. He was standing at the sink, had picked up a spatula—although he was holding it wrong, grasping it in the middle like it was a flashlight—and was hitting it against his hand.

"But?"

"But he's not Greg. Greg's my son. Martin isn't."

"I know, I know." I sagged down in my chair, suddenly— overwhelmingly—tired. As faded and tattered as the pajamas I was wearing.

"And—"

"And what?"

"I know you're tired, and this has been a long night, but I wanted to say one more thing. I don't want you going over there."

"Over where?" But I knew the answer.

"Over to Doctor Dan's."

"I know." I'd managed to convince Dan that I—Birdie—did not want my house cleaned by Super Mom, but that he, being a new bachelor, should take advantage of the opportunity. So I— Super Mom—had to go to his house tomorrow.

"I don't want you cleaning his house," Carl said. "I don't want you in his . . . things. . . ."

"He won't know it's me, Carl. That's the point."

"I'll know it's you. Isn't that the point, too?"

"I have to do this. I have to find out the truth."

"The truth about what? You were married. You got divorced. You're with me now. End of story." Carl walked over to the table and sank into a chair, his head in his hands.

"No, it's not—whatever just happened here proves that. It's not so simple. None of this is."

"It was simple before."

"It was just us before. Now it's so much more."

He nodded, head still in his hands, and I wanted to reach

across the table and smooth his rumpled brown hair and tell him it would be all right. But I couldn't.

"Tell me something. Would you know it was me? Even if I was in my costume and you didn't know about—well, you didn't know?"

"Of course." He finally raised his head, his brow tired and wrinkled like a puppy's. "How could I not know it was you? You think a mask and a funny dress can hide someone you love?"

"I guess I never thought about it before. . . ."

"I'd know you anywhere, Birdie. I knew you, even before I met you. Which makes no sense at all, and doesn't seem to matter right now."

"You're wrong about that." I found the strength to haul myself out of my chair and kneel beside him, grabbing his hand. I turned it over, traced the lines of his palms with my finger, brushed the fine hairs on his wrist, turned it back over and admired his long, muscular fingers, marveling at how strong he was, and how tender, too—the way he cradled me, with this very hand, as if I were an egg or a wish, something too fragile to disturb.

"It makes perfect sense. And you're wrong about another thing—it does matter now." Releasing his hand, I leaned against his chest and shut my eyes. "I think it's the only thing that's going to help us get through this whole mess. And I'm so sorry about tonight, about everything I've done—not just here, but with Bingo. . . ." I squeezed my eyes even tighter, stemming the flood of tears that was threatening.

"Shhhhh." Carl stroked my head, tenderly as any parent who had ever walked the floor with a sick child. "I'm sorry, too—and I promise I'll work on my eating habits."

"No, don't. You're perfect just the way you are."

"Liar. And a very bad liar, at that." He pulled me up, and somehow I was sitting on his lap again, and I was smelling pepperoni and basil and oregano and vanilla and wood smoke and sweat and salt and tasting it, too, the salt, the sweat, and his tongue, and his teeth, and more pepperoni and basil. . . .

And I closed my eyes, forgot about everything, and let myself just—be. With Carl, and his surprising arms and legs and other parts, his tufts of hair and his strong thrusts and gentle probes and determination to take care of me, in every way a woman would want to be taken care of, naked or clothed . . . until I had to bite his shoulder to keep from crying out, mindful of Greg, and he had to bury his face in my hair to hide his own surprisingly sudden, vulnerable cries . . .

And we astonished ourselves by both weeping, after. I didn't remember doing that before, not even the first time. But this was so much. This was so sacred, somehow—a seal, or a blessing, or a vow. That we were in this thing together, and nobody—not kids or ex-husbands or evil villains—could come between us. Not after what we'd just done to each other—for each other. *With* each other.

And that night, when I was finally in my own bed, all curled up on one side as if he were there, too, I dreamed again. Of a beautiful man with soft brown eyes and a funny way of looking at the world, a tentative smile upon his face, as if he was always trying to figure it out. And the only time he ever looked as if he *had* figured it out—the only time those brown eyes cleared up and that funny pucker disappeared, and his smile was broad and sure and constant—

Was when he looked at me.

CHAPTER 17

When both my children turned five, I'd enrolled them in soccer. We lived in the suburbs; I think it was required, along with driving a minivan and becoming addicted to home-improvement shows on TV.

Kelly had enjoyed it for a while. Not a star player, she still had a certain coltish gait that made it tough for other players to defend against her. She made friends with the girls on her team, but once she hit middle school she had other interests. And being a girl, the fact that these interests weren't athletic in any way didn't seem to hurt her social standing.

Martin, however, was a different story.

After his first practice, he came home with a note pinned to his sweatshirt asking us to work on his "running" skills with him. I wasn't sure what that meant—he looked okay to me, on the rare occasions I saw him run (from the TV to the computer and back again). So I ignored it. Next practice, another note— this time it was "kicking" skills. Every practice brought another revelation concerning Martin's amazing lack of coordination. But it didn't seem to bother him—he went to the practices dutifully, played in every game (if you call standing in the middle of the soccer field picking dead dandelions *playing*), and always looked forward to the snacks.

When Martin turned seven, though, Dan and I divorced, and frankly, I forgot all about enrolling him in soccer. I forgot about a lot of things during those first few months; simply paying bills on time was about all I could handle, and then only because I thought that if I didn't, someone would swoop in and take my children away. Even when I eventually found my footing and figured out how to be all things to my children, at all times, I kind of forgot about soccer. And Martin never said anything about it, because by then he'd discovered that he was something of a video game savant, which gave him a great deal of caché among a certain undersized subset of his schoolmates, and I thought everything was fine.

But apparently it wasn't. Apparently I had forgotten one thing: faint heart had never won fair maiden—and neither had Mad Video game Skillz.

So when I kept my promise to Coach Henderson and decided to check on Little League practice, following the mentholated fragrance of Ben-Gay, sweat, old gym shoes, and moldy socks—not to mention that increasingly rancid funk of rotten eggs—to the Astro Park-O-Dome Field, it was with more than a little trepidation and guilt. Guilt for having neglected my son's athletic training until now. Trepidation because I was there as Super Mom, not Martin's Mom—and I wasn't sure how well I could keep the two separate.

"One, two, three—again. One, two, three—again. One, two, three—again."

Walking out onto the field, eyes watering from the above-mentioned fumes, I beheld what looked like boot camp. For thirteen-year-olds.

"Drop and give me twenty," a large, muscle-bound man with

a tiny head yelled into a bullhorn. The Astro Park Jetpacks immediately dropped and started doing push-ups, huffing and puffing and trying their best to keep up with the pace set by their new "coach."

"One, two, three, four, five—don't be a weenie—seven, eight—Martin Lee, you're behind!—eleven, twelve . . ." I grimaced, watching my son's puny little video game-conditioned arms tremble as he raised himself then lowered himself to the ground. Greg snickered when he heard Martin singled out; I caught a quick flash of anger in Martin's eyes as he struggled to catch up with the rest.

"Jesus Christ," the new coach said, throwing his hat on the ground. "What a bunch of weenies! Greg Sayers, keep your nose to the ground!" This time Martin chuckled, while Greg flushed with anger.

"Hey!" I strode over to the coach. "Watch your language! And these are just boys, you know. It's only a game."

"What are you?" The man picked up his baseball cap and put it on his head.

"I'm Super Mom, protector and defender of all children everywhere. Even Little Leaguers. Especially Little Leaguers. Who are you?"

"This is Coach Bluto." Mayor Linseed suddenly appeared out of nowhere, clad in his enormous circus-tent-like Jetpacks baseball shirt, dress pants, and shiny loafers.

I couldn't help it; I laughed. "Coach Bluto? Are you serious?"

"What's so funny?"

"You know, Popeye. That big hairy guy—who, I have to admit, this person does resemble—was called Bluto. You know, the mean guy who was always chasing Olive Oyl?"

"I have no idea what you're talking about," Linseed said with a sniff.

"Me either," Coach Bluto said.

"Oookay," I said. "But seriously. You should watch Cartoon Network more often."

Coach Bluto grunted and turned back to the boys. Martin was bright red, his brown hair plastered to his forehead with sweat. Greg, I noticed, was just as red, but considerably less winded than Martin. Both boys wouldn't look at each other, or me.

"Okay, you weenies, run around the bases. Now! Run, run, run!" He started clapping his hands like a trained monkey as the boys took off—Martin immediately falling behind with only Brian Derringer to keep him company, while Greg ran backward right in front of them, a taunting grin on his face.

"I thought we had agreed that you would stay away from Astro Park-O-Dome Field, Super Mom." Mayor Linseed tucked his arm in mine and steered me away from the diamond, toward the dugout.

"I didn't agree to anything. And Coach Henderson asked me to look in on practice for him. Why did you remove him, Mayor?"

"Coach is a fine man, but it was time for him to retire. With a new stadium we needed a new coach. Coach Bluto is just the man to usher in this exciting new era in Astro Park competitive youth sports."

I shook off his arm. "I think you're making a mistake. Nobody loved those kids like Coach Henderson. And look at them—do they look happy to you?" The boys were on their sixteenth lap, tongues hanging out, desperate looks in their eyes. But at least I was pleased to note that Martin had caught up to Greg, who was no longer running backward, minding his own business.

"Happiness has no place in youth sports, Super Mom."

"That's the most ridiculous thing I've ever heard—" I froze, my neck tingling, hair standing on end—Super Mom Sense attacking my central nervous system with a vengeance. I turned around just in time to see Martin—my Martin—give Greg Sayers a flying push, knocking him flat on the ground, his chin digging grooves in the turf. *"Martin Stanley Lee!"* I couldn't help it; his name had left my lips before I could even think.

In a flash the two boys were rolling around on the ground, fists flailing, feet kicking. The other members of the team—led by Coach Bluto—circled around them, chanting, "Fight! Fight! Fight!"

"Boys! Stop that this instant! Boys!" I tore over to third base, where Martin and Greg were locked in mortal combat.

"You loser! Why can't you just leave me alone? Why did you have to join the team?" Greg was screaming as he pinned Martin to the ground.

Martin hocked up a giant loogey and spit in Greg's eye, and in a heartbeat their positions were reversed.

"I'm sick of you making fun of me! I'm sick of your face!" Martin had a desperate—dangerous—gleam in his eyes; I'd never seen it there before and it made me sick to my stomach.

"Then act like a man, you dweeb! Stop being such a baby!"

"I'm not a baby, you baby!"

"Boys!" The scream tore my throat, coming as it did from the most primal core of my being. *"Stop it! This instant!"* I stared at them, helpless, terrified of the intensity of my emotions— fierce mother bear protection of Martin, which translated to hatred of Greg, yet I would have protected him just as fiercely if it had been any other boy punching him in the shoulder, as Martin currently was.

"Stop them!" I turned to Coach Bluto, who was watching with a gleeful smirk on his face.

"They're just bein' boys," he snorted. "It's good for 'em."

"No, it's not." I reached down and grabbed both of them by

the backs of their jerseys, separating them with the laserlike intensity of my Merciless Gaze. Martin, with his father's defiant turn of his nose and set of his jaw, refused to look at me, irritating me so that my skin flushed with disgust. Greg, on the other hand, did look at me—and immediately burst into tears, crying so hard that it took every ounce of my superhero self-control not to start sobbing with him, wanting to take him in my arms and make everything all right. And I was stunned by the acrobatic reversal of my mother's heart—right now I was madder at Martin than I was at Greg. But I was also hopeful; if they could switch positions so quickly, each staking a claim to me, perhaps there was hope for us as a family, after all.

Still, my stomach recoiled at the evidence of so much anger, so much viciousness. They had been almost unrecognizable, for a moment. Not awkward adolescents with too much in common—but animals.

"I think we need some apologies here." I let go, watching them both fall to the ground with a thunk, dust flying up around them.

"No way," Martin muttered, rubbing his tailbone.

"I don't think so." Greg wiped his bloody nose with his sleeve.

Coach Bluto blew his whistle. "Drop and give me twenty!"

"Nobody's dropping anything until these two apologize to each other."

"Super Mom, I'm afraid I have to ask you to leave now. You're interrupting practice." Mayor Linseed tried to tuck his arm in mine again—so cozy and friendly—but I shook him off.

"I don't think so. I don't like the atmosphere around here— I don't like this coach encouraging this kind of aggressive beha— Hey! Let go of me!"

Coach Bluto had clamped his mammoth hand on my shoulder and was pushing me—not very gently—off the field.

"Hey!" He pushed too hard, and I tripped over a rut and fell, flat on my face, eating Tifway 419 Bermuda grass (which tasted like mint, by the way—more pleasant than the usual Kentucky Blue).

"Hey!" Martin yelled, running toward me.

"Watch it!" Greg was right behind him.

"You don't do that to my— You don't do that to Super Mom!" Martin confronted Bluto, who laughed.

"You gonna stop me? I said drop and give me twenty—but you can give me fifty."

"I'll take a hundred then, because you'd better apologize to her." Greg stepped between Martin and the coach. He and Martin exchanged looks.

"I'm all right, boys." Pushing myself up, I straightened my skirt and apron. "I think I've seen enough. Mayor Linseed, Coach Bluto, you're on notice. I don't like what's going on here and I will be back. If anything happens to these boys, you'll be sorry. Do you understand?"

"You've made yourself very clear." Mayor Linseed gestured grandly, pointing the way off the field. I was about to go when I felt a gentle tug on my skirt.

"Super Mom?"

"Yes?" I smiled at Brian Derringer; I couldn't help it, there was just something so sweet and appealing about his shy smile, his hesitant eyes.

"Could you tell Coach Henderson something?"

I nodded. He motioned for me to lean down; Brian was a very small thirteen-year-old. "Tell him we miss him. We don't like Coach Bluto. It's not fun anymore."

"I'll tell him," I whispered back. Then I allowed Mayor Linseed to escort me off the field while Coach Bluto started barking out orders again. But right before we got to the dugout, I whirled around, shook off the mayor's hand, and surveyed the stadium. The dome was rising, almost meeting in the middle. Workers were scurrying around painting and hammering and sawing and mowing; the grass was just about in, and the Jumbotron was being tested (it was currently tuned to ESPN). Out on the field—where Martin and Greg were doing their push-ups side by side, although resolutely not looking at one another—Coach Bluto called for a Gatorade break. One of the boys groaned, "That's the sixth one today."

"Gatorade is good for you. Suck it up!" Bluto barked.

"Is Gatorade sponsoring the team?" I asked Linseed.

"No." He shook his head, which began to shine with perspiration. Jasper—who suddenly materialized from thin air—handed him a handkerchief.

"Have you enjoyed your visit, Super Mom?"

"Not really."

"Then you won't mind me suggesting that you don't come back?" Linseed tucked the damp handkerchief into his pocket.

"You know, if someone asks me to stay away, I have to assume there's something they don't want me to find out. But I always do. Funny how that works."

"Super Mom, I'm a politician—I would never do anything that wasn't in the best interest of this town. The simple fact is, I have a stadium to build and a Little League team to manage. That's all. Read into it what you want, but I have nothing to hide."

"Famous last words for a politician." I smiled. He bowed, gestured at Jasper, and went back to the field. Jasper escorted me through the concourse, nodding when I informed him I wanted to get a Caramel Macchiato at the new Starbucks. But before I could, I ran smack into someone.

"Oh, excuse me—oh!" For that someone was Mr. Derringer. "What are you doing here? I thought I told you never to come to practice!"

The ferrety man laughed, wiping greasy hands on work trousers. "And you thought I'd listen to you?"

"All right, buddy, that's it. . . ." I grabbed his arm, but all of a sudden Jasper insinuated himself between us, wringing his hands.

"Mr. Derringer? I believe the mayor would like to have a word with you."

"Why?" I stared at Brian's father, who grinned, showing his yellow teeth.

"Well, Super Mom, it could be because I own the construction company building the stadium."

"You do?" I was stunned; how could such a horrible, horrible man own his own company? Then there was the fact that suddenly he was at the top of my list of people who might have tried to kill me at some point or another. (A very long list, by the way—longer than last year's Christmas card list.)

"Yes. Now if you'll excuse me. . . ."

And I did. Because I was so confused by this new information that I just stood there and watched as that weaselly little man cut in line at the Starbucks and got a quick latte before he sauntered out to the field, my Merciless Gaze following him. All of a sudden I heard a gasp.

It was Jasper, clutching his chest. "Oh—Super Mom, what happened to your knee?" He clucked his tongue, and it snaked out of his mouth long and narrow—I shuddered and concentrated on my bandaged knee.

"Just a little run-in with a car." I grabbed my Macchiato, leaving a nice tip.

"You should be careful. You're much too valuable an asset to the community."

"Hmmm. You're about the only one around here who seems to think that. Maybe you should remind your cousin." I stuck out my hand. He grasped it. And now that I could get a good look at his eyes, I shivered. They were light brown, almost yellow, the irises very narrow—reptilian, in a way, oddly gleaming.

I snatched my hand back, confused, certain that I'd seen that look somewhere before. But before I could decide just where, he left, his twisted, bent body slithering so, I almost expected to see him leave a trail of slime.

CHAPTER 18

"Mom, what do you think of this one?" Kelly emerged from the dressing room twirling around in a pink spaghetti-strap dress, modestly cut on top, although not so modestly cut on the bottom. Because it had a slit that went all the way up to her—well, you know.

"I don't think so," I said, rousing myself. I'd been staring in a mirror, shocked. Who was this middle-aged woman, and why did she have a pimple on her chin? (Which was one of the more frustrating contradictions in nature, as far as I was concerned. Either that, or some grand plot cooked up by cosmetic companies, forcing us to buy both Clearasil and antiwrinkle cream.) My brown hair was flat, hanging about my face like seaweed; when was the last time I'd curled it? I looked like a clown because I'd run out of blush two weeks ago, and lipstick, apparently, wasn't a very good substitute. So how was it that I had two middle-aged men interested in me? (Although Carl, I could understand. I was, after all, a tiger in the sack. But Dan? Ah, there was the rub.)

"I look like hell," I said, almost forgetting it was my daughter standing next to me. But she didn't appear to be shocked by my potty mouth.

"Yeah, you kinda do."

"Thanks. The only thing I like about this dress is that it matches the pink in your hair."

"I know! But I could always try a contrasting color. That might work."

"It might." I smiled as she turned and galloped into the dressing room, a frisky colt. "So, are you sure this isn't a real date? Are you all just going as friends?"

"Oh, yes. I am so over men right now. It's been fun just to hang out and be friends without all the pressure. You know?"

"I know." One small portion of the giant knot that was pressing itself against the base of my skull unwound and I relaxed, just a bit. "Is Chrissie part of that group?"

"No, not really." Her voice sounded muffled; she must have been pulling off or putting on a dress.

"Oh. But Vienna is?"

"Of course!"

"Oh."

"Mother." Kelly poked her head out between the dressing room curtains. "I know you don't like Vienna, but honestly, she's great! You don't understand her, that's all. And . . . well, she's not Chrissie. I think that's your main problem."

"It is not!" I was stunned. Stunned that my daughter knew me so well.

"Whatever." She shrugged and emerged from the dressing room in a long black dress, with a deep V-neck, sleeveless, gathered simply around the waist and then cascading in folds at her feet. She looked like a goddess—and I had to admit, the pink against the black did look smashing. "Do I look that good?" Those gray eyes studied my face; all I could do was smile.

"I like it, too!" Grabbing my hands, she spun me around and

around. I laughed until I had to catch my breath; we stopped and I put my hand on her shoulder, staring at the two of us in the mirror. Her eyes were sparkling, her cheeks rosy, her hair, although slightly damp at the forehead, a beautiful mess.

"Do you think I could get away with something like this?" I fingered the folds of her dress.

"What do you mean?"

"For the wedding. What do you think? Not exactly like this, but I do like the way the skirt drapes—what's wrong?" For Kelly had pushed me away, flouncing off toward the dressing room, her skirts gathered in her hand, just like Queen Victoria.

"I honestly don't have any opinion about that, Mother," she snarled as she yanked the curtains shut.

I stared at my reflection in the mirror, my arm still outstretched, holding only the memory of my daughter. But that wasn't enough—memories weren't enough. Not anymore. Memories like the videotape, like bits and pieces of dreams we all seemed to be having about our past.

Who could trust them, anyway? Memories were treacherous. They could betray you, trip you up so that you were unable to catch your balance, even fall flat on your face, if you weren't careful. It was time to figure out how to move forward, unobstructed, all of us—my children, most of all.

I turned around and looked at the dressing room, deciding that somehow it was easier to have this talk here, in unfamiliar surroundings, with only a flimsy curtain between us.

"Kelly," I began. "I never did say anything about that videotape the other day. I'm—I'm sorry. I'm sorry if you've been put in the middle of anything—I don't think it was fair of your father to do that at all. Do you?"

There was a silence. Then a muffled "No."

"I know you've been thinking—hoping—that with Daddy's divorce something might happen between him and me, but honestly, honey, it's not going to."

More silence, broken only by the rustling of expensive fabric. "I thought that was what you wanted," Kelly finally said, her voice thick and puffy. "At least you used to."

"Yes, I used to. But not anymore. And it's not just because of Carl, so I don't want you to blame him."

"Then who do I blame? Because I want to blame someone, and I used to blame you, and then I started to blame Daddy, but now that he wants you back, it seems like I should blame you again."

"You can blame me if you want, sweetheart. But I really think it's best if you try not to blame anybody. Because that won't change anything, will it?"

"But I just don't know what to believe anymore," Kelly sniffed, emerging from the dressing room in her jeans and sweater, the black dress draped over her arm. I smoothed her hair, which was a mess from trying on all the clothes. "I mean, you were the bad guy, then he was, now he's not—it seems like I don't know what to believe."

"I don't know, either." I sighed, sitting down in a chair and pulling her down next to me. I took the dress and folded it carefully so it wouldn't drag. "But what I do have to believe is that you and Martin will be okay. I love Carl, sweetheart. But I love you both, too, just as much as I always did, and nothing can change that. I don't expect you to love Carl back. I don't expect you to accept all this without any complaints. But I do expect you to treat him with respect."

Her face, which had been turned slightly away from me, flushed a delicate pink. She brought one of her fingers to her mouth to chew on the nail—her old habit—but then she stopped herself, with a visible effort. I watched as she studied the nail, which was just growing out to a decent length, squared her shoulders, and folded her hands on her lap.

"I know," she murmured. "I don't know what gets into me—I like him, really I do. I just like Daddy more."

"And you should." Reaching into my purse, I pulled out a comb and started untangling her hair; she closed her eyes, allowing me this privilege. "I'm not going to kid you—it's not always going to be easy. And heaven knows what we'll do with Martin and Greg. But I think if we all remember to treat each other with respect, we'll get through it somehow. And that includes your father—speaking of . . ." I looked at my watch. "Oops! We have to hurry, sweetheart, I have to be somewhere in an hour." I gave her hair a final tug, then gathered up the dress, my purse—and my daughter—and headed toward the cash register, wondering if I'd have to refinance the house in order to pay for the dress.

"Do you think you're worth it?" I showed her the receipt; she wrinkled her nose, above such earthly considerations as sales tax.

"Naturally. So where do you have to run off to?"

"It's—just a little housecleaning that I have to take care of. That's all."

She folded her arms across her chest and looked at me in that level, wary way of hers. "Housecleaning?"

"Yes. I'm not sure what I'll find, but I have a hunch I'll be throwing out a lot of old memories." I smiled, kissed her cheek, and pushed her out the door.

"You're late."

"Yes, I'm sorry, I had to . . . incarcerate a couple of evil villains." I fluttered my eyelashes even though they were mostly hidden by my mask. Doctor Dan frowned, but then stood aside to let me in.

"I have to say, I'm disappointed that my wife refused your services."

"Your wife?"

"My ex-wife, actually. I bid on you for her, not for myself. I hope you don't mind my being honest. But I don't like having strangers poking around my house."

"I'm not a stranger, I'm a superhero. And rest assured, any secrets I find will be safe with me."

"I don't have any secrets," Dan scoffed, brushing back his fine blond hair from his forehead.

"You know," I said, shocked at my boldness, but I'd been wanting to say this for years, "if you used a little hair gel, you wouldn't have to keep brushing it back. Plus, it would make it look thicker."

"I'll have you know my hair is perfectly fine the way it is! I don't know what you're talking about."

"Suit yourself." I shrugged, then walked into the living room. Looking around, I fought to keep my expression professionally neutral. But it was tough—Dixie's taste was so appalling. "Somebody likes white, I see." I shook my head at the white furniture, white rugs, white walls, and white tile. We could probably put one of the kids through college on what they must have spent on carpet and upholstery cleaners over the years.

"Not me, my wife. I mean, my ex-wife."

"The same one who didn't want me to clean for her?"

"No, my other wife—my new ex-wife, I mean."

"Two ex-wives?" I shook my head and whistled, having fun in spite of myself.

"Excuse me, this is getting a little too personal. Let me show you the house." Dan's face flushed, his eyes icing over, blue steel.

Then he marched through the house, barking out names: "Bathroom. Kitchen. Dining room. Other bathroom. Pantry. Den. . . ."

I followed, nodding professionally. Then we made our way up the wide carpeted staircase, where he paused at the door of his bedroom. His and Dixie's bedroom. One look at the king-sized bed and my hands got clammy. Suddenly this wasn't so fun anymore.

"Oh, that's your—bed," I said, my knees a little rubbery.

"Yes, it is. Your powers of deduction are impressive."

"It's just—I wasn't really expecting—" Gathering up my courage, I entered the room, strolling around the perimeter, until I came to a low cherry dresser with six drawers. I felt a little woozy then, afraid I was going to be flattened by the tidal wave of memories that rushed over me. This was the top of Dan's dresser—and it was exactly the same as I remembered it. The little ceramic dish, shaped like a seashell, that he'd gotten as a child on a vacation by the sea—he still used it to hold his change. The quaint, old-fashioned brush and comb set, in dark cherry varnish. Those were heirlooms, his grandfather's. I remembered going to his grandfather's funeral, when we were just married. That was the first time—the only time—I'd seen Dan cry, and I held him and felt very wise and patient and wifelike.

"Oh." I had to sit down; I plopped down on the bed, realized what it was—and jumped back to my feet again. I couldn't think straight—on the one hand, the dresser seemed like it was a part of me; it didn't belong here, it had belonged in my house, and when he left he took it with him and it was part of what I'd grieved for. I hadn't realized it until just this very moment. On the other hand—it was in the same room as this bed. Which wasn't my bed, or our bed—but *their* bed.

"Are you all right?" Dan—standing in the doorway, unaware

of all the emotions bound up in these two innocent-looking pieces of furniture—frowned.

"Oh, yes, I'm fine, really, so this is your bedroom?" I looked around, trying to find a neutral piece of furniture on which to concentrate, and finally I found it in the television perched on top of an otherwise empty dresser. "Nice TV!"

"Thanks." Dan turned to go. "You can start up here if you want."

"Okay," I said weakly, holding myself up by clutching the TV. As soon as he was gone, I sank to the floor, closed my eyes, and leaned against the dresser.

What the hell had I gotten myself into? What was I doing here? This was insane; I'd had some stupid notion that I could sneak in here and find out the truth, find out what Dan was up to, what his memories of our marriage really were. I thought that my superhero costume would make me invulnerable to everything—including this pain I hadn't expected, but which had risen up like a gargoyle and threatened to turn me to stone. What could I find here, anyway? Dust bunnies? Bathtub rings? What would that tell me—that Dixie was a terrible housekeeper? Like I didn't already know that—I frowned at a glob of lipstick on the baseboard and zapped it up with a disgusted flick of my fingers.

But then I pulled myself up. And I went over to Dan's dresser, picked up each object—and the tactile memory was just as strong; how many times had I dusted and polished these items?—until I realized that something was missing. Which was—

Anything that had to do with *me*.

It wasn't as if I had a shrine to him at my home. But as wounding as our divorce had been, I had never tried to deny that he had existed. For one thing, I couldn't do that to Kelly and Martin. For another, it had been such a large part of my life, and

I could never pretend that it hadn't happened. I could never cheapen it—and the kids, and *me*—in that way. So, yes, I still had an album of our wedding pictures. I didn't have it out on the coffee table, but I did have it in a drawer. And, yes, there were still some family photos with Dan in them that I kept out, mainly because they were pictures in which the kids looked adorable, but also because they were pictures that would one day mean something to Kelly and Martin—that would remind them that they did have a father who loved them, even when he was too busy to tell them that himself.

So I started pulling drawers out, looking. Looking for something about me. About *us*.

His sock drawer was a mess—it always had been; I took some time to match and roll his socks. But I didn't find anything.

His underwear drawer—was a little icky. I really didn't want to go rummaging through that. So I just kind of poked around it, my eyes half shut, rather relieved, actually, that I hadn't found any pictures there.

The bottom drawer of his dresser—the one he always used to shove all his weekend clothes, like running pants and long-sleeved T-shirts in—I rummaged around in that, too, and did have a nice moment when I found his old Kansas State sweatshirt, because I remembered wearing that on one of our first dates, a pep rally that had ended up being colder than I'd thought it would be. Dan had run up to his dorm room and brought down this sweatshirt, and I'd worn it. I pulled it to me now, inhaling it, trying to smell the autumn leaves that had fallen around us, the cologne he used to wear (Dakkar), the perfume that I had been wearing (Obsession).

But even with my Super Smelling Sense, the past wasn't in this sweatshirt; it had long since been laundered out. Maybe he'd kept this because of the memory of that date. But more likely, he kept it because it was simply an old college sweatshirt, and middle-aged people like to hang on to things like that.

Finally I stood in the middle of the room, drained. I had opened every drawer possible—including the ones in his office, across the hall—and I hadn't found anything that told me this man had been married before. There were no clues to the past—or hints of the future.

I started to leave, remembered the bathroom, zapped it up quickly—it was neat and tidy, because despite his sock drawer, Dan was not a messy man—and walked to the door. But before I left, I remembered something. I tiptoed over to the bed, pulled down the covers, and sure enough. There they were—those little half-moons, his toenail clippings.

I shuddered, remade the bed, and went downstairs. Dan was sitting in the kitchen drinking coffee and reading some medical journal.

"I finished upstairs," I told him. "I'll just be a second in here." I started in on the kitchen, zapping up the counters, the stove, the fingerprints on the cabinets—

"That's funny," he said, watching me over the top of the journal. "You remind me of my wife."

I froze. "Which one?"

"My first wife. She used to clean the kitchen just that way—well, with a sponge, of course, but still. In the same order—she always started with the stove, then did the counters, then the cabinets. Same way you are."

"Oh," I said with a nervous snort. "Well, that's the usual way, you know."

"No, I didn't know." He sipped his coffee again, his eyes following me as I continued to clean.

"So, your first wife—she's the one you were hoping to win this for?"

"That's right."

"Do you have a picture of her anywhere?" I paused in midswipe, my hand upon the china cabinet.

"I don't know, I'm sure I do somewhere," Dan said, sounding curious about it himself.

"Well, I'd love to see one. Is she—is she pretty?"

"Oh, I don't know about that."

"You don't?"

"More like cute, I think. She's very cute."

"Oh." I stifled a sigh. "Is she nice?"

"She has her moments," Dan replied. And I had no idea if that was a compliment or not.

"Well, she must be very nice, if you wanted to have her house cleaned for her. You must still be very—fond of her." I dragged a chair from the table over to the refrigerator, climbing up on the seat; as I did so, I felt two hands steadying the bottom. I twisted around to look; Dan was gazing up at me, a curious expression in his eyes.

"You know, she always had to do that, too. Use a chair to reach things. She's pretty short—about as short as you are."

"Small world." I zapped the top of the refrigerator, climbed down, took the chair out of his hands and pushed it back toward the table. "So, why did you want to clean her house? You never answered that."

"I just—wanted to do something nice for her."

"Really?" I spun around, looked into his eyes, and smiled.

"Yes, because I have hopes of winning her back."

"You do?"

"Yes. Now that I'm getting divorced again. . . ."

"What do you mean?"

He laughed. "I can't live alone. I'm not that kind of person. I need someone to take care of me, and Birdie—that's her name—is very good at that. Especially now that the kids are almost grown—she'll have more time for me."

I couldn't speak; couldn't think. Couldn't see, either, for the tears clouding my eyes.

"You missed a spot." Dan pointed at a smudge on the floor; I zapped it up, hardly looking at it.

"Have you—told her any of this?" I spoke very softly, as if my words were precious figurines that might break if I wasn't careful. "Have you told her why you want her back?"

"No, but does it matter? We're family. We have children. It's what makes sense."

"Family," I echoed, turning away from him and concentrating on an invisible smudge on the pantry door. Family. I thought of that dream I'd had, after the Second Horrible Swiffer Accident. I thought of how familiar, how right it had felt, to be back in that place, even in my dreams. He was right about that; we were a family. Once. "What does she think about this?"

"She has it in her head that she's marrying someone else. But she'll come around, because of the kids. She always does the right thing for the kids."

"Even if it's not the right thing for her?"

"Of course," he said dismissively. "She's a good mother. That's why I married her in the first place."

"You—you married her because you thought she'd be a good mother?"

"Well, there were other reasons—but it was so long ago, who remembers anymore?"

"Did you love her?" My voice was steadier now; I risked

turning around, remembering something that Carl had said. *You think a mask and a funny dress can hide someone you love?* "Did you ever love her?"

Dan didn't answer; he stood perfectly still, aristocratic head tilted quizzically, watching as I walked, step by deliberate step, toward him. Narrowing my eyes, I flexed my powerful hand, looked into those startlingly blue eyes, and prepared to fix him with my Merciless Gaze. Because I wanted to know the truth. Once and for all. I wanted to know . . . I needed to know . . . I *deserved* to know. . . .

I gasped—then looked away. And I realized, with a jolt—as if some piece of machinery within me had just clicked into place—that the only eyes I needed to look into, in order to see the truth, were brown. And soft.

And Carl's.

I started to laugh, tears rolling down my face—I was laughing and crying, and it felt very, very good to be able to do so. Especially while standing in the middle of Doctor Dan's kitchen.

"Are you all right?" He frowned, disapproving of the tears splotching all over his freshly cleaned floor. "You're going to clean that up, right?"

I started to nod, then decided against it.

"No," I said, with a little laugh. "I think I'll leave it alone. Just a little souvenir, since you don't seem to have any around here."

"What?"

"Good-bye, Doctor Lee." I grabbed his hand, shook it firmly, and started down the hall, toward the front door. "Good luck with everything."

"What do you mean? You're not finished here."

"No, I think I am."

"Wait—I paid good money for—"

But I slammed the front door before he could finish. And

I took my memories out the door with me—the good ones, the bad ones, the sweet ones, the painful ones. They were mine, and he couldn't rearrange them for me, not anymore. It didn't matter how he remembered the past. It only mattered how I did. Because it *was* the past.

And I wouldn't let it get in the way of the future.

CHAPTER 19

Dear Heloise,

Help! I have a pet that refuses to use the litter box. Instead, Mr. Fluffikins has chosen to use my prized Turkish rug as a bathroom. How can I get rid of the stain?

Sincerely,
Anguished in Arizona.

I took a sip of coffee—weak, in a foam cup—turned the page and continued.

Dear Anguished,

First, blot up what you can with a sponge. Mix one teaspoon mild dish-washing detergent in one cup warm water, dip a clean towel in the liquid, and, working from outside in, dab at stain. Do not over-wet. Rinse with fresh water and blot dry. Next, add one-third cup white vinegar with two-thirds cup water and dab on stain. Rinse with water and blot until dry. Once area is

totally dry, sprinkle entire carpet with baking soda or rug de-
odorizer. Vacuum after a few hours.

I looked at Janitor Bingo, all hooked up to tubes and machines, his eyes closed, mouth open, sleeping peacefully. A nurse
walked in just then with a fresh IV bag.

"Keep reading, Super Mom. They really can hear voices
when they're in a coma. It's good for them." She smiled and left
the room.

"Okay." I smoothed out my collection of "Hints from
Heloise" columns, picked another one, and began to read.

Dear Heloise,

My mother-in-law insists that the best way to get crayon marks
off the wall is to use a solution of bleach and water. I don't
agree. What do you recommend?

I shook my head and snorted. "No way! WD-40, duh!"

I wasn't one hundred percent sure, but I thought I could see,
on the monitor, Bingo's heart rate speed up just a little bit.

"So, how's our patient today?" A voice boomed out behind
me; I jumped, spilled my coffee, and spun around. Mayor Linseed
was in the doorway, the ever-present Jasper hanging just behind
him. But Jasper looked different today. His hair wasn't hanging
down in his eyes; in fact, it looked as if it had recently been
styled. His clothes, too, actually fit his crooked frame.

"Janitor Bingo is doing just fine," I said, zapping up the
spilled coffee with a quick flick of my finger. "Well, fine, that is,
for a person in a coma. But they think he'll come out of it."

"Good, good." Mayor Linseed stroked his many chins.

"Why are you so interested in his welfare, Mayor?" I asked, standing up, making sure to keep myself between Bingo and the mayor at all times.

"He's a loyal public employee, and we heard about his unfortunate accident. I can't imagine who would want to hurt him. Why are you here, Super Mom? Why are you so concerned?"

"Because—uh, I—that is . . ." Jasper, I noticed, was watching me intently. "Because Janitor Bingo's an old friend. A cleaning buddy. I just wanted to update him on all the latest housecleaning news." I held up my stack of "Heloise" columns. "What brings you here, Jasper?"

"I go where the mayor goes, naturally," he murmured, bowing and scraping in that obsequious way of his. But his eyes didn't seem submissive at all; his eyes seemed cold, and maybe a little disgusted.

"Of course." I nodded thoughtfully. "I understand. It's so nice of the mayor to have found you something to do, considering."

"Considering what?" He brushed away a fly that was buzzing around his head; I almost expected his tongue to come snaking out of his mouth and lasso it.

"Considering that you're cousins. It's so good of the mayor to take care of you."

Jasper's bent body went rigid. "Yes." His voice was cold and dead. "I'm very lucky. So lucky to have such a generous cousin."

Mayor Linseed put his arm around Jasper. "Blood is thicker than water," he said with a jovial laugh.

"Isn't it?" Jasper murmured. Just as he did, I happened to catch a glimpse of Janitor Bingo's heart monitor. It was racing, the screen looking like a line of mountains—up, down, up, down.

"Hmm, that's odd."

"What's odd?" Mayor Linseed was the picture of municipal concern—fat face puckered, eyes blinking.

"The heart monitor—Janitor Bingo—"

"We should be going, Jonathan," Jasper interrupted. "You have a news conference at eleven. And all those plans for opening day. . . ."

"Of course, of course," Mayor Linseed bumbled and blustered, laying down his bouquet of flowers—the fragrance threatening to overwhelm me with its sweet stickiness—and reaching up to his head, as if to tip his top hat, except that he wasn't wearing one.

"So will the Astro Park-O-Dome Field be ready in time?"

"Absolutely. The final inspection is—" The mayor stopped, confused; Jasper was gesturing wildly. "Soon."

"Soon." I nodded, pretending not to notice as the mayor and Jasper performed an elaborate pantomime of raised eyebrows, shrugs, and hand gestures.

"Well, I'm looking forward to opening day. The parade, the ceremony—it sounds like a blast," I chirped.

Jasper looked up then, his snake eyes gleaming. "You could say so."

"You wouldn't prevent Super Mom from enjoying the festivities, would you, Mayor?"

"Why no, not at all. Please join us!"

"I will then. See you on opening day!"

"Yes, see you then, Super Mom. But not before." He shook his finger sternly at me; I nodded innocently.

"Jonathan!" Jasper scurried to open the door for His Rotund Honor. "We need to go."

And they left, Jasper following a respectful two feet behind. As soon as the door closed I ran to it, ear pressed against it; Jasper was hissing at the mayor.

"What were you thinking? We don't want her at the inspection!"

"I know, I know, I'm sorry!"

I was surprised; Mayor Linseed sounded so scared and unsure, while Jasper sounded confident, in control, for a change.

"When is the inspection again?" It was Mayor Linseed asking.

"Five o'clock, the day before. Jonathan, you're slipping. We've gone over this a hundred times."

"I'm sorry. . . ." Their voices trailed away; I opened the door a crack and poked my head out, watching them walk down the antiseptic halls of Astro Park General Hospital in their usual way, Jasper trailing behind while the mayor waddled confidently ahead. Totally at odds with the exchange I'd just heard.

I sat down beside Janitor Bingo, frowning, then picked up my papers and continued to read.

Dear Heloise,

My husband spilled coffee all over my new white carpet. I tried using club soda to get it out, but that didn't work. . . .

Next to me, Janitor Bingo slept peacefully, his heart monitor showing a calm, steady rate again.

CHAPTER 20

"So is this where all the cool kids hang out?" Fiddling with my contraband PTA Volunteer badge, I looked around at the Jerome Siegel Junior High and High School library. Being a longtime PTA lackey had its advantages; I'd been able to call in a favor with Jennifer Barnes, organizer of the Hawthorne Valley MILFs (Mothers Interested in Library Fundamentals).

"Shhh."

"I'm sorry." I smiled at Lois Blane, who was pretending to study. She'd originally wanted to stick a flag in a flowerpot outside her house, then meet me in a parking lot in the middle of the night (I was supposed to be wearing a trench coat and smoking a cigarette). I told her she'd watched *All the President's Men* one too many times.

"So what do you need from me?" she whispered, frowning down at her book. But her pen was poised over her college-ruled notebook, ready to take notes.

"Let's talk corruption." I braced myself for her squeals of delight. But instead she just nodded, professionally cool, and started to go through her notes.

"All right. Mayor Linseed is getting kickbacks from the

construction company. He gets a cut of what the town is paying to Derringer, Incorporated. Which, by the way, didn't have any competing bids to contend with when they were awarded the contract."

"Okay. Seems like a clear-cut case. Do you have documentation?"

"Oh yes!"

"Then start writing that Pulitzer Prize—winning article, all right? I need some evidence before I haul this guy in. You said you overheard people talking about this at the dance—could you identify the voices if you heard them again?"

"You bet!" She grinned, braces gleaming in the fluorescent light.

"Oh, one more thing—Jasper. What do you think about him?"

"I think he's creepy," she said, consulting her notes. "But harmless."

"I think there's a story there, but nobody seems to know. Except the mayor, I suppose." I pursed my lips, thinking.

"I'd really like to talk to you about that salt company, though—the mayor's involvement there is very interesting, although not illegal. . . ."

"Lois, sweetheart, trust me on this. The mayor's investment in the land that the stadium is on isn't that important right now. If we can get the mayor and Derringer on corruption, I'm pretty sure we'll know who shot Janitor Bingo—and why he wanted both the mayor and me out of the way. When we're done, we'll look at the salt company, okay?"

"Okay, but I just think it might be important—"

"Mom?" I looked up. Martin was standing before us, his schoolbooks under his arm, a strained, horrified look on his face. He still had a shiner from his fight with Greg—which the three of us had tacitly agreed not to discuss with Carl, as long as it never happened again.

"Hi, sweetie!" That was the part I loved best about the PTA—being able to catch your children in their natural habitat, unawares. "How's my little guy—" But I stopped, for Martin had turned purple and was emitting strange, gargling noises. Lois, meanwhile, was sitting strangely still, as if she'd just been turned to wax. Her eyes were lowered, her face was pale, and the only thing on her that moved was her rapidly beating heart—I could see her chest rising and falling.

"I mean, um, how do you do . . . er, how's it hanging, dawg . . . um, anyone want a cookie?" I reached into my Apron of Anticipation—before I realized that I wasn't wearing it, because I was here as me, Birdie, perpetual PTA volunteer.

"You know," I said, my voice extremely cool and pleasant, "I think I'll just go help Mrs. Barnes stack books now. I'm so glad I was able to find you that book, Lois. See you, honey—I mean, sweetheart—I mean, *Martin*. I'll see you later." I jumped up and ran toward the front desk, where Jennifer Barnes was loading the library cart with returned books—most of them *The Catcher in the Rye*.

"Junior English project," she said with a sigh.

"Mom?"

I grimaced, turned around, and faced—an extremely angry young man who bore no resemblance at all to my son.

"Yes?" I squeaked.

"What—was that about?" He gestured back toward poor Lois, who was now hiding her face behind her book.

"I don't know what you're talking about."

"What were you doing talking to her?"

"To whom?"

"To her. Mom, she's the one. The gum girl. If Kelly told

you—I'll kill her!" He clenched his fists, his face pinched and dangerous (especially with all those cuts and bruises). And I was torn between alarm at his anger and delight that he had confided something in his sister.

"No, Kelly didn't tell me anything. I really don't know what you're talking about—Lois was just looking for a book and—"

Martin made a sound like he was gargling a goldfish.

"How do you know her name? If Kelly didn't tell you, how did you know her name?"

I opened my mouth, stared at this angry man in front of me, thought—briefly—of throwing my daughter under the bus in order to protect myself, then decided the gig was up.

"Okay." I sighed. "Come here." I motioned to a far corner of the library—the poetry section—where I knew no one would bother us. I grabbed a book and pretended to read it while I explained things to Martin.

"Lois is a reporter for the school newspaper. You know that, right?"

He nodded. "She's the sports reporter."

"She's also an investigative reporter. She's been nosing around the new stadium, and somehow—accidentally—discovered my secret identity."

Martin's nostrils returned to their normal shape, and he looked reluctantly interested.

"And I also discovered *her* secret identity—that she was the girl you were telling me about. Because you were right. Her hair does smell like peaches."

A quick, radiant grin beamed itself across Martin's face before he could catch it. Then his eyes grew wide and horrified. "You didn't—you didn't tell her I liked her, did you, Mom? Oh, God, please tell me you didn't tell her that!" He actually grabbed his stomach, as if he were in physical pain.

"No! No, honey, I didn't! I never let on that you'd told me about her at all."

"You swear?" He let go of his stomach, the color returning to his face.

"I swear. Now, the thing I can't understand is—if you like her, and from what I can tell, she likes you, why are you over here talking to me? Why aren't you over there talking to her?"

"I don't—I don't know," Martin said, as if the idea had never occurred to him. Which, knowing men the way I did, it probably hadn't.

"Honey, if I know women—and I think I do—she likes you. I don't need my Merciless Gaze to see that—all I had to do was watch her face when she saw you." I didn't know why I was telling him this; it was almost as if I *wanted* the two of them to get together. I wasn't sure about that; I was only sure that I wanted my child to be happy. That had been the driving force behind a thousand hours spent standing in line at the toy store in order to get him the newest action figure or video game; I couldn't shake it off, even though now the prize was a girl.

"Well, okay, I guess I'll go." But he didn't, not right away; he spent a good two minutes staring at her, his skin pale and clammy. I watched him, equal parts fascinated and horrified, before I finally gave him a shove toward his eighth-grade paramour. As he lurched over to her table, I crouched down behind the *W*s—*Leaves of Grass* hit me on the forehead—and watched, unable to stop myself from shedding a few maternal tears. Because my son asked, politely, if he could sit down next to a girl who was not me, who was not his sister. And when she said yes—barely raising her head—he smiled that dreamy, lovesick smile and sat next to her, very smoothly, almost as if he'd practiced this many times before. And then—

And then I had the good sense to disappear before I started

rending my clothes and tearing my hair out. It was self-preservation—and something else. I felt I had already seen too much—more than a mother was supposed to see. And for that, I felt both guilty and privileged.

The only thing left for me to do was to say a quick prayer that I had raised a good and gentle man, one who would treat a woman better than his father had.

In other words, a man who wouldn't confuse need with love.

CHAPTER 21

There's nothing that restores your faith in the youth of today more than being around a bunch of marching band geeks.

There may be bad kids in the world. There *are* bad kids in the world—I meet them on a daily basis. But there are good kids, too, and in my experience, many of them can be found in the performing arts. Orchestra, band, drama club—most of these kids are shy overachievers, who seek out similarly shy overachievers, and want nothing more than to sneak through high school unnoticed by the alpha students, graduate from college, and then take over the world.

So when they're in high school they tend to travel together in packs for protection. Such as the pack that Kelly was going to the prom with—other marching band members, foreign to me out of their faded military-type band uniforms with the gold braid and funny hats. In unaccustomed finery—long dresses, tuxedos, and bare heads—they looked touchingly young. Which wasn't quite the effect they were going for, I'm sure.

"Smile!" They faced a lineup of paparazzi: parents with digital cameras, all gathered at Tommy McFarland's house. "Turn this way. One with just the girls. Now the boys. Okay, the whole group this time. . . ." They turned patiently, practiced—a lifetime of being photographed by indulgent parents.

The only one who didn't have a parent snapping away was Vienna. She didn't appear to let it bother her—in fact, if anything, she was louder and flashier than usual. Her dress was a vibrant red, compared to the more muted colors of the other girls'. And it didn't really fit; too tight in the chest, too big in the hips.

"Now, who's driving?" I asked. Two boys raised their hands; I nodded, because I knew them and their parents, and none of them, so far, had any traffic tickets.

"Be home by midnight," I told Kelly. "What time do you have to be home, Vienna?"

She shrugged. "No particular time."

"Hmmmm."

"Mom, we'll be fine. We're not going to do anything stupid."

"You're right about that, because I won't let you," I whispered in Kelly's ear, carefully hugging her, trying not to crush her corsage. They all trooped out the door, the girls wincing and tottering in their new high heels.

"I've got wine and cheese for the parents," Mrs. McFarland chirped, handing out glasses.

"No, thanks, I have an errand to run." I waved my good-byes, then ran out the door to change into my own prom outfit, confident of only one thing.

After so much practice fighting crime in them, I could definitely walk in heels better than Kelly and her friends.

"So how's it going?" I asked Police Commissioner Borden.

"Quiet so far." We both shivered in the night air; we were standing at the intersection of Main Street and Vine, where the first roadblock had been set up. "But the dance just ended, so I'm sure business will pick up."

Sure enough, a car came squealing around the corner, two teenagers hanging out the window going, "Woo-hoo!"

"I'll handle it." Striding out into the middle of the street, I held my hand up. The car screeched to a halt. I walked around to the driver's side and motioned for the driver—a junior, Jeremy Myers—to roll down the window.

"Hey, Jeremy."

"Hey, Super Mom."

"What's up?"

"Nothin'." The rest of the car—five other kids in rapidly crumpling finery—giggled.

"Out of the car." I opened the door. He grinned at his friends, got out, and stood before me. "Exhale."

"What?"

"Exhale. Breathe out. You know—" and I demonstrated.

"Oh." He exhaled; I sniffed. I stood back, calculating, processing, my nostrils flaring with the effort. "Onions, Tic Tacs, french fries, Three Musketeers bar . . . fruit punch. No alcohol," I said, surprised. Jeremy grinned.

"Can we go now?"

"Just a minute." I leaned into the car and sniffed, loudly and rapidly. Pine air freshener, lots of perfume and aftershave, sweat, the sweet, sticky odor of hairspray, makeup, a couple of Odor-Eaters (for the boys' shoes, I imagined), gum—and no illegal substances of any kind. Not even cigarettes. "Okay, you're clean. Be careful tonight, though. You never know where I might show up! And buckle those seat belts! No more hanging out of car windows." This was for the two boys in the back.

"Yes, ma'am!" Jeremy saluted, got back in the car, and drove off, very slowly.

"Well, there's one," I told Borden, who nodded. Then the cars started coming through in earnest—this was only one of two roads leading to the high school—and I got very busy.

"Eight ounces of Corona Light." I sniffed Tabitha Warren's

breath. "Over there, sweetheart." Tabitha giggled as one of the police officers escorted her over to the official Operation Super Mom tent, where they had coffee and tables and chairs ready for offending teens. My Mom Mobile was nearby, ready to take kids home when they were sober.

"No alcohol, you guys are clear to— Wait a minute. . . ." Oregano . . . something smelled a lot like oregano, and I was fairly sure neither of these teens was planning on making any pizza tonight. I opened the door to Travis Fishburne's Jeep, sniffing violently, reaching under the glove box and producing a bag of marijuana that had been taped there. "Sorry, kids. All of you— out of the car." The police officers escorted them to the tent.

"When will you guys learn?" I shook my head at an entire van of seniors who had each consumed four glasses of very cheap red wine—from a box, I could tell, by the paper smell that accompanied it. "Boys, round 'em up." The seniors were escorted to the tent; they giggled and staggered until one of them bent over and threw up. Then they all became very, very quiet.

In between sniffs, I could hear the police radio chirping over in Borden's car—so far, so good. No accidents, although there were quite a few blown stop signs and one near miss with a mailbox over on Elm.

"I think it's gonna be a good night," Borden said during a lull. I looked at his watch—it was eleven thirty. We still had a few hours to go.

"I'll just go get a cup of coffee, if you don't mind. Let me know when you need me." I waved and walked over to the tent, poured some coffee, and handed out a few necessary antibacterial hand wipes to the teenagers, who were starting to understand what was in store once their parents found out. This realization was a much more effective vomit inducer than cheap wine.

I started back to my post when I heard agitated, staccato

sounds from the police radio. I walked toward it, sipping my coffee.

"Accident at Dover and Pine. Two cars, one driven by teens. Two girls . . . ," and then the frequency filled with static. I froze, coffee cup halfway to my lips. "Two girls . . . Astro Park General . . . ambulance on its way . . . parents need to be notified. . . ." More static. Still I couldn't move. Dover and Pine was near my house. And it had to be close to midnight—the time when Kelly was due home.

Finally the static cleared, and the dispatcher was saying, ". . . identified as Kelly Lee and . . ."

But then I didn't hear anything else. I dropped the coffee, spun around, somehow made my rubbery legs propel me to my Mom Mobile amid shouts and calls from the police, and I drove. More recklessly than any teenager could drive; later, when it was all over, I had no recollection of the drive itself, of stoplights or stop signs or other cars on the road. Because I didn't see them at all; all I could see was Kelly's face, and that ridiculous pink streak in her hair, and I wondered how pink hair would look if it were caked in blood. And then I pulled over to the side of the road and threw up. And then I drove some more.

"Super Mom, can I help you?" The nurse in the emergency room looked so calm and pleasant. How could she be? Didn't she know something terrible had happened?

"My . . . oh . . ." I stared down at my costume, forgetting who I was, forgetting everything other than that my baby was inside somewhere, and I didn't know if she was alive. "There was an accident, and . . ."

"Oh, yes." The nurse's voice took on a serious, concerned tone. "Yes, it's a shame. But until the girls' parents are notified, I'm afraid I can't let you—"

"Excuse me?" I turned around to see Doctor Dan running up behind me. "I'm Doctor Dan Lee, my daughter was in an accident. . . ."

I just about passed out, right then, to hear him say it. Because then it must be real.

"Oh, Doctor Lee, follow me," and the nurse turned and bustled Dan—who hadn't even glanced at me—into the emergency room. I ran in behind them, dashed into a bathroom to tear off my costume and pull on regular clothes—thank God for my Jolly Green Giant tote bag—then I ran back out, looking up and down the hallways, but I couldn't see where they'd gone.

"Oh, God, please, somebody help me. . . ." I ran up to an orderly—who didn't speak English. I ran up and down the halls of the ER, until finally that nurse came out of a room, her rubber-soled shoes squeaking on the bright, antiseptic linoleum. "Please, help me—I'm Birdie Lee, the mother of—"

"Oh, yes, Mrs. Lee, come right this way . . . your husband is already here."

"He's not . . . how is she? How is my daughter?"

The nurse didn't say a word. Which made me want to hurt her. But I didn't have time to because all of a sudden I was being shown into a room full of bright, fluorescent light. It took me a few seconds to adjust my eyes, and when I did I saw that Dan was standing next to someone on one of those doctor's tables—and the someone was Kelly.

Who was sitting up, pale and trembling, but somehow, miraculously, alive.

"Kelly!" I ran to her, knocking Dan aside, hugging her so tightly even I couldn't breathe but I needed to *feel* her, feel her bones, her skin, her amazing, beating heart against my heart . . . and then I burst into tears.

So did she.

"What? What happened? Are you all right? Are you hurt? Are you all right?"

She just nodded, tears rolling down her face, streaking the makeup she had spent so much time applying earlier in the evening. Her dress was crumpled up in a corner of the room; she was wearing a hospital gown and one of those hospital bracelets. Her right leg was bruised and bandaged, the ankle wrapped, her foot in some funny thick sock. But other than that she looked fine. And finally, for the first time in about an hour, I could breathe.

"So what happened?" I turned to Dan. "Oh. You're here."

"Yes, of course." He looked worried, too—his eyes small, his hair all over the place. "They couldn't find you at first."

"Right. Martin! Where's Martin?"

"He's in the waiting room."

"Okay." I turned back to Kelly. "What happened?"

"Mom, it wasn't her fault, you have to understand—"

"Vienna? It was Vienna, wasn't it? What was she doing driving? Where were you going? Why weren't you with the rest of your friends?"

"Vienna wanted to go—"

"I knew it! That's it. You are not seeing her anymore, do you hear me? She's no good. She almost got you killed!" I was so angry at this girl, I wanted to hurt her. I wanted to throw her against a wall; I wanted to make her cry.

"Mom! Don't you even want to know how she is? She was in an accident, too—"

"Which was all her fault. Was she driving?"

"Yes, but—"

"Then I don't need to hear any more."

"Birdie." Dan put a hand on my arm, but I wriggled away. "Calm down, you don't know—"

"What do you mean, I don't know? I'm the parent here,

Dan. I'm sorry, but you're not really qualified to say anything about any of this. Not right now."

"Kelly's as much my daughter as yours. We're a family, remember?"

"Right. Such a family—you don't even have any pictures of us at your house, do you? What kind of a family is that? What are you up to, anyway, Dan?"

"Right now I'm not so sure, to tell the truth—"

"Just because you want someone to take care of you? How selfish is that? And suddenly you want to be back in our lives? Just because Dixie left you, that's all this is about—"

"*Stop it!*" Kelly screamed, sobbing great, choking sobs. "What are you talking about? What about me? What about Vienna? Doesn't anybody care? Where is she, anyway? Why won't they let me see her?"

"Honey . . ." I ran over and gathered her in my arms, soothing her, kissing her forehead. I looked at Dan, who was trembling, pale, his pajama top sticking out through his oxford shirt—the buttons all lined up wrong. "I'm sorry," I told him. "Now's not the time. . . ."

"No," he said. And then he sat back down on one of the chairs against the wall, suddenly middle-aged and tired.

"You don't understand about Vienna." Kelly sobbed until I thought she would split in two. "She wanted to go home because they were making fun of her—making fun of her dress. She wanted to go home because she was sad, Mom. And it wasn't her fault—the other guy ran the stoplight. That's what the police said. I just want to see her, Mommy, I just want to make sure she's all right. . . ."

"Shhh, honey, shhh. I'll go see. You stay right here with Daddy, okay? I'll go see about Vienna." Kissing the top of Kelly's head, I felt eerily calm and in control—and generous. So generous that I stopped to pat Dan on the arm—an apology—before I left the room.

I stood in the hallway full of doors, branching off in a thousand directions, and I had no idea what to do next. I started to walk, trying to find someone in charge.

"What did she do now?" an angry voice was demanding, down the hallway to my right. I followed it. "What did my idiotic daughter do now?"

"Mr. Derringer, calm down," someone said in a soothing, professional voice.

"Mr. Derringer?" I ran down the hall, turned a corner, and came face-to-face with that weaselly little man, purple with rage.

"You're Vienna's father?" I was shocked. So shocked I pointed my finger right at him and held it there.

"Who are you?" He glared at me. "You look familiar."

"I'm Kelly's mother. Kelly? Vienna's friend?"

"No, you're that do-gooder at the grocery store," he snarled with his yellow teeth.

"Well, yes, but I'm also Kelly's mother, and the girls were together tonight, and Kelly's very worried about Vienna—"

"She's fine," the doctor told me with a tired smile. "She's a little bruised up but she's fine. Those girls were both very lucky. They had their seat belts on, and the other driver wasn't going very fast."

"Whose fault was it?" Mr. Derringer demanded. "If my insurance premiums have to go up—"

"Mr. Derringer! Your daughter was in an accident tonight, don't you understand that?" Now the anger that I'd felt for Vienna was directed entirely at her crooked, obnoxious father. And everything I'd ever said about Vienna—about her hair, her clothing, her intentions—filled me with shame. That poor, poor girl!

"The girls were not at fault. The other driver ran the red

light." The doctor was reading from his chart. "That's what the police report says."

"Can Kelly see her? She's so worried—is that all right?"

"Of course, Mrs. Lee. She's in examining room A."

"Thank you, Doctor." I turned to go back to Kelly—but down another hall I saw the waiting room—and two giant sneakered feet poking out from behind a wall.

"Martin!" I ran to him—

But when I got there, I saw that he wasn't alone. Carl was with him. And Greg. I started to cry when I saw them there, sitting on either side of Martin like two slightly nerdy sentries.

"Oh!" was all I could say before I gave in to sobs, holding on to the wall for support. But then I didn't have to hold on anymore; Carl was holding me up and pushing me toward Martin.

"Sweetheart, are you all right?"

Martin looked up, his eyes red-rimmed. He nodded.

"Is Kel going to be okay?"

"She's just fine." I smiled at him, brushed his floppy hair out of his eyes, and gave him a huge hug. I felt him let out his breath, stifling a little sob, then trying to hide it by coughing.

"That's good." He gave himself a manly shake, then wiped his eyes with the sleeve of his raggedy old army jacket.

"How did you guys get here?" I looked at Carl, then Greg. Greg was paler than usual, his black hair in such contrast. I smiled at him, and he smiled back.

"Martin called us," Carl said, his brown eyes shining, a shy grin on his face.

"He did?" I looked at my son, who merely shrugged.

"Well, I thought they ought to know . . . ," was all he said. Which was enough for now. More than enough.

"I'm very glad you did." Unable to stop myself, I wrapped my arms around him again and kissed his forehead. "I need to go see Kelly now, and then I guess we can go home—I'm not sure. We'll probably have to fill out some paperwork."

"We'll stay as long as you want." Carl put his strong arms around me, and I clung to him, my rock, my strength. The one sure thing in my life.

"Thanks." I rubbed my face against his sweatshirt, then started down the hall toward Kelly's room. But before I turned the corner, I looked back.

Martin and Greg were sitting on the floor next to each other, watching cartoons on the waiting room television, Carl lounging on a chair behind them, his hands on each boys' shoulders. And I smiled at them through my tears.

"Can Vienna come home with us?" Kelly buttoned up my jacket, her flimsy little shawl, bought to match her dress, not warm enough for her. At least, that's what I had decided.

Vienna and Kelly had had a touching reunion, crying and hugging and making sure the other was all right. Mr. Derringer had hung around in the background, scowling, reminding everyone how stupid Vienna had been. My fists were clenched the entire time, or else I might have been tempted to fling cleaning fluid into his beady little eyes.

"Of course Vienna can spend the night," I said, too quickly. Vienna could live with us the rest of her life, as far as I was concerned.

"Thanks, but I'd like to go home and see my brother," Vienna whispered. And that's when it all came together for me—Brian Derringer, that sweet little boy, was Vienna's brother. The brother that Kelly had said her father neglected her for. Although, from what I could tell, Vienna was probably lucky he had—the kind of attention that Mr. Derringer paid Brian wasn't what I would wish on anyone.

"Can I spend the night at Vienna's, then?" Kelly turned to me.

"No! No, honey. You should rest tonight. You girls can see each other tomorrow." I was worried about Vienna and Brian— but there was no way I was going to let my own daughter go home with that man. My need to keep my family safe and warm overshadowed my superhero's concern for other children tonight. And again—Vienna didn't look physically frightened of her father. Neither had Brian. Still, I wished there was a way they could be rescued from the situation—a way they could have a loving home. Because they were both good kids—even Vienna, underneath the purple stripe and loud clothing, cries for attention, I could see now. I gave her a hug, ashamed of how I'd treated her in the past.

I steered Kelly toward the waiting room. Dan followed behind us; when he saw Carl and Greg, he stiffened. When Carl saw Dan, he did the same.

"Could you walk the kids out to the car?" I asked Carl. He nodded, then shepherded them all out the door. I turned to Dan.

"I'm sorry for what I said back there."

"That's all right." Dan's face was bleached white under the harsh lights.

"I know that you were worried about Kelly, and of course you're her father, her parent. That will never change."

He didn't say anything; he just shifted his coat from one arm to the other.

"But I want you to forget about this idea you have, that we can be together again. We can't. I've moved on, Dan. You should, too."

"But—"

"You don't want me, anyway. I annoy you so much, Dan! I always did. And I haven't changed—well, maybe I have, but I think I'd still annoy you. More than ever." I smiled to myself; he thought that all I was capable of was taking care of him? How little he knew about me, after all.

And that was the way I wanted it. After all.

"Birdie, you don't know what you want . . . the kids want us to be together . . . we're a family, we belong together. . . ."

"Define family."

"What?"

"Define family. What does it mean?"

"Birdie, really." He shook his head, giving up. "Okay. A father. A mother. Kids. A family."

"You left out one important part." I put my hand to his cheek.

"What?" His blue eyes were startled; he started to put his hand up to grasp mine.

"You left out love," I told him. And removed my hand, just in time.

"But, Birdie . . ."

"Good-bye, Dan. Take care."

And I really meant it. I hoped he would. Take care—or find someone to do it for him. Because he obviously needed it, so very much.

CHAPTER 22

I stood in the parking lot, my hand shielding my eyes from the bright sun. The brand-new Astro-Park-O-Dome Field sparkled like it was in a TV commercial—like someone had dipped it in gold, to make it shine. It was huge, taking up several city blocks; yellow-painted brick on the bottom, where the big sign reading ASTRO-PARK-O-DOME FIELD, HOME OF THE JETPACKS hung over the mammoth entrance. There were other signs, too. WITH THANKS TO THE GENEROUS DONATIONS MADE BY THE PEOPLE OF ASTRO PARK hung over the ticket window. And MADE POSSIBLE BY SPECIAL FUNDING COURTESY OF THE ASTRO PARK SHRINERS AND THE HAWTHORNE VALLEY SCHOOL DISTRICT PARENT-TEACHER AS-SOCIATION welcomed patrons to the outside entrance of the new Starbucks.

Carrie was *not* going to like that.

The dome rose like the wide end of an egg against the blue sky. It was closed right now; someone had said that rain was pre-dicted for tonight.

Striding through the bustling concourse, I surveyed all the new businesses. Starbucks, the gourmet pretzel place, the sushi place, the burrito place, and the usual hot dog and hamburger vendors. Although I was sad to note that the frozen-chocolate-dipped-banana-on-a-stick place—my personal favorite—was not yet up and running.

After first stopping for a quick Macchiato, I continued out to the field, which was carpeted by emerald green Tifway 419 Bermuda grass. A baseball team was out there, hitting the ball into the outfield more often than not, shagging flies (and only dropping half of them), jogging from base to base with almost athletic grace. I thought that the Smallville team had arrived a day early. But no. Because suddenly, on the Jumbotron, I saw Jimmy Denton flash a pearly white smile—underneath a faint mustache on his lip. I stopped, stunned. His muscles rippled beneath his shirt, and his neck was thicker than it had been just a couple of weeks before.

"Oh my God," I said, and wished that I'd been paying attention to what Carl had said about José Canseco. Because all of a sudden I knew that whatever he was referring to was here, on this field—even to my unpracticed eyes, I didn't think that the Jetpacks could have improved so dramatically merely through calisthenics.

My scalp hummed, sang, tingled—up and down my spine shivers ran, kicking my Super Mom Sense into full gear.

"Lois!" She was sitting in the dugout, her college-ruled notebook clutched to her chest. She gave a little wave and trotted out to meet me.

"Hi, Mrs.— Super Mom!"

"Lois, how long have you been here?"

"About an hour. Why?"

"Have you noticed anything unusual about the team?"

She consulted her notes. "They do a lot of exercises, and the new coach yells at them a lot, and they yell back, and they don't seem very happy, but they're awesome, aren't they? Do you think they'll win tomorrow?"

"I don't care about that. Look at them! Don't they look different to you?" I watched Martin—who I thought looked the same, but all of a sudden I couldn't trust myself anymore. He seemed to grow overnight these days—but I'd always thought that was normal teenaged boy behavior. Now, I wasn't so sure.

Suddenly Coach Bluto called out, "Gatorade break!" And the boys ran, elbows out, jockeying for position, to the dugout.

"That is the one thing that's puzzled me," Lois said. "They take a lot of Gatorade breaks."

"They said that the other day." I looked at the Gatorade, in one of those bright orange coolers, sitting on a table in the dugout. The boys were reluctantly raising cups to their lips, just pretending to drink.

Until Coach Bluto walked by. Then they guzzled it down like they were dying of thirst.

"That's the third one in half an hour."

"Okay." I looked at my watch; it was almost five o'clock. "I don't have time to look into this now, but do me a favor. Smuggle some of that Gatorade over to Mr. Sayers's house—he's at three twelve Dundee Avenue—and ask him to analyze it for me. Tell him to remember José Canseco. I think he'll know what you mean."

"Okay!" Lois sped away, excited; she hopped off toward the dugout, her brown hair bobbing up and down. I sniffed. I didn't smell peaches, though. In fact . . .

I sniffed. And sniffed again. Then I sniffed some more. Then I got a really sharp headache.

Because the overwhelming smell wasn't of peaches or Gatorade or turf or sweat. It was that rotten egg smell again, only more pungent than ever. Nauseating—I clutched my stomach, shook my head to clear the fumes, then looked around for Mayor Linseed and Jasper.

I spotted them up near the Jumbotron, backs turned to the field. And so I made my way up the endless steps, pausing once to look down, to where the baseball team looked like tiny ants. The stadium was enormous; you could fly an airplane in it.

Finally I reached the level where the mayor, Jasper, and two unfamiliar men were talking, nodding, shaking hands.

"What's up, Mayor?" I strolled over to them, hands on hips. "How's the inspection going?"

"Super Mom!" Mayor Linseed sputtered. "What are you doing here?"

Jasper didn't say anything; he simply hung back and watched.

"I thought I should be here to make sure this testament to our fine young athletes was properly inspected before opening it to the public."

The two men—both holding clipboards—looked guiltily at the mayor.

"I'm sorry you missed it," Mayor Linseed clucked. "But the inspection's over. Not to worry, we passed. The structure's sound as can be. Tomorrow, we play ball!"

"Funny, I'm not surprised at all. How long did this inspection take, by the way? It's a big place. It must have taken quite some time."

Jasper insinuated himself between the mayor and me. "It took as long as it needed to. There's no time limit for inspections."

"Hmmm." I grabbed one of the clipboards before anyone could stop me. "Looks like everything's on the up-and-up. . . ."

"Of course it is, Super Mom. . . ."

"All right, buddy. Spill it." I tossed the clipboard aside, grabbed one of the inspectors by the collar, and threw him into a nearby stadium seat. "Tell me the truth. How much are they paying you?" I fixed him with my Merciless Gaze.

Squirming, fidgeting, he looked right, then left, then right again, until I grabbed his chin and held firm.

"All right . . . all right, Super Mom . . . I'll tell . . . just stop

looking at me like that . . . we didn't do a regular inspection . . .
Jasper paid us off . . . five hundred dollars each . . . but I'm sure
the structure is sound anyway. . . . I'm sorry, I know I did a bad
thing, I'm really sorry . . . I'll be good now. . . ."

"Of course you will. But in the meantime, I'm going to
have to ask you to hand over the money. As for you—" I
whirled around, fixing Mayor Linseed with my Merciless Gaze.
"I need to hear the truth. Now. About the kickbacks you're getting from Derringer and Company." I advanced toward him,
hands on my hips.

He shrank back, eyes widening, mouth open. It looked as if
he was trying to speak, but nothing came out. I narrowed my
eyes even more menacingly, intent upon making him talk. . . .

Never noticing the soft tread of someone sneaking up behind me. For all of a sudden I was whacked on the head with a
heavy object; I heard the crack of wood on skull before I felt it.
But when I felt it, my eyes exploded from the pain—

And then there was nothing. Nothing but blackness.

I heard voices first. Whispered voices—Jasper's. And the mayor's.

"Why did you do that? What are you going to do with her?
She looks like—she looks just like—she looks dead! Not again!"
Mayor Linseed's voice oozed panic.

"We have to keep her here until tomorrow. We can't let anything go wrong. The whole world will be watching tomorrow,
remember, Jonathan? Your lifelong dream."

"Yes . . . but I can't have a dead superhero on my hands . . .
not again . . . not now. . . ."

"Leave everything to me, just like before. And she's not
dead, she's just unconscious."

I tried to open my eyes to see if this was true or not. But I
couldn't; I blinked, felt heavy fabric against my eyelids, and knew

I was blindfolded. From the cottony taste in my mouth—seasoned with a little basil, so it must have come from somebody's kitchen—I knew I was gagged.

And given the way my wrists and ankles were painfully twisted together in unnatural positions, I figured I was bound, too.

Sniffing, I tried to figure out my location; the horrible, rotten egg odor was even more overwhelming. So I knew I was still in the Astro-Park-O-Dome Field.

"How will we keep her quiet?"

"Jonathan, you're panicking. We've been through this a hundred times. Don't worry. What time is it, anyway?"

"Five o'clock— Oh!"

"That's right. Don't you have an errand to run?"

"Oh, my, yes." Feet scuffled, fabric flapped, and a door slammed.

Jasper cackled. "Idiot. This has been far too easy."

Afraid to move a muscle, I wondered how long I'd have to play dead. Metal scraped against concrete—a chair? A rustle of plastic, the rich, sweet scent of tobacco, a brushing sound followed by a quick jolt of sulfur—followed by an explosion of expletives.

"Jesus Christ!" Jasper stamped his feet. "That would have been stupid." Then he cackled again. "Almost as stupid as my cousin. Yes, go ahead, run your little errand, you idiot. Go ahead and make your last payment. All this time, you have no idea I'm the one blackmailing you? Who's the brains of the family now?"

Blackmail??? I would have gasped, had I not had a mouthful of cotton. But I must have made some kind of noise, because all of a sudden I felt a sharp kick to my ribs, and I couldn't help but moan.

"Oh, so she's awake now, is she?"

I didn't move.

"Stop playing possum." He grabbed an arm, hauled me up,

and maneuvered me to a sitting position, my back against what had to be a wall. The floor beneath my skirt was icy cold—concrete, I figured. All of a sudden the cotton was ripped from my mouth, and I spit fibers out.

"Ugh . . . ," I sputtered.

"Go ahead and scream if you want, Super Mom. No one will hear you. That's one good thing about this monstrosity—plenty of places to hide the bodies."

"What . . ." My throat was dry and cottony, and I had to swallow several times before I could speak. "What are you going to do with me?"

"Keep you out of the way, until you're not necessary anymore."

"When will that be? Because I need to fix dinner and do some laundry and—"

"Sorry. Not tonight, Super Mom. I'm afraid you'll have to stay here tonight." I swiveled my head, trying to follow the sound of his voice as it moved about the room.

"Why did you hit me?"

"Because I couldn't get rid of you the other night. So I had to try again."

"You! You were the one who shot Janitor Bingo? Why? Why did you put him up to all that Phantom stuff?"

"Oh, come now, I'm not foolish enough to give one of those end-of-the-movie confessions, just in time for you to break through your shackles and take me into custody."

"Stupid Hollywood." All those superhero movies—while good for JLA publicity—have really made it hard on those of us actually fighting crime. Without the assistance of screenwriters and stunt doubles.

Jasper laughed, hissing in his reptilian way. "You'll have to figure it out for yourself."

"You wanted me out of the way for some reason. . . ."

"You give yourself too much credit. You were a decoy. If people were focused on you—particularly if my idiotic cousin was focused on you—nobody would be paying any attention to what I was up to." He laughed again, evilly. My skin crawled.

I was stumped. With the blindfold on I couldn't put him in a Super Time-Out, or use my Merciless Gaze. I wriggled my hands, wondering where they were pointed. . . .

"I wouldn't try that, Super Mom. How would you like to be burned with your own cleaning fluid? There's no way you can shoot that stuff out your fingertips without burning your own flesh."

Damn. He was right. Shooting my fluid would be suicidal. However . . . I concentrated, frowning, my hands straining—then relaxing. Straining, relaxing, over and over . . . until I had a drip hanging from one fingertip. I let it fall, holding my breath; I felt a drop on the back of my skirt, a tiny hiss as it ate through the fabric. So I tried again, maneuvering my fingers, working up a drop, trying to aim it at my wrists, to whatever was binding them. It wasn't fabric; it was metal. This was going to take a while—a long while. But it was the best I could do. Strain . . . relax . . . strain . . . relax . . . my hands began to ache, but I had to keep going. Meanwhile, I concentrated on keeping Jasper talking.

"Jasper, I'm curious. This is between you and me—and let's face it, I'm totally at your mercy. So tell me the big secret. What did you do, that the mayor has to keep you on such a short leash?"

"This town is full of fools. I didn't do anything—he did. He slept with a little girlie once, long ago, and that girlie turned up dead. I was the only one who knew. . . . Now, he's never stopped twice to figure out how it was that I knew. Mistake number one. Mistake number two—trusting me to keep my mouth shut.

Without payment. So he pays. But not enough. So I've had to scare him a little bit lately, pretending to blackmail him. Why do you think he was in such a rush to get this stadium built? He needs the revenue—he's getting kickbacks from the construction company. . . ."

"Well, duh. Even a junior high school reporter knew that."

"And where does the money go? To me."

Through the whole speech I was maneuvering my wrists, until finally I was able to drip my cleaning fluid onto the heavy chains binding my hands. (And only occasionally missing and burning my skin, which caused me to wince, but fortunately Jasper wasn't paying any attention.)

Finally his voice remained in one place, directly in front of me. I stopped dripping.

"That's it for tonight's confessional, Super Mom."

"Wait a minute," I said, remembering something else Lois had said. "What about his interest in the salt company? What's that about?"

"Nothing financial, if that's what you mean. But here's something for you to think about. Underneath this structure lie salt mines. Lots and lots of salt mines. That's all I'm going to say. You have to figure out the rest, and you have the rest of your short life to do so, Super Mom. Sleep well!"

He gave me a farewell kick to the ribs, then opened and shut the door.

And I resumed dripping my cleaning fluid, drop by drop. Waiting impatiently for it to eat through the shackles binding my wrists. Thinking about salt mines.

I must have fallen asleep. I heard scurrying sounds, like mice, which jolted me awake, my heart racing; the last thing I wanted was to become a jungle gym for rodents. My eyes were dry from rubbing against my blindfold; my head ached, my ribs throbbed, and my hands were raw from straining. But still I kept trying.

I had no idea what time it was. I strained to hear something . . . anything . . . but all I got was ominous silence. I sniffed and sniffed . . . but all I smelled were the basil from the fabric, my own smells of fabric softener and bleach and ammonia and Swiffer. And that heavy, pungent odor of rotting eggs, getting more rotten by the hour.

I started in on the straining . . . relaxing . . . straining . . . relaxing . . . drip by drip. I twisted my wrists; nothing seemed to budge. Whatever metal was holding them together didn't seem to give in any way, and finally I hung my head, giving up.

"Oh, please, somebody," I whispered, my throat dry. "Mr. Clean, where are you when I need you?"

All of a sudden I heard a happy little *chirrup.*

I raised my head.

Purrup!

"Scrubbing Bubbles?" I croaked.

Something fell over in a corner; I swiveled my head toward the loud clank. All of a sudden something soft and bristly was tickling my leg.

"Ow! Stop . . . stop!" I couldn't help myself; I started giggling, even as I prayed that I wasn't being tickled by a giant mouse.

Chirrup, whirrup—wheeee!!! Lots of bristly things were tickling my leg, swarming up, over me, over my shoulders, down my arms, concentrating on my wrists. They whirred and whirred, and finally my arms were free.

"Thank you! Thank you!" I tried to swing my arms around to their normal positions but almost passed out from the pain, my shoulders, elbows, were so locked and rusty. But I managed to pull the blindfold off—though for a minute I wasn't sure I had, because I was still totally in the dark. Gradually my eyes adjusted, and when I looked down, prepared to see myself surrounded by a band of Scrubbing Bubbles—

I saw that I was alone.

"But—I don't understand." I quickly unbound my feet, threw off my metal shackles, then slowly, painfully, rose. Hobbling, I stumbled around until I found a light switch and flipped it on, my eyes burning from the sudden light.

"Little dudes? Where are you? I know you saved me—I just want to thank you!" My eyelids felt heavy, almost as if the blindfold was still pressing against them, as I lurched around what appeared to be a storage room full of boxes and cast-off furniture and an autographed poster of the San Diego Chicken. But no Scrubbing Bubbles were in evidence. Just when I was about to give up, deciding that I must have been delirious from all the pain and confusion (either that, or those mice had some nasty chompers), I spotted a bucket upended in a corner. And spilling out of that bucket—

Was an aerosol can of Dow Bathroom Cleaner. I grabbed it, staring at the happy little guys on the label, begging them with my tired, crusty eyes for a sign—any sign. A sign that I was not, actually, losing my mind.

But the Scrubbing Bubbles did not make a sound. Nor did they wink. They simply remained what they were—computer-generated one-dimensional images stuck on an aerosol can. And I couldn't help it—I started to cry, cold, lonely, every muscle in my body feeling like it had been pulled as far as it could go and then snapped back in place, like a rubber band. I needed to know I wasn't in this alone. I needed to know that someone had been looking out for me, after all; I was tired of being the strong one—the superhero.

Blowing my nose on a faded cloth, I tried to pull myself together by tugging on my costume, making sure my cape was in place, and my mask back around in the center of my face (it had gotten twisted in the blindfold). My panty hose were in shreds. (Typical. I've yet to find a brand that can hold up under ordinary crime-fighting circumstances, although L'eggs Sheer Energy comes close.) But I straightened my shoulders—not feeling any more confident but at least knowing I looked it— and started toward the door.

Just then I heard a commotion in the corner. Spinning around, I saw the overturned bucket—with the Dow Bathroom Cleaner inside it—suddenly, magically, set itself right-side up again.

"Aha!" I couldn't help it; I started to laugh, relief tickling my body the same way the Scrubbing Bubbles had.

Chirrup!

"Thanks, guys!" I gave them a smart salute as I prepared to open the door, although I had no idea what—or who—I would see when I emerged. . . .

Although I think it's safe to say that the last thing I expected to see was a member of Astro Park's finest, seated on a chair sound asleep with a rifle across his lap. I almost screamed—the sound was about to tear through my lips when I remembered, just in time, to clamp my hand across my mouth and take a step back. The officer's head was lolling about, his tongue sticking out. He stirred, snorted—I held my breath—then resumed snoring peacefully.

I tiptoed down the dark corridor, not knowing where I was within the stadium—only that I needed to go down, because the top of the dome wasn't too far above me. I figured I was somewhere near the skyboxes. So I searched for a staircase— careful to tiptoe quietly, which is almost as hard to do in high heels as running—finally located one, and opened the door leading to it. . . .

Which had to squeak, naturally. Which must have woken the officer up, because I heard a sound very much—at least to my vivid imagination—like a rifle dropping to the floor, followed by a very distinct, "Son of a bitch, that bastard'll kill me."

I threw myself down those stairs as fast as my short, stubby little legs would carry me. Heavy footsteps followed closely behind, accompanied by expletives and threats. "Damn you, Super Mom, get back here. I'm not supposed to let you escape!"

"Too bad! And you should be ashamed of yourself—does Police Commissioner Borden know about this?" My legs felt like rubber, but still I ran—until I spotted a metal sign hanging in the stairwell—CAUTION, KEEP STAIRWELLS CLEARED AT ALL TIMES IN CASE OF EMERGENCY. "That'll do." Yanking it off the wall, I heard the policeman's steps getting closer and closer, aimed both of my hands and fired—streams and streams of cleaning fluid, making the stairs below me as slick as possible. Then I jumped on the sign, said a desperate prayer, tried to channel my inner thirteen-year-old skateboarder, and went flying down the stairs.

"Oh . . . my . . . God!" I screamed, terrified—and thrilled beyond normal maternal reason. I was surfing down those stairs, my feet absorbing the bumps from each step, but I was so gnarly, dude! I was hanging ten, or eleven, or whatever it is you call it— my cape was streaming behind me, and I figured out—just in the nick of time—how to lean into the turns at the end of each flight so that I didn't run flat into the wall in front of me.

I took one look behind me as I rounded a corner. The officer's feet were flailing like a cartoon figure's. I heard a gigantic thump, almost a crack, and I winced, my tailbone smarting in sympathy.

"That's gonna leave a mark!"

"Super Mom!" he screamed. "Stop!"

"Sorry—whoa!" as I almost fell off my sign. Then I fired more cleaning fluid as I surfed and surfed down the stairs, finally coming to a stop at the ground floor. I grabbed my sign, looked around, didn't see anybody, and crept out a side door. The first rosy glow of sunrise was on the horizon as I strolled away, makeshift surfboard under my arm, costume tattered and torn—and a giant grin on my face.

I didn't risk getting into my car; I had no idea who might be watching. So I crept along the side of the enormous stadium, careful to remain within its shadow, and ran home, darting down side streets, cutting through yards, zapping the occasional dirty linen hanging on a clothesline.

And I finally reached my destination—a certain absent-minded professor's split-level house. My old dented minivan was parked in front, and all the lights were on, and when I opened the door the house was abuzz with activity—Kelly and Martin seated at the kitchen table with Lois, Greg running around with the phone, Carrie making pancakes at the stove . . . and Carl, standing at the kitchen counter staring out the window, his face all worried and puckered.

"Hey," I shouted, closing the door behind me. "Am I too late for dinner?"

All heads turned to me. Nobody moved. At least not right away. Carl was the first one who recovered enough to speak, although what he said wasn't very intelligent at all.

"You—what—where—oh!!" And I'll leave it to your imagination to figure out what he did when he finally reached me.

CHAPTER 23

"Lois came over around four o'clock. She said you'd sent her, and she had that Gatorade. Well, I ran all the tests, and then we waited for you. We waited, and waited, and waited. We called Commissioner Borden. I couldn't get through to him; his line was busy all night, but we finally got his deputy, and he was going to send some men over to the Astro-Park-O-Dome Field, but Mayor Linseed said he had his own special force there looking for you. Then Kelly and Martin called, worried, so I had them come over here. We called Carrie. And then all we could do was wait. And I'm officially sick of wringing my hands on the sidelines while my superhero loved one is out there being tied up by evil villains." Carl slapped his hand on the table, startling us all.

"Me, too," I said, grabbing his hand. My other arm was around Kelly. "But it is part of the job description, you know."

"I know. Stupid superhero job hazards."

I smiled at my fiancé. Then I asked the one question that had been on my mind all night.

"Did everybody get their homework done?" I looked at my children. Who rolled their eyes and sighed.

Then it got quiet. Suddenly no one was looking at me; Carrie was concentrating on the dishes in the sink, Kelly was extremely interested in her pink hair, and even Carl appeared enormously concerned about a tiny speck of jam on the table.

"What? What is it?"

"Birdie," Carl began. Finally he did look at me, and his face was so sad—I noticed, then, how tired he looked, his face rumpled and sleepy.

"What?"

"Janitor Bingo—he died, Birdie. It was on the news last night. I'm so, so sorry."

"He died?" All I could do was repeat the words. "Janitor Bingo died?"

"Yes, sweetheart."

"Janitor Bingo?" Gruff, ornery Janitor Bingo—whose desire to bring order and cleanliness to a chaotic world rivaled my own, whose job, whose very reason for living, I had thoughtlessly taken away from him—was dead? Before—before I had a chance to right my wrongs?

"But it wasn't your fault, Birdie."

"Would everyone stop saying that?" I yanked my hand away from Carl's. "It *is* my fault! I'm the one who got him shot, I'm the one who put him out of a job in the first place, and now he's dead. And it's my fault." I started to shake, from exhaustion, hunger—my stomach was gnawing on itself—and despair. "I wish everyone would let me take responsibility for it! I wish . . . I wish . . . I wish I didn't have to do all this," I whispered. Carl put his arm around me and let me cry, softly, all over his sweatshirt.

The kids and Carrie were silent. Then Martin whispered something to Kelly, who shook her head vehemently.

"What?" I wiped my nose on my apron and sat back up. "What did you say?"

"Nothing." Kelly glared at him.

"It's all right, you can tell me."

"No, trust me, Mother, you do not want to hear what this Neanderthal just asked."

"*What?*"

Kelly sighed, shuffled over to me and whispered in my ear.

"I am *so* over people asking me that!" I fumed to the room—the world—in general, wanting to take out an advertisement in *People* just to announce that it was not, in fact, that time of the month.

But surprisingly, it was the exact thing I needed to hear at that moment, because it fueled the fire necessary to keep going, finish the task at hand, avenge Janitor Bingo's death—show the world that I was a superhero who was not ruled by her hormones.

"So what was in that Gatorade?" I looked at Lois. Greg looked at her, too. Then he smiled at Martin, gave him a thumbs-up, and whispered, "Sweet!" in approval. Martin blushed, but nod-ded, and returned the thumbs-up. And I wished I had my camera so I could have captured this Kodak moment—the moment two awkward outsiders took the first step to becoming friends. Maybe even brothers.

I squeezed Carl's hand, then asked the question again.

"Well, you won't believe this," Carl said, shaking his head. "Steroids. Oral steroids."

"Jesus Christ!"

"I know. I can't believe that the mayor would do this just to get a championship team."

"How are you two?" I jumped up and ran over to both Greg and Martin. I had to touch them, feel their flesh, just to make sure they were all right.

"It's a very small amount. I don't think they'd had enough to do any permanent damage. Yet. But we need to take them all to the doctor just to make sure."

"I can't believe we didn't know—we should have known. I'm Super Mom! I should have trusted my Super Mom Sense, but I just thought you were being a teenager, all moody and surly." I hugged Martin, so tight.

"I didn't drink as much as the other kids," Martin said. "I wasn't that thirsty."

"I wonder if this had anything to do with the fight?" I looked at Greg and Martin, who both hung their heads.

"What fight?" Carl stood up.

"Nothing. There was just a fight at practice the other day— between Jimmy and Johnny." I rumpled Greg's hair, for the first time—it felt sleek, silky, like a wet seal. He grunted, but flashed me a look of gratitude.

"But don't you think somebody else would have noticed?" Carl asked.

"Not if the team was winning," I said with a sad sigh.

Carrie tugged on her bangs, jerking her little arms all over the place. "If I find out any of my PTA parents were willingly giving their children steroids, they are out. Out, I say. I will personally tear up their PTA membership cards."

"Settle down, General Patton. I really doubt they knew, consciously. Remember, that coach was also putting the boys through a lot of calisthenics and weight training."

"We'll see." Carrie's bright blue eyes gleamed dangerously.

"Right now, though, we need to talk salt mines," I told Carl.

"Huh?"

"I knew it—the salt company! I told you the mayor owned stock in that!" Lois started flipping through her ever-present college-ruled notebook.

"It's not a financial thing, though. That's what Jasper said. He said, let me think . . . he said, underneath this structure lie salt mines. Lots and lots of salt mines. He said to think about it. And I have, but I have no idea what he means. So there are salt mines? Aren't there a bunch of those on the other side of town, too? Who cares?"

"Well . . ." Carl leaped up and started pacing, his hair standing up on end, like it always did when his brain clicked into overdrive. And I relaxed, just a little, knowing that I had an absentminded professor on my side. "Salt mines by themselves don't mean anything. And, yes, there are ones on the other side of town. I thought, though . . . I thought that all of them had been sealed off."

"Why?"

"Because salt mines can trap natural gas. And if they're not contained—if they leak—they could, theoretically, start a fire. Or an explosion. But tests are done nowadays before anything is built on a site like that. And mercaptan has to be added so that any leaks can be detected, because natural gas is odorless. So there would have been a noticeable smell, and nobody's mentioned that. I've never noticed it. And of course the gas company had to have inspected the site. . . ."

"Unless they were on the payroll, like the inspectors I saw yesterday. But wait a minute—you said there wasn't a smell. Well, I've been smelling something from the beginning. That smell, like Martin's gym socks—"

"Mom!" Martin hissed, nodding at Lois.

"Sorry. Anyway, it's been getting stronger every day."

"I don't know why it would be stronger. It's not like it can increase in volume. And besides, I've told you before, natural gas is odorless. It's an absolute."

"Wait a minute!" I jumped up. "You have that little pillbox

thing in your lab! I told you I smelled something—and you told me then I was crazy. But was that natural gas?"

"Well, yes. . . ." Carl tugged on his chin.

"Let me smell it!" I ran down to the basement, followed closely by Carl. Who was wringing his hands like a little girl, yelling at me not to touch anything.

The kids and Carrie scrambled behind us, Carrie holding them back on the basement stairs as Carl and I ran to his pool table.

"Is this it?" I reached for that metal box, knocking over a couple of test tubes.

"Birdie!" Carl shouted. "Stop! Don't touch anything!"

"Why?"

"Because these are highly flammable materials! I've been running some experiments with natural gas, trying to find ways to trap it because—and I really believe I'm on to something here—if I could come up with a viable, inexpensive way to contain it, I could change the future of the entire world! Think of it—a cheap, unlimited alternative fuel! Why, the possibilities are—"

"Yeah, yeah, yeah, whatever. First things first. Let me smell that."

Carl sighed. Then he handed me that metal pillbox thing.

Everyone held their collective breath. I sniffed. And reeled back, eyes watering.

"Rotten eggs and old gym socks and a little bit of compost—exactly what I smelled at the stadium."

"That's incredible." Carl shook his head. "Do you know that you are possibly the only person on the face of the earth who can detect natural gas—naturally?"

"I'm a woman of many talents."

"But why would the smell be getting stronger at the stadium?" Lois piped up from the stairs. Martin looked at her, so proud.

"Yeah, Mom?"

"I don't know . . . except . . . the dome?"

"What?" Carl turned to me, a wild gleam in his eyes.

"The dome is up. It was supposed to rain last night—did it?"

"No."

"Funny, that's what Jasper said. Anyway, they put the dome up, a couple of days ago, I think. Could that trap the gas in some way?"

"I suppose so, if it was up long enough, and there was enough gas. I mean, it could get like a powder keg in there. And one spark—"

"One struck match!" I pounded my fist on the pool table, remembering how Jasper had cursed himself and put that match out right away.

"Please don't do that again." Carl pulled me away from the table. "Well, more than one, most likely. But—yeah."

I looked at the clock hanging next to the St. Pauli Girl poster. Ten o'clock.

"What time is the parade?" I asked, trying to keep my voice calm.

"Oh, man!" Kelly jumped up. "In an hour! I need to get my band uniform!" She started to climb the steps.

"What time's the game?"

"One o'clock," Greg said. "We should get going, Martin. Coach wanted an extra practice." He, too, got up to go.

"Hold it," I said, my voice low and terrible. Everyone turned to look at me.

"Nobody's going anywhere. Because if I'm not mistaken, at one o'clock, there's going to be . . ." I started to laugh; I was so tired and overwhelmed I couldn't help it. I couldn't help but re-member what Jasper had said the other day in Janitor Bingo's hospital room.

"He said it's going to be a blast," I gasped, laughing hysterically. Holding on to Carl for support—

Until I stopped, abruptly. And started to do what I did best. Which was figure out a way to clean up this gigantic, explosive mess.

CHAPTER 24

"Why can't I reach Borden?" I slammed the phone down, looked at the clock, and realized that I couldn't waste any more time trying to call the authorities.

"We couldn't get him, either, while you were missing. And by the way—how did you get untied? You never told us that." Carl grabbed the phone and returned it to the wall.

"Oh! It was the Scrubbing Bubbles!" I beamed at him.

He turned around and glanced at Carrie—who frowned.

"Oh, Birdie." She shook her sad little head. "I really wish you hadn't said that."

"Why not? Aren't you happy for me—I wasn't crazy, after all!"

"More than one verifiable instance of hallucinating, and I'm obligated to turn you in." She blinked, furiously, trying unsuccessfully to stop a few tears from rolling down her cheeks. "I'm so sorry."

"Well, whatever—do what you have to later."

"No, Birdie, I have to do it now. It's my job—I'm sworn by the JLA."

"Carrie—Carl, you believe me, don't you?" He was standing between Carrie and me, mouth open. Meanwhile, Carrie reached for the phone.

"Carl? You believe me. Don't you?" I couldn't believe my eyes. Or ears. Because the right words weren't coming out of his mouth.

"Believe you? Why, actually, the truth is . . ." He backed away from me—toward Carrie. Siding with her.

"No, no—this isn't happening. You have to believe me—you're my—"

Carrie was dialing the phone, shaking her head sadly. "I'm afraid you need to remain here until a JLA administrator arrives to evaluate you. Meanwhile they'll send another superhero out to pinch-hit for you."

"No! This is my responsibility! This is my town—my evil villain! Carl, you can't possibly be on her side!"

"I'm so, so sorry," my (former) fiancé said, wringing his hands. "I'm so sorry I have to do this!"

And I gasped. For with a smooth, rather impressive judo chop, Carl knocked the phone out of Carrie's hand and grabbed her arms, wincing as her little feet kicked him in the shin.

"Run, Birdie! Run!"

"What?"

"Go, Mom!" Martin gave me a shove. "Go!"

"Oh! Okay! I love you, you know!" I smiled at my (current) fiancé.

"I know."

"All right—listen up, people, it's up to us to stop the parade. Kelly—you go tell the band director and try to get him to stop marching. Lois—you try to find Commissioner Borden. Greg, Martin, you need to find Coach Bluto and keep the team out of the stadium. They'll be on a float or something, I'm sure. Carl—"

"Go. I'll take care of Carrie."

"What?" Carrie yelped. "Don't you hurt me—I have friends in high places. . . ."

"Oh, please." He rolled his eyes. "It's not like I'm going to throw you in the river. I'm just going to let Birdie get a head start. What are you waiting for?" he shouted at me, jolting me into action. "Go—save the world! And take my car—yours is out of wiper fluid." He threw me the keys.

"Thanks!" And I went, followed by the kids.

"Can I drive?" Kelly tugged on my arm.

"Kelly, now is not exactly the time to—"

"Please, Mom? I need more practice driving in traffic."

"Oh, all right." I tossed her the keys and got in the passenger side. "Don't forget to adjust the rearview mirror."

"Don't worry!" She released the parking brake, stepped on the accelerator, and sped off in the general direction of the Astro-Park-O-Dome Field. She hadn't driven three blocks before we spotted a roadblock ahead.

"I don't like the looks of this," Lois piped up from the back, where she was seated—quite contentedly—between Martin and Greg.

"Me either." Martin frowned. "Quick, Mom—down on the floor!"

"Wha—?" But Martin and Greg were already pulling me into the backseat, shoving me down on the floor of Carl's station wagon and covering me up with everything they could find— an old picnic blanket, paper bags, an old folding lawn chair. They kept piling stuff on top of me until I couldn't breathe, but I also couldn't afford to let them know that, because I heard Kelly roll down her window.

"What's going on, Officer?" She sounded extremely confident for a newly licensed driver who was smuggling her superhero mother in her future stepfather's car.

"We have all the roads leading to the stadium blocked, due to security."

"Security?"

"For the parade, and the opening day. You can't be too careful these days, you know. Terrorists and all."

"Oh."

"Can I take a quick look in your car?"

"Well, we're really in a hurry—I'm supposed to be marching in the parade. I'm in band. I play clarinet—first chair this year!"

"It won't take a minute."

I felt Martin and Greg step on me, patting me down with their feet. Then I think they both crossed their legs on top of me—all I know is that a heel nearly punctured my eardrum. And also? I still couldn't breathe. I heard the passenger doors open, shut, open again. Then—

"How long have you had your license, miss?"

"A month!"

"Should you be driving this many minors, then?"

"Oh, but they're my brothers and sister!"

I was impressed by Kelly's ability to lie under pressure. Impressed, and more than a little alarmed.

"Well . . . all right, you're clear. But you can't get any closer to the stadium. You'll have to turn around."

"Okay!"

I felt the car lurch, turn around—tires squealing, but I couldn't yell at Kelly because I didn't want the officer to hear—and then we drove away.

Finally Martin pulled the blanket off me; I gasped, gulping air.

"Sorry, Mom." He shrugged.

"It's all right."

"I think they were looking for you!" Lois's eyes were sparkling with excitement. "Terrorists? As if!"

"I know. Jasper must have them in his pocket. Well, now what?"

"Hold on!" Kelly shouted, suddenly swerving off the street and down a little alley—at higher speeds than they teach in driver's ed.

Everyone in the backseat—including me—screamed.

"Kelly Maria Lee! You stop this car right now!"

"Just a little farther!" she chirped, grinning.

"Watch out for that little old lady!" Martin shouted.

"Don't hit that puppy!" Greg yelled.

"Oops!" The driver's-side mirror hit a mailbox and snapped off.

"That is coming out of your allowance, young lady!"

"Mom!" But she continued to drive like we were in a video game—lurching left, then right, speeding down side streets and alleys and lanes. Finally she screeched to a stop behind an abandoned building. "Here we are!" she trilled, unbuckling her seat belt and swiping her lips with a tube of lip gloss.

The rest of us were slightly green in the face. "I think I'm gonna be sick," Lois groaned, stumbling out of the car.

"Kelly Maria Lee, when I am done keeping the world safe for democracy, you are going to be grounded. Do you understand? You didn't use your turn signals once!"

"Mom!" She pouted.

"All right." I surveyed my troops. "Be careful, don't talk to strangers, and look both ways when you're crossing the street!"

And we scattered like bowling pins, tumbling toward our separate destinations along the parade route.

Crowds of jubilant Astro Parkers lined Main Street—the street that led directly to the Astro Park-O-Dome Field—eating cotton candy, popcorn, peanuts; spilling Sno-Cones. My hands itched and burned to start scrubbing and cleaning up, but I promised myself I could do that tomorrow. If tomorrow ever came, that is. I pulled my gaze away from the awful spills and litter that were accumulating, and reminded myself there was something more important to do. Like, oh, SAVE THE WORLD.

I started to slip through the crowds, trying not to be overcome by all the parade smells—popcorn, exhaust from the little floats that were putt-putting down the street. Not to mention elephant poop. Balloons kept escaping from crying toddlers, flying up and dotting the bright blue sky. I ran in the direction of the stadium, which loomed over the end of the street like a giant mushroom cloud. There were police everywhere, probably on the lookout for me; the only thing I could do was pray they were too busy watching the Rockettes, who were now in the middle of Main Street kicking up a storm to "You're a Grand Old Flag."

I kept running, passing drill teams and bands and the float carrying Kelly Clarkson (who had a *huge* head, by the way). I caught up to the high school band, which was standing at attention, performing "Love Will Keep Us Together."

On the sidelines, Gloria Tubwell smiled and clapped along with the music, pure agony in her eyes.

"Stop the parade," I shouted to Mr. Vandercliff, the band director.

"Yes, it is!" he yelled over the blaring tubas—the brass section never could stay in tune. He smiled, continuing to conduct the band—earplugs in his ears.

I turned and started running again, hoping Kelly could make him understand. My side was aching now; my feet, having long since poked through my tired panty hose, were blistering and burning in my high-heeled pumps. But still I jogged, passing the 4H float with their usual papier-mâché farm—a silo that leaned too far to the right and a cow with only three legs (the fourth a casualty of an errant firecracker during last year's Fourth of July parade), clowns, policemen mounted on horses. . . .

Policemen . . . whom I was no longer sure I could trust. Mounted on horses . . . which could run faster than I could. . . .

"Look, there's Super Mom!" one of them shouted.

"Get her," said another, as he turned his horse and started galloping—straight toward me.

I yelped, tried to run faster, tried to see a way I could cut through the crowd somehow, heard pounding hooves, like the devil's very own, closing in on me—and suddenly spotted my salvation.

"Shriners!" I ran up to the contingent of large men in tiny cars, with those funny little fez hats on their heads. "Quick, I need to borrow your car."

"Excuse me?" A particularly enormous man, wedged somehow into a tiny Corvette, gaped at me.

I flashed my JLA card. "In the name of the Justice League of America, I'm commandeering this car!"

"Okay! Okay!" He slammed on the brake and tried to get out, but he was really stuck, the steering wheel cutting into his huge belly. I pulled and pulled on him as he huffed and puffed—meanwhile those galloping hooves were getting louder and louder . . . finally the man got free, tumbling against me, nearly flattening me.

"Thanks," I wheezed, jumped in the car and took off, looking over my shoulder. The police—on their frightening steeds—were gaining on me.

"Stop her! Stop that—tiny car!" one of them shouted.

I floored the miniature Corvette, whirring around the other Shriners, who were driving in crazy patterns, confused and aghast. I sped past them, past other floats, past—

Carrie. Who was standing next to Carl, up ahead on the right. Her face was scarlet, her mouth open in horror, but all I could do was wave as I darted by.

Ryan Seacrest—who was in the head car as grand marshal, seated next to Mayor Linseed, saluted.

"Why, hello, Super Mom," Ryan Seacrest called. "You forgot that autograph last time!"

"I'll get it later!" I shouted. The mayor—who was turning red, eyes bulging—said nothing.

Police Commissioner Borden was standing at the end of the parade route, right by the entrance to the stadium, and I floored the tiny Corvette, squealing to a stop about a foot away from his shiny police shoes. I unbuckled my seat belt and sprang out.

"Finally! Thank God! We've been trying to get in touch with you! You have to evacuate the area. You have to make sure nobody goes in there." I pointed at the looming Astro Park-O-Dome Field.

"I can't," he said, shaking his head.

"Look, do you want me to put you in a Super Time-Out? You have to evacuate this area—"

"I can't because I was relieved of my duties yesterday by Mayor Linseed. I'm fired. The new police commissioner is—"

"Me," Jasper said, emerging from the shadows twirling Borden's old nightstick. I gulped.

"Nice of you to make this so easy, Super Mom. You delivered yourself right into our hands. Men!" He beckoned to a bunch of deputies. "Arrest this woman!"

"Why? You have no warrant! He has to have a warrant, doesn't he?" I looked at Borden.

"Not since the Patriot Act," he said sorrowfully.

"Damn!"

"I'm arresting you on suspicion of terror. That's good

enough for the Justice Department these days—they'll throw you in a cell, forget about you for a while. That's all I need."

"Terrorist? Me? I'm not the one who's planning to blow up this stadium!"

"What?" Mayor Linseed came trundling up, Ryan Seacrest in tow. "What does she mean? Blow up the stadium?"

"She's deranged," Jasper said, his long tongue snaking out of his mouth.

"You're deranged!"

"You are!"

"No, you are!"

"Wow, it's just like Paula and Simon!" Ryan Seacrest broke in. I glared at him.

"Jasper, I found out about those salt mines—I know what lies beneath this stadium. And I can smell it—I can smell the natural gas. It's filling up the stadium right now." I turned to Linseed, who was sweating, pulling out handkerchief after great white handkerchief. "Didn't you wonder why the dome was up on a beautiful day like today?"

"I thought you said the forecast was for rain." He stared at Jasper.

"I just wanted to protect the grass. I'll open up the dome as soon as everyone's inside."

"No! He's going to blow it up! Don't you see? He wants to ruin you—he wants to ruin the town. You've been paying him hush money, and now he's got enough, and he doesn't need you anymore. Don't you see? He doesn't need you anymore." I grabbed Mayor Linseed's sausagelike hand. "Now, who do you believe? Me—or him?"

Mayor Linseed blinked, his little eyes reddening. "No, Jasper said he'd always take care of me—he said he'd take care of everything. He always did. Even—"

"I know all about the girl. Did you ever stop to figure out why Jasper knew, before you told him?"

"He—you?" Linseed turned to him, his jowls quivering. "You did it? You framed me?"

"Now, Jonathan," Jasper hissed, curling his wiry body around the mayor, hooking his arm around him. "Don't get upset. Don't think too much. Just trust me. Everything will be the same, everything will go on as usual. Haven't I always taken care of you?"

"I guess. . . ."

"Now look at me, young man," I thundered, striding over to Linseed, grabbing his shiny lapel. "Look me in the eye. Would I lie to you? Don't I only want what's for your own good? Haven't I always kept your best interests at heart? Don't give into peer pressure—" I glared at Jasper. "Trust me to know what's best for you."

"I—but—" Linseed swiveled his puffy head around, looking from me, to Jasper, to me. His lower lip started to tremble.

"Don't listen to her, Jonathan. She's just a Girl Scout with a cape."

"I know about the steroids," I told Linseed, who paled. "You're already in big trouble, mister. Do you want to make it worse on yourself?"

"Oh, for God's sake!" Jasper hissed. "Arrest her already! And get this show on the road!"

"Officers!" Mayor Linseed beckoned to them.

"No, don't you understand—he's going to blow up the stadium! With you in it! And the entire town—even scrawny little Ryan Seacrest!"

"Arrest this man," Mayor Linseed instructed the officers—pointing to Jasper.

"Oh!" I said, blinking.

"Jonathan!" Jasper screamed, his reptilian eyes cold and dangerous. "You don't know what you're doing!"

"I'm doing what I should have done a long time ago, Jasper. I'm sorry, but—"

A shot pierced the air. The mayor gasped, looked at his huge belly, clutched it, and pulled his hand away. It was dripping with blood. "Jasper—why—you?"

"I had no choice, Jonathan. I'm sorry. Now it's your turn, Super Mom—"

I froze, my hands in front of me. I wondered if I could stop a bullet with my cleaning fluid. I realized I was about to find out.

Jasper aimed—I shut my eyes, anticipating the blow—but then the ground started to rumble beneath me. I opened my eyes, looked around—the trees, buildings, and streetlamps were shaking and swaying.

"Look!" someone yelled. "It's a bird!"

"It's a plane!"

"No! It's Mr. Clean!" I almost cried with relief. That great, gorgeous bald genie was walking through the crowd, which parted like the Red Sea in front of him. Behind him, clutching Super Secret Super Duper Swiffers—a field of green cleaning machines—was my little band of scientists, led by Dr. Septavius.

"All right, boys!" he squeaked. They tittered, shushed each other, then held their Swiffers at attention. "Ready, aim—fire!"

And with astonishing precision, waves of lethal cleaning fluid zinged through the air, landing right on the intended targets—the guns clutched by the policemen surrounding me.

One gun remained pointed, though. But not for long, as Jasper suddenly dropped it, screaming, clutching his arm. Commissioner Borden was standing over him, grinning, his hands in a karate chop position.

"Wow, that was terrific!" I told him. "Where did you learn that?"

"I've been taking some lessons on the side," he said, kicking at the ground.

"And you guys!" I addressed my valiant band of scientists armed with Swiffers. "Thank you so much! My heroes!"

"We've been practicing," one of them said, his eyes shining proudly.

"That's what the new Swiffer is for—part of a top secret project called Operation Super Mom," Dr. Septavius informed me. "Funded by the Pentagon—although technically we report to the Department of Homeland Security, when we're not supposed to be answering to the director of FEMA—it gets a little confusing."

"I'm sure it does." I nodded in sympathy.

All of a sudden Mr. Clean unfolded his arms and pointed, his massive biceps glistening in the sun.

Jasper had disappeared, racing into the stadium with astonishing speed, just as the parade crowd surged toward the entrance of the stadium. It was too late—if the stadium blew now, it would still take out most of the town.

"Try to evacuate the area," I told Borden, who nodded. "Get Mr. Clean to help. And get him an ambulance." I nodded at the mayor, who was crying and clutching his stomach. "I'll take care of the rest!" Then I turned and followed Jasper, running right inside the gas chamber known as Astro-Park-O-Dome Field.

As soon as I entered, I reeled—the smell was noxious. My head felt like it was going to remove itself from my body and float up to the sky. But I pulled out my Febreze and sprayed myself, praying it would keep me conscious until I'd finished the job at hand. Then I ran out to the middle of the baseball field, searching up, down, all around for Jasper.

All of a sudden I heard a crackling sound—static interrupting radio waves. Then "Roger that. Timers are all set and have been initiated." It was Derringer's voice.

"Stop it!" I shouted, spinning around, looking for him. "Why are you doing this? Why do you want to blow up the town?"

"Because!" His voice floated down from a far-off corner of the stadium, behind the scoreboard. I whipped around, my hand shielding my eyes from the bright stadium lights. "They kicked me out! They didn't start my son! They deserve to die! Besides, I've got my money—I don't care what happens to this place!"

"Are you nuts? It's only a game!"

His unbelieving laughter filled the stadium. "Only a game? Do you even hear yourself?"

"Have you stopped to think about what you're doing to your own kids? Brian and Vienna?" I kept talking even as I raced across the field and up a flight of stairs, heading toward the scoreboard. But it was a long way away. And all of a sudden my Super Electronic Ears were filled with an ominous ticking sound.

"Coach Henderson humiliated me!" Derringer screamed. I paused, catching my breath—I was getting more lightheaded by the minute. The ticking continued, I couldn't find Jasper, and I knew I had to do something before I passed out. I craned my head up at the very top of the dome; the only possible way out of this was to open it up somehow. But I had no idea where the mechanism was.

More radio static crackled in the atmosphere; Jasper's voice oozed over the airwaves.

"Overriding timers . . . manually detonating. . . ."

"What?" Derringer screamed. "You said I'd have time to get out—get my kid out—"

"There's been a change of plans. . . ." Jasper cackled.

"Super Mom?"

I spun around, heart racing, eyes searching for Jasper, for a way to stop him. But there, standing in the middle of the baseball field, was Martin.

"Martin! Get out of here! Now!"

"Remember the other day?"

"What?"

"The other day when you wanted to go out and fly? And I didn't want to?"

"Yes, sweetheart, but—just get out of here! There's no time!"

"Ten . . . nine . . . ," Jasper started to count down.

"Martin, leave!" I screamed with all my might.

"There's time if you fly!" Martin pointed up. Up toward the heavens. The top of the dome was probably seven hundred feet above my head. Martin was approximately five hundred feet below. Either way, I didn't have time to run. I had to do something. Now.

"But . . . I'm afraid," I said.

"Me, too," my son revealed. He was standing on the pitcher's mound, his hair flopping into his eyes, his old green army jacket too tight around his shoulders. "But I don't have to do it. You do. And I know you can." His brown eyes shone encouragement, lighting the path in front of me.

I shook my head—loving him so much. Proud of him—and proud of myself, for raising such a good son, a good man. Who believed in me, always—even with doors between us. Maybe he didn't tell me that as much as he used to, but I had to learn to trust that he always would. For both of us, from now on, actions would have to speak louder than words.

And there wasn't any better way for me to show him this

than by climbing up on a rail, prepared to fly. I held my hands out—claiming my balance, claiming my destiny. I looked at my son, my trusty sidekick once more, who nodded. Then I raised my head to the sky—the white sky of the interior of the dome. I took a breath, threw off the memories I didn't need anymore because this was one flight that required as little baggage as possible, and reached with all my might toward that sky, toward the next exciting phase of my life. Who knew that at age forty-two I'd still be finding out such amazing things about myself? And I was unstoppable. I was Super Mom. I was—

Flying.

"Ohhhh . . . shit . . . ," I screamed, forgetting about Martin. I squeezed my eyes shut, then realized that flying blind the first time out probably wasn't so smart; I opened them and watched as the seats, the concession stands, the skybox, the scoreboard, Derringer, his eyes wide with astonishment, rushed by—I watched as that tight stretch of white material, the very tip of the dome, came rushing toward me. I pointed my fingers toward it, aimed, fired cleaning fluid in jolting, burning waves, tearing a hole that got bigger and bigger as I flew nearer and nearer; I kept firing, widening it, just in time for me to burst through the top of the dome, my eyes squeezed shut, shards of some kind of material falling about me. I hoped to God that Martin had taken cover.

". . . six . . . five . . . ," Jasper continued counting, cackling gleefully.

I opened my eyes then; I was suspended over the Astro Park-O-Dome Field like an angel on a Christmas tree. Catching a wave of air, I swooped down toward the crowd below and had time to make out an astonished Carrie, perched coyly in Mr. Clean's arms, before I remembered Jasper and the bomb. I tumbled over in a somersault—tugging at my skirt—and spotted him in the farthest section of the parking lot, on top of a T-shirt vendor's stand, his coiled S of a figure giving him away. Slicing through the air, I hurtled myself at him, firing fluid at Jasper just before his finger hit the button, knocking him out, knocking him off the top of the stand. I grabbed him as I sped past, looping in the air—I could see my house from here!—and winging back to the stadium, where we shot through the hole in the dome, diving toward the Tifway 419 Bermuda grass.

"Super Mom!" someone down on the field called out, but I couldn't see who it was. Because all of a sudden the only thing I was aware of was that brown dot of a pitcher's mound racing toward me, faster and faster; the grass was so green, I remembered thinking. It looked so soft. Maybe it wouldn't hurt as much as I thought it would—

Because I didn't know how to stop myself. I could get up, but I couldn't get down, and that's when I realized what the hardest part of flying was. Figuring how to set yourself free, to reach for the sky, the stars, all your dreams, even the ones you haven't had yet—that was the easy part.

Figuring out how to come back to earth without hurting yourself—without hurting the ones you loved—well, that was trickier.

I fell, we fell, Jasper and I—he was limp in my grasp—tumbled and plunged. I didn't know how to stop us; I didn't know how or where to land.

And then I saw Carl. Running out on the field, his arms outstretched, as if he could catch me himself. And I laughed. I laughed at the stupidity of this man thinking he could catch a tumbling superhero and land her safely on the ground. I laughed at the dearness of him. The way he tried, always, to keep me safe when I was on the ground—

And the way he cheered, proud and happy, when it was time for me to fly. I wasn't a little brown bird to him, to be set out on the limb of a tree now and then, allowed to test her wings, but always brought back to her cage; that was who I was to Doctor Dan.

But to Carl, I was a wild bird, an eagle, a soaring superhero who could do anything while he waited on the ground, ready to catch her if she fell—but just as ready to propel her back up again, when it was time for her to go.

"I can catch you," he shouted, still running, arms outstretched. "I can catch you!"

"You don't need to," I yelled back at him, drawn to the ground, safe and sound, just by the love in his eyes. I floated down, touched ground gracefully—on point, actually, like a ballerina—and tossed Jasper unceremoniously toward home plate.

"Well, good," Carl panted, holding on to his side like he was about to collapse. "Because to be honest, I really didn't think I could."

I laughed, reaching out to hug him—then jumping away as applause filled the air. The stadium was filling up with astonished onlookers—Borden, various police officers, Carrie (still flirting with Mr. Clean), Lois, Kelly, Greg, Dr. Septavius and the troops—and Martin, who was jumping up and down and clapping like a little kid.

"Again!" he shouted. "Do it again!"

I looked at them all, and laughed, then walked over to Jasper lying on home plate. I put my foot on him, struck Classic Superhero Pose #1, and smiled for the crowd.

"Three strikes, you're out!"

"Aww," someone from the crowd moaned. "I liked 'Cleanup on Aisle Four' a lot better."

"Really?" I surveyed the crowd. "I just thought with the baseball setting and all, that . . ."

"No, no!" the crowd chanted. "We like the old catch-phrase!"

"Okay." I shrugged, struck Classic Superhero Pose #1 again, and beamed. "Cleanup on Aisle Four!"

And the crowd, as we say in baseball, went wild.

CHAPTER 25

"What's that you've got behind your back?" Janitor Bingo eyed me suspiciously, then started to cackle. Heartily. Especially for a man so recently declared dead.

"I still don't understand!" I sat on his hospital bed and grabbed his gnarled hand—stripped and bleached by decades' worth of good, honest work. Cleaning up after the world.

Commissioner Borden grinned. "After Mayor Linseed removed me from duty, I figured something was up. So I leaked it to the papers that Bingo was dead, and we moved him to another room. Just to keep him safe."

"That's brilliant! I don't think I could have come up with anything better myself."

"So, now what?" Bingo scratched his chin. "What happens next?"

"Well . . ." I stepped into the hallway, crooked a finger, and beckoned. I looked at Bingo, sitting there in his faded janitor's clothes, ready—and eager—to go back to work.

"Jumping Jehoshaphat!" Bingo yelped, rubbing his good eye. "Who's that young whippersnapper?"

"Mr. Clean, I'd like to introduce you to Janitor Bingo."

Mr. Clean, standing in the doorway with his arms crossed and earring gleaming, grunted politely.

"You'll see." I smiled at Bingo. "I know a place where you'll be happy. Do you trust me?"

"Well . . ." Bingo stroked his stubbled chin. "You did sort of put me out of work, and then almost had me killed. . . ."

"But you almost killed me yourself. A couple of times," I reminded him.

"True. Okay. Where's this magical place?"

"I'll leave you in his hands." I patted Mr. Clean on the biceps, suppressing a lustful shudder. "Don't forget the blindfold, and watch out for the White Tornado."

And I left my friend, my fellow soldier in the war against dirt and grime. I had the feeling that he was going to be very, very happy. Especially if Martha Stewart came back from the Betty. I thought they might make a cute couple.

The headline in the *National Enquirer* trumpeted:

SUPER MOM SAVES THE DAY

by special correspondent Jimmy Nelson

AFTER DISCOVERING a potentially deadly gas leak under the brand-new Astro-Park-O-Dome Field, Super Mom flew to the rescue once again, punching a hole in the dome and eliminating deadly gas vapors before enemies of the town could ignite them.

Jasper Linseed, cousin of Mayor Jonathan Linseed, was arrested, as well as his accomplice, Terrance Derringer. Both will be arraigned in court tomorrow and are expected to receive long jail terms.

"I'm just glad to have been of service," Super
Mom said when asked how she felt after saving the
town, once again. "I don't want any thanks, really.
Just knowing this town is safe is thanks enough."

"Ha!" I snorted. "Thanks enough, my foot. If I don't get
something better than a trash can out of this, I will be so pissed."

A customer placed three oranges on my conveyor belt, then
noticed the paper in my hands. "Can you believe that Super
Mom?" She shook her head. "They have to tear down the stadium now because of the salt mines. She put everyone out of
work again!"

"Well, but . . . it was for their own good," I pouted, keying
in the oranges.

"Hmmph." The woman paid up, took her oranges, and left.

"I cannot believe this town!" I fumed at Carrie. "Nobody
appreciates anything I do!"

"Of course not. You're a mom—a super mom."

"Well, I had better get one heck of a Mother's Day present
this year, that's all I'm sayin'." I continued reading the paper.
" '*For more information about the corruption in the mayor's office, please
turn to page twelve for an exclusive scoop by our newest junior reporter,
Lois Blane.*' Oh, that's so nice of Jimmy to give Lois her own by-
line! I think she's going to love interning there!"

"They're a regular Woodward and Bernstein."

"I know! Oh, and listen to this!

'SCIENTIST ON THE VERGE OF MAJOR
BREAKTHROUGH

CARL SAYERS, Astro Park scientist, is considering several offers of major funding for his pursuit

of a way to convert natural gas into energy. "It's all because of the near tragedy at the Astro-Park-O-Dome Field. The situation there, combined with my own experiments, have led me to a major discovery that may change this nation's dependency on foreign oil."'

"You know what?" I folded the paper with a sigh. "He'll get a statue, just you wait and see."

"But aren't you proud?"

"Of course!" And I was. Proud as could be.

"Think how it will be to have two celebrities in the family!"

"It should be interesting." I smiled.

"You know, Birdie, I owe you an enormous apology."

"Go on." I crossed my arms and stared at her.

"I took my job too literally. I was drunk on my own power—I let it get in the way of what I knew about you. I should have trusted you."

"Yeah, well, I should have trusted myself." I shook my head. "Sooner, at least. About a lot of things."

"Will you forgive me?"

"Done."

"I'm still your matron of honor?"

"You bet! And you'll watch all three kids while we're on our honeymoon?"

"Can all three kids manage not to kill each other?"

"Well, we can only hope. But I think they'll manage. I think they'll manage just fine." Groceries started rolling down my conveyor belt—TUMS, Rolaids, Pepto-Bismol . . . "Hi, Coach!" I chirped, not even looking up. Cheerios, peanut butter, carrot sticks, bananas, Oreos, a *Seventeen* magazine . . . lip gloss . . . "What on earth?"

Standing before me was Coach Henderson—and Brian and Vienna Derringer. I grinned.

"Hey, guys!"

"Hey, Mrs. Lee." Brian smiled shyly, his features back to normal—no longer the thick neck, dark upper lip from the steroids. Vienna waved, twisting her purple streak—although I couldn't help but notice she was wearing more modest clothes.

I looked at Coach Henderson, who was beaming. "How's it going, Coach?"

"Well, we have our ups and downs." He gestured at the Rolaids. I nodded. "But so far, so good."

"I'm so glad you were able to be a foster parent for them. I'm so glad it worked out that way."

"Me, too, Birdie. Me, too." He stood back and watched as the kids loaded the bags into the cart. I shook my head, watching this new family, and I thought that in a way, I'd saved the three of them. Vienna and Brian were in good hands, despite the trauma of seeing their father being led away in handcuffs. And Coach Henderson—well, he looked happier than I'd ever seen him. He had his job back as head coach. But best of all he finally had someone of his own to take care of; I knew that he would be the best father in the world.

And that's when I realized that I hadn't saved them. They were in the process of saving each other.

"Can Kelly sleep over tonight?" Vienna asked.

Coach paled. "Sleep over? What's that involve?"

"Oh, you know. My friends come over and we stay up late and talk and try new makeup and maybe put more streaks in our hair. . . ."

Coach Henderson groaned and grabbed his stomach.

"Here you go," I said, handing him an extra roll of TUMS.

"On me. Because you have no idea what you've gotten yourself into."

The sand was warm beneath my bare feet. So was the water, lapping gently at my toes. The hem of my dress was wet, but I didn't care.

I was standing on the beach. With my husband. And I still couldn't get used to calling him that.

"Mrs. Sayers." I sighed. "Birdie Sayers. It sounds good, doesn't it?"

"It sounds perfect," Carl said, holding my hand.

We were on our honeymoon at Club DC, *the* premier timeshare and vacation club for superheroes. I'd finally given in to all their direct-mail pieces and rented a week in one of the "luxury condos overlooking the ocean." And really, it was perfect for a honeymoon. Security was tight; no evil villains could mar our bliss.

"What do you think the kids are doing now?" I allowed my husband to keep my hand in his as we strolled along the beach, still in our wedding finery. Carl was wearing a light gray suit, but his shirt was unbuttoned and his tie had gotten lost somewhere between the reception at Wally's Pizza Station and check-in at the condo.

My dress? Vera Wang, naturally. (She designs for all the biggest superheroes; she has my measurements on file now, just in case I ever go to the Emmys or the Oscars. Or the upcoming PTA Night in Monte Carlo dinner dance, scheduled for June.)

"They're probably all in sugar shock. Did you see how much cake Martin ate?"

"I didn't think he was going to wait for us to cut it." I giggled. "Did you see Greg dancing with Chrissie? They were so cute."

"That's my boy. Dancing with an older woman." Carl smirked. I elbowed him in the ribs, and we kept walking. The sun was sinking gently into the ocean—it was that perfect hour between day and night. That hour when the sweetest of dreams was just a sky full of stars away.

For the first time, really, it was just the two of us; neither of us trying to squeeze into the other one's remnant of a former life. This was it—this was life. Our life. The way it would be from now on—I would always have this man beside me, holding my hand, waiting on the shore—watching me.

"You told me we'd dance at our wedding," I reminded him. "But we didn't. We were too busy taking pictures of the kids. We're such *parents*."

Carl didn't reply. He just took my hand, pulled me to him, put his other hand on my waist, firm, yet gentle—I never knew how he managed to be both at once, but he did. And we began to dance. Right before we started, I looked up; his eyes, shining softly down at me, two beacons of light in the fading day. They showed me all I needed to know; they showed me how to come back, no matter how far away I might fly.

Then he started twirling me, our feet heavy and awkward in the sand.

"Oops." He laughed, so boyish and handsome in the twilight that he took my breath away. "This isn't as easy as it seems on TV!"

"Nothing ever is, but I have an idea." I grinned, raising an eyebrow.

"What? What are you up to . . . whoa!"

For I was flying—my feet off the ground, tracing circles in the air. I was still holding on to him, still letting him guide me. But suddenly I was graceful, more graceful than I ever was on earth—part air, part sea, part sand—

All his. Forevermore.

"Do you know why I can fly?" I teased. He was still pretending that he was leading. And I let him, although right then I was more powerful—I was the wind pushing us gently forward. And he didn't mind. He never did.

"No, why?"

"Because you're here. Waiting for me. I have someone to come back to."

"Always, heart of mine. Always."

I laughed, the wind tickling my bare feet. He laughed, too—and we waltzed on the beach, spinning around and around to the accompaniment of waves crashing, hearts pounding, two rare creatures, one of earth, one of sky—

Both of joy.

Acknowledgments

Again, I'm blessed to have my own personal Justice League to swoop in and help me out in a crisis:

Thanks to Laura Langlie, as always, for her support, belief and friendship. Also Laurie Chittenden, for her insight; Claire Zion, for the same; and Erika Kahn, Tina Brown, Lisa Mondello, Kathleen Schmidt, Bill Contardi, Beth Scanlon and Tooraj Kavoussi, for all their hard work.

To the many writers I've been so fortunate to meet over the past year, thank you so much for your friendship and inspiration. But in particular I'd like to thank Nicole Hayes, Tasha Alexander, Joe Konrath, Henry Perez, David Kedson, Sachin Waikar, Karen Dionne, Eileen Cruz Coleman, Timothy Schaffert, Karin Gillespie (and the rest of the Girlfriends). Also thanks to Sue Petersen of BrainSnacks, and Jane Stroh of The Bookstore in Glen Ellyn.

Thanks also to Lisa Whitaker, who has sold more of my books than I have, I'm sure. Also to Lori Bales, for her unending enthusiasm. And to Charlie Kondek and David Binkowski, for wrangling me an invitation to my first—and probably only—Hollywood party.

And to my family, thank you for always acting interested, even when you're not: Norm Miller, Pat Miller, Michael Miller, Mark Miller and Stephanie Miller.

A big sloppy Mom-hug to my sons, Alec Hauser and Ben

Hauser—you guys are the best. (And no, Ben, I'm sorry—I'm still not going to pay you for your idea for the next book.)

Finally, last but not least, to the best husband a girl writer could ever have, Dennis Hauser. I love you always. That's all.

Photo by Dennis Hauser/Michael Miller Studios

A former member of the PTA, **Melanie Lynne Hauser** is a prototypical Super Mom. She lives in Chicago, Illinois, with her husband and two teenage sons, and is the author of *Confessions of Super Mom*. Visit her Web site at www.MelanieLynne Hauser.com.

SAVES THE WORLD

Melanie Lynne Hauser

Dear Reader,

I'm often asked why I chose to write women's fiction from a superhero's perspective. Contrary to popular belief (my family's, anyway), it's not because I wanted to be Wonder Woman when I grew up. (Queen of the Universe was my actual goal.) Although I do think that if you grew up in the United States during the 1960s and 1970s, you can't help but have absorbed a lot of superhero mythology. Batman on TV, the Wonder Twins on Saturday mornings, and yes, of course, Lynda Carter as Wonder Woman—pop culture icons, all.

But the truth is, I just wanted to write women's fiction, period. I wanted to write about the issues we all face as women: juggling work, kids, spouses (ex or otherwise). Much of the "mommy lit" that I was reading at the time tended to place the heroine in a high-powered job with personal assistants and nannies at her disposal. I wanted to write about more of a working-class mom—the kind of woman I knew personally. But the truth is, writing about people you already know can be just a little, well, boring. What's the fun in reading about characters who are exactly like the people you see at PTA meetings? I wanted to give readers something a bit more—characters whose everyday lives were very much like theirs. But who had an element of fantasy, of fun, that mere mortals can only dream of. What better way to do that than write about a superhero? Better still, a mom. A Super Mom.

And what fun it all turned out to be! Daydreaming of powers that would make a real difference in my boring ol' soccer-mom life—now that was exciting! It's fine to be able to see through steel (Superman) or swing from building to building (Spider-Man). If you're an idle bachelor who has nothing better to do. But if you're a woman, a mother, with a messy house, no time for a personal life, and kids growing more distant by the year, swinging from building to building doesn't really help out, you know? But being able to clean with the power of ten thousand Swiffers? Knowing exactly what your teenagers are up to, no matter how hard they try to hide it? The ability to put grown men into Super Time-Outs with just a glance? Much more practical!

And the more I wrote about this part—the fun, superhero part—the more resonance it provided to the "real" part. I understood that there were many parallels between the journey that a superhero takes, and the journey that we women experience. Gaining new powers, juggling secret identities, learning to embrace our strengths—I ended up realizing that women really are the true superheroes in life. Only we don't always take the time to rejoice in it. Until now.

So that's why I don't really think that I'm writing

women's fiction from a superhero's perspective. I'm just writing women's fiction. Period. Exploring issues that women face, trying to find humor in the ordinary events of our lives. So what if my heroine wears a cape, Spandex and leaps over tall buildings at a single bound?

Sooner or later, don't we all?

Obviously, I could go on and on about these parallels—in fact, I think there are lots of things to talk about here, as in all women's fiction, and I hope that you do, too. So if you're in a book club, or just looking for some things to ponder, I've put together a few discussion questions for *Super Mom Saves the World*.

1. Considering all the other unsung heroes out there, why do you think a superhero honoring mothers was necessary in today's society? Or do you think that mothers should be celebrated in this way?

2. As the book begins, Birdie is beginning to feel as if the town doesn't appreciate all she does. Do you feel that women are typically underappreciated in this way, in the workplace and at home? Or do you think that Birdie is too sensitive about this?

3. The friendship between Carrie and Birdie is a very big part of these books, yet they're both worried that it will change as their daughters grow apart. Do you feel that their bond is real, or was it a friendship that grew out of convenience and will fade as their lives take them in different directions?

4. Blending families is an important theme of the book. Do you feel Birdie and Carl are too honest when they admit to each other that their own children will always come first? Will Carl replace Dr. Dan in Kelly's and Martin's lives, or do you believe Birdie will try to keep her ex-husband involved as a parent?

5. Dr. Dan's attempt to win his ex-wife back fails. How selfish were his motives? Do you feel there was any genuine feeling or attraction on his part? Was Birdie ever truly tempted, or was the feeling she once had for him truly dead?

6. Birdie admits that her fears over her son dating are stronger than they were when her daughter was the same age. Why do you think this is? What role does gender and birth order play in her different approach to her children?

7. Despite her hatred of Mr. Derringer and the way he treats his son, Birdie is reluctant to truly intervene until the end. Do you feel she should have stepped in sooner, as Super Mom? Did the fact that she had no evidence of actual physical abuse make up for the obvious psychological damage she witnessed? What exactly is the line between abuse and poor parenting?

8. While the entire town is involved in the building of the new stadium and the excitement of competitive sports, academic and music funding is slowly taken away. Do you think this is a true reflection of our society today?

9. The fund-raising competition between the PTA and the Shriners is one of the more humorous parts of the book. However, do you think that school fund-raising is an issue that needs to be addressed? Is the depiction of the PTA really that exaggerated in the book? Are the parents of Astro Park well-intentioned in their zealousness?

10. Who is the true villain of the book: Mayor Linseed, Jasper, Janitor Bingo, or Dr. Dan? Are any of these innocent of bad intent? Or is there some flaw in all of their characters?

11. Why do you think Birdie is so quick to overlook the fact that Janitor Bingo initially wanted to do her harm? Beyond their connection through cleaning, what is the bond that ties them? Why does Birdie feel so responsible for him?

12. Birdie and Carl talk about the fact that they were so busy being parents, they didn't even remember to dance at their own wedding. Is this an indication that they need to do a better job balancing parenting with being in love? Or have they found a way to do that already? What do you think is the underlying strength of their relationship?

13. The end of the book suggests that Carl will soon be celebrated in his own right. How do you think they'll manage a marriage between two celebrities? How will Carl react to his fame? How will Birdie?

14. When the book begins, Birdie is unable to fly. What is it that gives her the confidence to do so at the end? What in her life has changed? What do you think flying symbolizes to her? To all women?